GW00707268

THE
EQUATION
OF MURDER

THE
EQUATION
OF MURDER

J. L. SEED

Copyright © 2008 J.L. Seed

The moral right of the author has been asserted.

Apart from any fair dealing for the purposes of research or private study,
or criticism or review, as permitted under the Copyright, Designs and Patents
Act 1988, this publication may only be reproduced, stored or transmitted, in
any form or by any means, with the prior permission in writing of the
publishers, or in the case of reprographic reproduction in accordance with
the terms of licences issued by the Copyright Licensing Agency. Enquiries
concerning reproduction outside those terms should be sent to the publishers.

This novel is entirely a work of fiction. The names, characters and incidents portrayed
in it are the work of the author's imagination. Any resemblance to actual persons,
living or dead, is entirely coincidental.

Matador
9 De Montfort Mews
Leicester LE1 7FW, UK
Tel: (+44) 116 255 9311 / 9312
Email: books@troubador.co.uk
Web: www.troubador.co.uk/matador

ISBN 978 1906510 206

A Cataloguing-in-Publication (CIP) catalogue record for this book is available
from the British Library.

Mixed Sources
Product group from well-managed
forests and other controlled sources
www.fsc.org Cert no. TT-COC-2082
© 1996 Forest Stewardship Council
FSC

Typeset in 12pt Bembo by Troubador Publishing Ltd, Leicester, UK
Printed in the UK by The Cromwell Press Ltd, Trowbridge, Wilts, UK

Matador is an imprint of Troubador Publishing Ltd

To my friend Tomm Brooker

Chapter 1

I grab her from behind, clamping my hand over her mouth and pinning her against me in one quick movement. My other hand thrusts the case of a penknife against her neck. "Just do as I say" I whisper "and you won't get hurt."

She freezes as she lets the fear get to her. And then she starts to struggle. Her body stretches and lurches, her head jerks back and forth, and her elbows thrust against my ribs. But she cannot get away.

I move the knife until it is within an inch of her eyes and then flick the blade. So that she gets a good glimpse of it, so that she can witness the cold, hard steel, so that she knows I'm serious, that I'm not someone to be messed around with. A ray from the mid-morning sun breaches the forest and hits the tip of the blade. I warn her once more.

"I don't want to use this, so don't be silly."

As soon as she sees the weapon, the woman stops fighting.

I don't want to use the knife, but I'm prepared to do whatever it takes, I'm prepared to slit her throat if she doesn't comply. I press the knife back against her neck, angling it into the groove at the front of her jugular vein, so that it doesn't cut her, but so that it's ready, in the vicinity, waiting, just in case. With that, I drag her sideways through a gap between two trees and into the shelter of the late summer bushes.

Once through, I move my thumb, releasing her nose so that she can breathe but keeping my hand clamped firmly over her mouth. She snorts loudly as she draws in air and then shudders and begins to cry. The tears flow freely.

I wonder what she's thinking now, I wonder if she can sense that these are her final seconds. I wonder whether she's thinking about one particular person, or aching for all the things she promised herself she'd do once she had the time. I'd like to ask her if it's true that your life flashes in front of your eyes before you die and if this is what she's experiencing at the moment, but I don't want to alarm her more than necessary. She stumbles, but cannot fall, as I drag her through the dense bracken into the depths of the woods.

I push her forward, over mangled roots and past big trees towards the centre, where the bushes are at their thickest and the pathways are furthest away, steering her towards the spot that I chose a long time ago. To the place I've visited many times since, but will have no further need of after today. My pre chosen spot. Right off the beaten track. A little way up a hillside. A dark point in the middle of nowhere. There, I snatch her bag from her shoulder and push her to the ground.

She slumps into a pitiful heap, her hair flopping forward as her body curls into a ball. Her tears break into loud sobs

"Shut up" I snap at her angrily.

A few more whimpers escape before she manages to contain the noise. She wipes her face. And then looks up, fear glistening in her eyes, terror mingling with despise she so evidently feels. In spite of that she manages to look up and hold my gaze.

"What do you want?" she asks.

I have no answer that she would welcome.

"Why are you doing this?"

I spring her bag open and tip the contents onto the floor. Then bend to pick up her phone.

"I'm ill" she blurts out, "I am… I am… ask anyone… they'll tell you… ring someone… ring my friend… she'll tell you… "

I switch the phone off and then hurl it into the bushes. She gasps in dismay as she watches it disappear. But it doesn't stop her.

"I've got money" she pleads. "I can get you any amount you want, just say the word… name a figure"

"I don't want it."

"You don't have to do this" she cries.

But she doesn't understand. She thinks she knows but she doesn't.

I press the recoil button on my knife and the blade snaps shut. As I slip it into my pocket, her eyes only widen.

"If you let me go I won't say anything to anyone, I swear I won't" she says, dragging a finger across her chest to form an invisible cross.

I watch in mild fascination, finding her naive gesture strangely touching. She thinks that forming a cross will save her, that god and religion will step in and sort this mess out. And I'm betting that she's never stepped foot in a church before, not really, not for the right reasons, maybe she was christened and maybe she got married in one, but I'm betting that she's never been a proper worshipper. No, that cross won't save her now. And I should know.

"Just let me go"

Her eyes plead. But I've seen it before.

"Is it sex you want?" she says, the tone of her voice becoming more acute, more anxiety ridden. "Look, if it is, I won't make it difficult, I'll let you, I don't mind"

Watching her, watching the wretchedness on her face, reminds me of the last time. It reminds me that I've killed before.

For a fleeting second I switch off. Like with everything I do, the reason why I'm here, it follows me everywhere, no matter what I'm doing, or who I'm with, it's with me, always with me, lurking in the background, ready to pop up at any given second. Ready to ruin my day. And ruin my life. She's just offered me sex, but she's wrong, she's so wrong.

"I've got children," she says, interrupting my thoughts and bringing me back to reality, "do you have any?"

Her face softens as it takes on a new expression. As if her thoughts are turning elsewhere. She looks into the distance. Not focusing on anything in particular. Her mood shifts, as if she's finding an inner strength. She no longer cowers, and no longer shakes. And I know that I've taken far too long.

"Do you have any children?" she asks again.

I shake my head. I've not come here for conversation and I haven't got the time.

"My husband will be looking for me" she says, her voice squeaking as I close in.

I bend over her.

"Let him come."

I put my hands round her neck. And in those final moments she knows. She knows that she's not going to be able to walk away from this, that she's not going to be able to say goodbye to anyone she loves, that she's not going to go to sleep tonight nor wake tomorrow, that she's never going to shop again, nor eat in fancy restaurants, never going to kiss or make love, never going to laugh or cry, never going to love or hate, never going to feel the cold, nor go through the seasons. That her season is being brutally cut short, that the only way she's going to leave this spot is in a body bag. I see it in her eyes. I see the terror, then the realization. And I squeeze a little harder.

Her hands rise, her long nails clawing in an awkward search for somewhere to grip. They scratch the leather of my gloves, but it doesn't concern me, by this time tomorrow I'll have disposed of them properly and there'll be no connection that leads back to me.

Her head jerks backwards and I get to look straight into her face. With her pale blue eyes and her upturned nose, with her thinning lips and her eyebrows that have been over plucked. I see it all. It's funny when looking at a person from a closer angle, how it all changes, that some people are prettier from a distance and some look better close up. The woman in front did look better from a closer angle. She did until I started to squeeze. Now her face begins to swell.

Watching someone die is surreal. I feel detached, and at the same time, I'm curious. I'm curious because I'm looking for a sign. I want to know if she is passing on to somewhere else, to heaven or hell, I want to know if it's true, that we all get to face our makers, and pay for our sins. But I've already taken the time to consider this and if I do have to face my maker then I'm living on a tab. I'll pay later, thank you.

Her body relaxes. Her eyes take on a glazy stare. She gives in. I hold on for a few more seconds, but know. There is something different about a corpse, the skin is different, it takes on a plastic look, the look of a mannequin. Her face is no longer contorted, no longer afraid, her soul having departed, she's become nothing more than a casing.

I push her back across a clump of ferns and reach into my pocket.

I take out some scissors and set to work. Her light blue top cuts neatly and falls aside, exposing her white lacy bra. I pull at the front of it and then cut through the centre. With the support taken away, her chest is soft and limp.

I move to her trousers. The black jeans are tight and have pinched her skin around the waistband, leaving angry red lines.

Even though I know that she's dead, I'm still wary of hurting her unnecessarily. I don't want to cut her, or to graze her. I don't want to draw blood or mark her in any way that could be construed as being part of what I'm doing here.

I put the scissors down and dig my fingers into her waistband, forcing the top button open, then unzip and pull them down. They slide awkwardly over her thighs and on past her knees. I bring them to rest on her shins

Under the trousers is a tiny pair of black knickers with stringy sides. They cut easily.

I pull the knickers away, and then pause to look at her. She is early thirties, pretty, and not a natural blonde. Her body shows the signs that she is a mother after all, I wasn't sure whether to believe her but those marks across her stomach can only be caused by one thing. She is plump, but curvy in a nice way. Her pubic hair is black and has been neatly waxed. Her nipples are the colour of dark coffee. Her suntan is limited to her face, chest, arms and legs, and outlines the shape of a full swimming costume.

I consider sex.

I know that the crime I have just committed will see me locked up with the key thrown away forever and so to have sex wouldn't make a difference to any punishment if I'm caught, because let's face it we're talking about life term here, and at my age, life would certainly mean life. But I don't intend to get caught.

I brush the idea away. Sex has never been a part of my plan and to deviate now could throw my whole system out of order.

The clock is ticking and time is marching on. Or at least for some people it is.

I reach into my left pocket and bring out a plastic bag. The bag is the type that usually contains sandwiches, with a seal running across the top. Only mine contains something different. I open the seal and extract one dark hair. This I place on her right shoulder blade, near the crease of her neck, aside her own hair and contrasting with the colour. I then select a second hair and scan her body for a suitable place to leave it. Just like with everything else, this has to be precise. Everything counts when you're a murderer. It's all about being exact.

The spot I select is in the gap between her thighs, just above her knees. I place it carefully, then reseal the bag and slip it back into my pocket. I ruffle her hair. And wipe her face and ear, where I had hold of her earlier, with an antiseptic cloth. I take out the bag from my right pocket, open it and extract the contents. I place them into her bellybutton.

The woman is exposed, the contents of her navel giving her body a strange absurdity. It's almost a cult image. She is spread across the floor, her nakedness, having lost its sexual appeal, is overshadowed by a set of deep blue rosary beads.

I pause. I mentally run though my list of objectives. Once I'm satisfied that I've done everything correctly, I know that I'm done here.

I take one last look to see me through. One last look to soothe away any doubts which might pervade my thoughts. One last look to carry me through when things are bad. One last look. And then walk away.

Chapter 2

Murder, it's an equation. It's the calculation between do and don't, it's the mathematics between risk and reward. Everything we do is a choice between what we think might be the best option for our own personal circumstances and the rejection of what we suspect to be the lesser deal. We weigh up the options, we ponder the implications, we even consult outside forces, be it tarot cards or clairvoyants or horoscopes, all in the quest of reaching the right conclusion. Ultimately though, it's us who have the final say. And it's we who have to live with the consequences. I know that. But I also believe that my equation is relatively straightforward. It's as simple as the two questions which I ask myself every morning as I study the bedroom ceiling before getting out of bed. Does what a person stands to lose equate with what they stand to gain? And does the risk of getting caught and being thrown into prison for a long time seem preferable to life at the moment?

I, Charlie Scanlon, think I know the answer. I think the solution is simple. I've spent ten months of planning to get to this point. I've spent time and I've spent money, but most of all I've sacrificed a part of my life, all in the quest to pull off the mother of all getaways. I'm a complicated creature and I don't say that lightly. The plan that I've set myself is no less so. I've come up with a crime of stages. So it seems that I've consigned myself to the long haul. The idea is to commit eight crimes in all. No more. No less. Just eight. And then I'll give up. I'll give up and I'll revert back to the guy I was before any of this ever began. Now, as I make my escape from the second crime scene,

I'm more convinced than ever that all my plans are foolproof, that I have got what it takes, that I am the one to pull it off, that I am a serial killer who will blow this country, and this life, apart.

I leave the crime scene and head north in the opposite direction from the pathway where I met with her. I do not panic nor move with haste. I am in control. There is nothing about my situation that gives me cause for concern. My attire is that of a hiker and I look the part. I wear a woollen hat which is pulled forward, partly to hide my face and, more importantly, to keep my hair tucked in. My shirt is made of cotton and has long sleeves that conceal my arms and slip nicely into my gloves. My waistcoat matches my tweed trousers, my trousers are tucked into socks, and my socks sit inside sturdy boots that cover the terrain easily. I stop briefly to pick up an old gnarled twig, to give added emphasis to my look. And then continue. The route that I take, like everything else, has been pre-planned. I zigzag between the trees, staying away from the beaten routes. One hundred metres to the north, I meet with a brook. I keep to the right of it, tracing its curves downstream. On several occasions I come close to people, couples taking dogs for walks, children, in Wellington boots, shouting with excitement, families on afternoon strolls. None of them spot me; my training in the Territorial Army when I was younger ensures I stay out of sight. I pause, I swerve, I look, and I listen.

It's been twenty years since I was in the Queen's Infantry. First Battalion, C Company, 8th Platoon. I still have the knowledge. It's something that stays with me. I live on autopilot, I duck, I sneak, I move in the shadows. Put me in any hostile environment and my actions will be the same every time. I let my senses guide me and my training kicks in. It's part of who I am. It's been ingrained into my very being. I am the unseen.

Three hundred metres downstream, I come to a bridge. I stop short of it and reconnaissance the area. The woodland is quiet and no-one is around. I move out and cross to the opposite side. There, several pathways split into different routes. Beyond them, an embankment leads upwards. I skip the pathways and scramble up the hillside. I get to a big oak tree and pause. I check my surroundings once again. The coast is clear and so I continue.

I reach the top of the embankment in record time. There, just as it has on the many trial runs in the past, awaits a wooden fence. Beyond it, an open field stretches into the distance. The crop is as I expect with the strands of barley almost ready to harvest. The field is a six foot high swaying mass of golden camouflage.

I climb over the fence and walk within the dirt track which plots its circumference.

On the far side is a quiet country road. I stay within the fields, keeping the road within my sight. A mile to the west, then I reach the car park where I left my car several hours before.

My Ford Fiesta is parked amongst a dozen other cars. It is just another vehicle. There's nothing about it that attracts attention. It's an average family saloon, an average car and an average colour. Blue. Except for the dirt. Thick grey globules of baked earth are sprayed along the wheels, the bumpers and the registration plate.

My eyes sweep the parking lot. Nothing. All the cars are empty. The area beyond is still. I cross to my car, slip into the driving seat and put my keys into the ignition.

I drive to a secluded spot ten miles away, stop the car and switch off the engine.

It's as I ease back into my seat that I catch my reflection in the rear view mirror. My eyes, with the aide of contact lenses, are brown instead of blue, my eyebrows are pencilled in to match, and my cheeks are smeared with a tan coloured make up. I'm even wearing mascara. The reflection that greets me looks strangely alien, almost foreign in fact. Which is my intention. At the same time it strikes me as weird, looking into a mirror and not seeing the person that you're used to staring back. I wonder whether the man in the mirror is what it's all about, that I'm only able to commit my crimes by taking on another persona. But would I be able to kill without my disguise?

Deep thoughts, I have them at the most unsuitable moments. Like I know I should be somewhere else now, but all I can do is look in the mirror. All I can do is analyse myself. Only it doesn't matter how many questions I ask, the answer remains the same.

I snap myself out of it and set to work. I take out the holdall from underneath the back of the passenger seat and place it onto the seat next to me. I take off my hat and tuck it away. Next I take out my lenses. I drop each lens into separate pots, top up the saline, then replace them into the inside pocket of the holdall. I remove my make-up using a strong cleanser, and wipe my face with a moist flannel. After drying it with a towel, I splash on some aftershave. I empty my jacket pockets. The scissors are put into their sheath, the penknife is tucked away and the bag containing the hairs is placed into a black bin liner.

I start to strip. I take off my gloves, and then swap my shirt with a vest, my tweed jacket with a patterned jumper, my corduroy trousers with beige chinos, and my hiking boots with some black slip on shoes. The removed clothes are thrown into the bin bag.

I stop momentarily, and think. The girl is my second victim and the impact of my actions is no less shocking than after the first. I feel sad. I feel sorry for what I have done. Guilt plays its part too. But the truth of it is that I have no choice, that, in order to fulfil my plan, I had to kill. And I'll have to continue to kill as well. I'm sure that people think murderers don't have a conscience, but I do. I'm aware that two people could've had longer lives if it wasn't for me. But let's get real here, they could've had longer lives but that doesn't necessarily mean that they would've been happy, or fulfilled, they still might've had problems to deal with. What is life? It's a messy path littered with all sorts of issues. There's adultery, lies, miserable partners, cancers, illness, redundancy, unemployment, and poverty. Life is harsh. And I'm not trying to absolve myself from what I've done but any one of these things could've been waiting for them in their future, had they lived. Anyway it's not about them, it's about me. Sometimes a person has to do what is necessary in order to make a difference. Which is what I intend. I intend to make a difference.

The reflection in the mirror has changed; the man in it looks no different to anyone else. Which is what I am. I'm the type of person you wouldn't look at twice if you saw me walking in the street. I'm mister average. I'm a face in the crowd. I could be anyone, I could be a father, a husband, an uncle, a butcher whom you speak to over a glass counter, a plumber called out to fix a leak, a member of the neighbourhood watch, anyone. I don't have madness in my face. I don't have murderer tattooed on my forehead. Outwardly I don't show any signs of being what I am. You could walk past me a hundred times and not know.

But inside, well that's a different story.

Chapter 3

The house is in its usual state of disrepair, the green and white bamboo patterned wallpaper has faded and is peeling in several places, the carpet running down the middle of the hall is threadbare, with its former colours now indistinguishable, the floor tiles, which are visible around the edges of the carpet, have long lost their sheen and serve only to collect dust. The small entrance is overcrowded and claustrophobic. Coats bulge from a wooden rack. Dishevelled rows of shoes sit beneath. A Welsh dresser stands next to a Stannah stair-lift in order for the occupant to lean against it to manoeuvre herself into the chair. One corner of it is dust free from when she last went upstairs. The rest of the dresser is cluttered with an eclectic array of items. A letter-holder, which doubles as a barometer, clutches a stack of yellowing letters. Beside it, ornaments of many descriptions are crammed together in little groupings. Porcelain plates sit next to a pewter coffee set. Toby jugs intermingle with crocheted cloths. Picture-frames cradle sienna coloured memories. Empty candleholders stand forgotten. A display of plastic roses poke out from a small vase. Above it all is the smell of a stale environment. It hits you as soon as you open the front door. It's a musty aroma due to the shortage of fresh air. The house is barely lived in any more, the oxygen a testament to the lack of movement.

I walk through the hall and step into the back room to find her sitting in her high winged chair, which dwarfs her tiny frame and at certain angles looks like it's consuming her. Only her legs remain visible, they stick out of the front and are always snugly wrapped into a blanket. Today it's the turn of her pink summer blanket.

I slip my holdall onto the floor behind her seat and then move forward so that she can see me without having to strain. I stand beneath the cross on the chimney breast, and then put two shopping bags onto the hearth rug. She looks up at me and smiles.

"Everything alright?" I ask.

"Yes" she nods.

"Sorry I took so long, but I had a lot of things to do this morning."

"It's alright" she replies "I'm not going anywhere." Mrs Gibson pulls up her blanket and tucks it across her chest as if to stress the point.

"I picked up your prescriptions and I got your shopping, then I washed the car" I tell her, explaining my absence since leaving her house early on. "I stopped off at a couple of garden centres on the way back. I thought I'd be back before now, but I must've lost track of the time."

"You've no need to explain to me, it makes no difference to me how long you take" she mutters.

"I thought you'd be worried."

"It's not me who'll worry, it's your wife," she replies, cautioning me "she'll think that I've kept you here all morning."

"Maureen's working today" I tell her "it's her weekend to work so she won't be thinking about me at the moment, she'll be too busy."

"Ah, I didn't realise" she says understandingly. "But if you had the day to yourself then you shouldn't have spent your time running around after me."

"It's no trouble" I reply.

I bend forward and take a small white bag out one of the shopping bags and then stand up. "I got your prescriptions here" I say, opening the bag and emptying the contents onto the table at the side of her seat. "The pharmacist has marked them, she's put a W on your water tablets, she's marked your blood pressure tablets with a P, and the anti- inflammatory tablets are marked with an A."

"And the painkillers?"

"Got them" I say, bringing out a brown medicine bottle. I untwist the lid and reach for her pillbox. "I'll put them into your pot."

Mrs Gibson lets out a sigh. "It all makes me feel like a child" she says sadly.

I look at her. I look at her pitiful figure bent forward, her back arching involuntarily. I see the way her hands tremble. I see her head which nods with its rhythmic gesture and her white hair which sprouts from various parts of her face as well as her head. I see her concave cheeks which exaggerate the bones beneath and her wrinkled skin which falls away from her body. I see her hands, with their gnarled fingers, twisted from the ravages of arthritis. I see it all.

"But I shouldn't be complaining" she adds lightly "as it could be worse."

"It's okay," I reply "say whatever you want, sometimes it's better to voice your feelings, it's what I'm here for as well."

And it is. When I signed up with the Salvation Army to do some voluntary work it was a calculated decision, I needed a place to store my stuff and I also needed an alibi, an excuse to tell Maureen where I was going and what I was doing without getting too many questions in return. Somehow I've ended up with more than I bargained for along the way. Over the past year I've forged an unlikely relationship. Now she is in front of me. I can't deny that helping Mrs Gibson has touched me in a way that I never thought possible, that she's reached a part of me that I thought was long time barren, so much so that I can hardly bring myself to acknowledge it.

"You do too much as it is, you shouldn't have to listen to me" she says.

"No, it's not true," I insist "I don't do any more than I want to and I'm happy to spend time with you. I wouldn't do it if I didn't want to."

Mrs Gibson smiles.

It's a smile which makes me feel bad because it reminds me that my holdall is only a few feet away. And that inside that holdall is the knife and all the other necessities which I had need of earlier on. That beyond this house, and beyond the window that she looks out of, is the garden shed. And that inside that shed is the key to all of my planning. She's no more than part of the equation, I tell myself. But deep down inside of me I know it's not true.

"You are good" she says gratefully.

Seeing her gratitude makes things worse.

I empty the last of the tablets into the porcelain dish, crumple the bag and throw it, and the empty bottle, into the paper basket under the table. "Better put these away, before the butter melts" I say, picking up the shopping bags.

I escape to the kitchen, thankful for the excuse to leave the room.

I pop the butter into the butter dish and stock up the fridge with some milk and yoghurts. I open the packet of digestives and empty them into a container with a spring lid. Then I put the bread into a blue and white striped metal breadbin. I rip the lid off the box of cup-a-soup and then store them at the back of the worktop, next to a pair of scissors. I open the bag of sugar and fill the sugar bowl, then open the packets of cereal and clip them with a peg to keep them fresh. I unseal the lid of the jam and put some into a pot.

"Do you want a drink?" I ask, through the kitchen doorway.

"I wouldn't mind a glass of water as I could do with taking a painkiller."

It's as I'm putting the glass under the running tap that I catch sight of my hands, which remind me that only an hour before they were tightly wrapped around the neck of my second victim. For a second all I can think about is her coffee coloured nipples and the way her torso was softer and rounder with her clothes cut open. All I can think about is her nakedness and the dark curls at the top of her thighs.

There in Mrs Gibson's kitchen, I'm transported back to that forest, back to the sunshine hitting me in the face as it broke through the tops of the trees, to the forest with its distant echoing sounds. Inside my head I'm checking and double checking that I didn't make any mistakes and that I didn't leave any traces, that I followed everything that I set out to do correctly. Beneath me the water from the glass overflows onto my hand, bringing me back to my senses.

When I re-enter the back room, Mrs Gibson has her tablet ready. I hand her the glass of water and sit on the couch nearby. She pops the tablet into her mouth. Her face immediately crumples into a thousand lines as the bitterness gets to her. She crunches loudly, wincing all the while, and then washes the residues down with a couple of gulps of water.

"Nasty things" she says once she's finished. She reaches over and gingerly places the glass onto the side table. After wiping her mouth with a tissue, she turns to me. "I don't see why this medicine has to come in tablet form" she says, tapping the medicine box, "how is someone like me supposed to swallow those huge things?"

"You'd think they'd make them as a syrup" I reply.

She looks at me intensely with her watery red rimmed eyes caught in hesitation, as if unsure of whether to continue talking. Her mouth, in the middle of her indecision, hangs half open, the yellowing of her dentures on show, along with her tongue which glistens with the excess moisture that her mouth seems to produce.

I look away, not wanting to stare. I look around the room with all its clutter, I look at the pile of old newspapers sitting next to the black hi-fi in the corner, and then at the stack of jigsaw boxes propped up against a bureau along the side wall, I notice the kitsch ornaments which spring from the 60's, collecting dust on top of the tiled fireplace, and the old knitting box sitting on the hearth. I look up to the picture of The Mona Lisa in its cheap plastic frame, and then feel embarrassed for noticing it. I turn and focus on the black ash bookshelf, in particular, the line of Reader's Digest books on the second shelf down.

"I sometimes wonder if it's worth taking them" she says quietly. I turn back to her. "Don't."

"No, I know you don't want to hear this, but it's been on my mind and I've had these thoughts for a while. You're the only person I can talk to…"

"When I said you can talk to me about anything…"

"I know."

"I didn't…"

"I know" she whispers, her voice emotional and terse.

I nod, not wanting to, but giving her the go-ahead to continue anyway.

"I've been thinking about things… and I've come to the conclusion that I'm not much of a benefit to this world anymore. I've had my time here and I've done all the things I ever wanted to do… the trouble is I'm stuck between two difficult places, if I don't take my medicine then I'll end up in a lot of pain, but if I do, then I'm overstaying my time…"

"No, you're not" I protest. "You're not overstaying…"

"It must be difficult for you to comprehend," she says kindly "you being so young and active, you've got years ahead, and more importantly, you've got your health and that is the biggest blessing of all, health is the biggest asset anyone can have. You'll understand when you get to my age."

"I understand now, I know how difficult it is for you and I know how limited you are."

I fall silent.

"I'm getting worse" she says sadly, "the painkillers don't seem to have the same effect they once had, I'm on the highest dose possible and it still doesn't take the pain away, all they do is make me feel groggy."

"What does the doctor say?"

"He says there's nothing more he can give me." She pauses and studies her hands, inspecting them. And then rests them on her lap. "I'm thinking of stopping my medicine altogether."

"You can't do that!" I exclaim.

"Why not?"

I scramble for an answer, but the only one I can come up with sounds feeble.

"I don't want you to."

Mrs Gibson looks at me in surprise, and appreciation.

"Nobody lives forever" she says.

"No they don't, but that's no reason to stop taking your pills."

Her eyes flicker over to the cross on the wall. She studies it intensely. And then looks guilty.

"Yes, you're right" she says. "It's just me being selfish."

"No it isn't" I retort. I know it isn't. There's only one selfish person in this room. And I know that it's me. If I were a bigger person then I'd help, she's spoken like this before, I'm aware of how much pain she's in, if I were a better person then I'd find a solution. But that's something I can't do. I can kill for hate but I cannot kill for love.

"I shouldn't be talking like this" she says, bowing her head.

"It's ok" I respond. "I understand how you must feel and I know that it can't be easy but ignoring your medicine isn't the solution."

"You're right. It's just me being silly. But sometimes I feel that I've had my best days and now all I'm waiting for is the inevitable."

"No, you've got your trips to the bingo, and you get to see your friends. I visit. And I want to visit…"

"That's kind of you, and I do appreciate your visits, don't take what I'm saying to mean that I'm not grateful, it's just sometimes I feel like I'm in a waiting room."

I nod with understanding. Her words strike a chord; they have meaning to me too.

"Life can be like that, whatever your age" I tell her.

Mrs Gibson looks thoughtful now, wistful even. Her eyes wander over to the row of photographs on the mantelpiece, "true" she whispers solemnly. She brushes a strand of her hair away from her face. The thick white coil bounces straight back to the front of her forehead. She wipes it away again, tucking it behind her ear. But it doesn't stay there.

"Yes. I suppose you're right" she says, finally ignoring the errant hair, "there were times when I was younger when I felt like this, times before Stanley passed away even." Her eyes wander over to the picture of her wedding day "I suppose there were many times over the years."

"I feel like that at times. There are days when I feel like I'm waiting for bigger things to happen…" I stop myself before it's too late. I'm only too well aware that every conversation I have might become significant at some point, that all the things I say, or have said in the past, might end up being seized upon and then pored over and dissected. Only sometimes Mrs Gibson draws me out, sometimes I can't help but talk. Mrs Gibson doesn't wait for me to finish my sentence, as she's long used to me turning silent in the middle of a conversation.

"I suppose everybody must have these feelings at some point it their life" she says.

"I'm sure they do."

Mrs Gibson's cat, Smoky, appears at the doorway, walks across the room and then springs onto her lap. "Smoky" she laughs heartily. "I forget about him sometimes. Now where would he be without me?"

"Exactly!"

"Exactly" she repeats. "Fancy forgetting about you!" she exclaims, stroking his back lovingly. "I am a silly person." He rolls into a ball and purrs contentedly, unaware of the meatier points of life.

"I only wish there was more I could do" I tell her.

"You do enough. Take no notice of me," she replies, "I was being silly, I shouldn't grumble, I'm in my own home and I have help, especially from you, you're such a good person. It could be worse" she says firmly. "It can always be worse."

"Everything can be worse" I say. And more as an afterthought, I add "and everything can be better."

Mrs Gibson smiles "you're completely right again."

We both sit in silence, pondering what's been said. The sound of next doors television can be heard through the wall, it transmits the tune of some funky music. I recognise it as the advert where the car turns into a robot. Mrs Gibson leans forward and reaches for the plate of biscuits on the table. "Biscuit?" she asks, as if the conversation a minute ago was insignificant.

"No thank you" I reply, glancing at the clock on the mantelpiece, "I'm going to have to get home soon. I said I'd be back in time for when Maureen finishes work."

"Of course" nods Mrs Gibson "don't let me hold you up."

I stand awkwardly.

"I've just got to tidy some things away in the shed and then I'll be off. That's if there's nothing else you'd like me to do before going?"

"Can you switch on the television for me? To save me from getting up"

"Sure."

I walk to the television and switch it on, then move the remote control closer to her. Once she's settled, I head for the back door, pausing momentarily to collect my holdall.

Chapter 4

When I get home, Maureen, having heard my car, is waiting in the hall.

"Where have you been?" she asks, as soon as I step through the door. I take a deep breath. Close the door. And place my keys on the top of the cupboard which houses the electric meter. I want to tell her about the events of today. To see her face. To let her know that she can follow me and question me. That she can nag and complain. And that the only reason I go along with her demands is for an easy life. She thinks she knows me but she doesn't. She's spent the last twenty years with a stranger. I am not the person she thinks I am. Lurking inside me is a hatred so raw, it beggars belief.

"I've been helping Mrs Gibson" I reply solemnly.

"What? All day?" she snaps.

I slip my coat off and hang it on the wooden Ikea rack, then take off my shoes and swap them for a pair of tartan slippers. I line them against the wall next to a pair of flat black, passionless shoes and move passed her and up the stairs.

"I got there late… then I had to go out and collect her prescriptions… by the time I'd waited at the surgery… and at the chemist, it was gone lunch. I stopped off for some food, and then went to a few garden centres… I washed the car… and I had a cup of tea back at Mrs Gibson's…"

I skip the last two stairs and enter the one safe haven of the house, the only room with a lock on the door, the bathroom. I walk in, close the door, and click the lock. But, even in doing this, I know that she'll be waiting outside, ready for when I emerge. Once inside, I sit on the edge of the bath and steel myself, grabbing a few minutes of privacy to gather my thoughts together. Nobody knows what my life is like. Or how clingy Maureen can be. I try to get my space, but it's hard, she follows me everywhere and there are few places left where I feel safe anymore.

I look over to the reflection in the mirror. The sight that greets me is worrying. The man staring back looks tired and worn, which is what I am, I am forty three, my fine sandy hair is receding, my belly is portly, my skin has started to sag and I'm sure that I am shrinking. My 5'8" frame is no longer as imposing as it once was. Lately, there have been times when I've caught sight of my reflection and I don't recognise myself anymore. Instead, the person I see looking back is a stranger to me. He's a middle aged man who has got caught up in a situation which has spun out of control. I'm not thinking about the murders now; I'm thinking about my life, in particular my life with Maureen. She's the one that has aged me. For she suffocates. She fills our house with her overbearing ways and there are few places left to hide anymore. I ran out of excuses to avoid her a long time ago. The solitary excuse is that I'm using the loo.

I reach over and flush the toilet for the benefit of the ears beyond the door, then lean over to the basin and turn the hot tap on. I put the plug in and watch as the water fills up. I know that I'm stalling, that I'll have to face her eventually, but I need to prime myself first of all. There are times when I try to tolerate Maureen, but mainly I can't. And it's been this way for years. The problem with something that irritates is that it begins to fester, like an open wound that hasn't been treated properly; Maureen is a visual reminder of something gone wrong. She's the scab on my life.

I switch the tap off and sink my hands into the steaming water.

One thought of her stirs the deepest animosity inside of me. I know it's not completely her, and that I am partly to blame, which is why I try to keep my distance. Only the more distant I am, the needier she becomes.

I splash my face with water.

Over the years I've tried all sorts of approaches, sometimes I turn things into a game, just to lighten the stress which I feel whenever we're around each other, to show myself that I'm strong, that I have levels of tolerance beyond an average man's. But, it's always the same in the end. I have this one game where I move from room to room knowing that she is one step behind and I try and see how long I can keep it up for and how many rooms I can enter, or sometimes I bounce between two rooms, kitchen…lounge, lounge…kitchen, before one of us gets bored. She beats me every time. It's true. Every time I give in. This is my life and this is how it has been for years. My life is a constant set of manoeuvres of trying to escape. Only sometimes I don't know what I'm trying to get away from.

A cough penetrates the door.

I pull the plug out

The man in the mirror inhales a deep breath.

I reach for the towel and wipe my hands and face slowly.

When I exit the bathroom Maureen is there, sitting at the top of the stairs, waiting, patiently, but waiting all the same.

"Did you find the list?" she asks.

I move swiftly passed her and down the stairs.

"Well? Did you?" she asks, as she gets up to follow me.

I start to take the stairs two at a time. Then hop the last three.

"I take it, you didn't then" she snaps breathlessly over the banister.

I head into the kitchen.

The white melamine worktops shine pristinely, the smell of bleach still lingering in the air. The tea and coffee caddies are perfectly arranged with the labels facing to the front. The mug tree is full. The teapot is under its floral cover. The toaster is sat on a clean crumb tray. The dishcloth is folded and hung over the mixer tap. On the message board, a sheet of A4, covered in copper plating, hangs from a bulldog clip. I walk by it to the far corner of the room.

"Here it is" she rasps, as she unclips the list and comes over to place it in front of me to make a point. I look away. And reach for the kettle. "I mustn't have seen it" I mutter.

"I'll do that" she says, forgetting about her list in her haste to nudge in and take over. She unplugs the kettle and moves to the sink to fill it up.

I move out of her way. I round the breakfast bar and pull out a stool on purpose.

"Wouldn't you be more comfortable in the lounge?" she moans, plugging the kettle back in and flicking the switch, "I've just finished cleaning this room and I don't want it messed up again."

I get up and push the chair back, lining it up with the one beside it. But I know that however careful I am at replacing it, she will have to straighten it herself later on because that's the way Maureen is. Our house is a museum to angles which have been worked out in precise detail. Everything has to be aligned. Everything has its exact position. Everything has its rightful place within these walls. Including me.

When I exit the kitchen, Maureen is shadowing me.

I go to the lounge and as I sink into the comfiest armchair, she is hovering at the side.

"So" she says tersely "you didn't see the list?"

"No" I reply, reaching for the newspaper.

"Did you get any shopping?"

"I didn't know what to get."

"So what have you done all day?"

"I've told you" I reply, turning to the sports pages at the back, "I've been busy."

"Busy for who?" she asks sarcastically, as she sits on the armrest of the nearby chair. She then leans across and tilts her body to invade my space, whilst her head twists in order to peak at the pages I'm looking at. "Have you been helping her all day?" she asks.

"Not all of it."

"What else have you done?"

"I told you" I sigh, moving the paper higher to block her out, "I went to some garden centres."

"I would've liked to have gone too."

"You was working."

"You could've waited."

"Waited for what?" I ask.

I put the paper down, having read the same line several times.

"You could've waited until I had some time to go with you."

"Like when?"

"Like tomorrow, for instance."

"We can go tomorrow, if that's what you want."

"What's the point" she says, "you've already been."

From the kitchen, the sound of the kettle boiling and then clicking can be heard. She gets up. "Tomorrow's Sunday" she states, before exiting the room.

I pick up the paper again, but am too distracted to absorb the words.

From behind, I hear the swish of the serving hatch opening.

"I wanted you to collect some shopping for me" says Maureen, shouting through from the kitchen, "We're getting low on sugar."

I don't speak.

After half a minute without a response, Maureen prompts me. "Did you hear me?" she asks.

"Yes."

"We're almost out of sugar."

I give up on the paper and put it down, then stand up and walk over to the triple set of occasional tables. I uncouple them and spread them around my chair, to act as a barricade and sit back down.

Maureen re-enters the room and immediately moves two of the tables, then she walks over to the hatch in the dining room, picks up a tray and brings it across to me. She slides it onto the table in front. As she does, she takes the time to say her mantra. "Don't make a mess".

On the tray is a steaming cup of coffee and several slices of cake. I pick the knife up from the cake plate to chop a bit off the Madeira slice. I am a murderer and by rights I should not be able to hold a knife and have Maureen in the same house as me without plunging it into her, but, as I've said, I'm in control. Anyway it would mess the carpet up. I don't like mess. I suppose that's the one good thing that living with Maureen has done, it's taught me to be tidy. My killings are tidy, there's no blood, no gore, just a few bruises around the neck, there's nothing too unpleasant for the forensic team and the detectives to have to deal with. I'm not interested in being brutal. For me it's not a case of getting off on killing. Nor do I run home and aim to have sex with Maureen afterwards. That's not what it's all about either. It's not about having to claim some control because I don't have any at home. Psychologists will look for all kinds of excuses for what I have done; they'll sift through my life searching for an explanation. Did I have a bad childhood? Am I lonely? Have I got repressed anger? Did I not bond with my mother at birth? But there's only one reason.

Maureen goes over to the serving hatch to collect her tray and then joins me. She puts her tray down, drags her chair closer to mine and sits down heavily. "There's a film on the T.V. later" she says "it's one of your favourites, True Grit with John Wayne in it."

I've yet to tell her that I don't like westerns and even more that I can't stand John Wayne. I don't know why I haven't, but Maureen got it into her head a long time ago that that's what I like and there seems little point in telling her any different now. Anyway I'm sure that if I were to tell her, she wouldn't listen and so I've not bothered.

I try not to focus on the sound coming from Maureen's direction as she slurps her drink. Instead I mentally line up the porcelain figurines on the mantelpiece and think about shooting them. I get to eight and then stop. Eight. Eight is my destiny. I'm going to kill eight women in total. And stop.

So that's two down. And six to go.

I pop another piece of cake into my mouth. And pick up the paper again. I open it and pretend to read. But all the while my thoughts are in a different place. And all the while, I'm aware of what Maureen is doing; Maureen is watching me intensely, like she always does. She's always trying to fathom what I'm thinking. It's as if she can never quite work me out, she can't get inside me or be privy to my thoughts, and it upsets her, my thoughts are something that she has no access to. And I'm damn well sure that she wouldn't be sat next to me right now if she knew of the things that tip through my head, I'm sure that I wouldn't see her for dust if she knew what I'm thinking about right now. I'm comparing the first murder with the last. And then comparing the women's bodies. The first being younger and more firm, she was around the age of twenty five, whereas the woman this morning was a good ten years older. But I'm not just thinking about their bodies, I'm thinking about whether once the woman today has been found if the police will realise that they have a serial killer on the loose. I left rosary beads in each women's navel to give them a clue, it's my symbol, my calling card, if you like, I placed beads into each of their bellybuttons and will carry on doing so until I've completed my mission, to let the police know that there's a link. But here's the clever bit, I struck in two different counties, to give myself some breathing space. I want to be able to carry out several murders before they pick up on my trail. So, I ask myself, at what point will they link the murders? And at what point do I make it obvious? I feel that the halfway point is a good indication, that by victim number four it should be clear that I've struck before. And that I'll do it again.

"The film is starting in a couple of minutes" she says.

I look at her. And hate. She's wearing her hurt expression. She knows that I was deep in thought. But she doesn't know why. So every time I get to thinking, she has to talk and interrupt because she can't bear it; she can't bear for me to have anything private, not a letter, not a phone call. Not even a thought.

She switches the television on and then picks up the remote control and changes the channel to the station of her choice.

"I'm going upstairs for my cardigan" I say, standing up and stretching.

"I'll put the paper away and then we can relax and watch the film together" she replies, eying up the gap between our seats.

I leave the room and heave a sigh of relief when she doesn't follow. Once upstairs, I perch on my side of the bed. From below, the twanging starting notes of the film begin.

Maureen calls up.

"It's starting."

But I'm not interested. I linger in the bedroom, thinking about my future and thinking about my life. But, as I do, I'm aware that I can't be away too long otherwise she'll come looking for me. I pause just long enough to feel the freedom of not being in the same room as her, just long enough to absorb the calmed atmosphere. Even now the serenity is peppered with interruptions.

"Charlie?" she calls.

It doesn't jolt me.

"Charlie?" her voice getting more strained.

I ignore her.

I find myself staring at the picture of Maureen on my bedside cabinet. She placed it there a long time ago. I bet myself that she put it there so that I'd wake up to see her regardless of which way I'm facing in the morning. I have a habit of sleeping on my back now. But it still gets to me that she did it. That it was her choice to put her photograph on my side of the bed. Now, every time I see that picture, it gets me thinking about what a sham it all is. That relationships are just a sham. That my relationship is. It's just a long winded pretence where I'm pretending to be what she wants me to be, and where I'm pretending to have feelings that I don't really have. This relationship doesn't have any room in my life anymore. But no one tells Maureen that. No one tells her anything she doesn't want to hear. Life for my wife only revolves around herself. She only notices the things that make her happy and is blind to everything else. I sold my soul a long time ago for the sake of peace and quiet. Now my life isn't my own and I can't even nip upstairs without knowing that she's waiting for me to come back down.

And if anyone were to ask me why I am what I am. Well, the answer is simple.

She is on the third rung of the stairs when I move.

Chapter 5

The first is something different, it's like standing on the edge of a cliff and you know that all it takes is one small step, only that step is so significant, it's so life changing, that it scares you like never before because you know that in choosing to make it, you're going to be instantly transported from one level to another. And there's no stop gap in between. There are no shelves waiting to scoop you up, there's nothing in the middle to pause and say 'I did a little'. It's all or nothing. It's like the biggest fear in the world combining with the biggest high. And the impact of those two feelings, the mixture is so huge, it's so damn intense, that it really blows your mind. So there I stood. I was rooted to the spot like a magnetic power had a hold of me and was in grip of my entire being. In my mind, the thoughts. Oh those thoughts. Rattling around in that cavernous system inside my skull. My head felt like it had been hijacked by some alien force which was throwing all the doubts of the world at me. The what ifs, the can't, the anxieties and the fears all came to visit me on that sunny afternoon, so much so that I nearly didn't go through with it. I remember that all I wanted to do was to throw up. And all I wanted was to go home and live the rest of my life in nothingness. Only the image of that depressed me so much that it kept me rooted to the spot. Even now, I've no doubt that it was the thought of going home, to sit alongside Maureen, and to have yet another pointless conversation, which in the end impelled me to do what I did. So I stood. And I saw out my concerns. The day seemed to stretch on, the heat was stifling and intense and there wasn't a cloud up above to break the humidity. The sky was the palest of blue and the trees, with their olive coloured leaves, were no break from the weather. But the pathway was a mere stride away. I stood and I watched at least a dozen go by. All of them coming inches from death. All of them oblivious to the fact that their lives could have ended in those very seconds had I chosen it. But you can bet your bottom dollar that they won't be relieved about that, that they won't suddenly find that life is worth seizing, that there's so much out there waiting to happen, that life has to be snatched before someone or something takes it from you. No, they all went on their merry little way, all of them probably tottering off home, maybe to bicker with their partners, maybe to sulk, maybe to fall out with the neighbours, maybe to do the same job and the same routine for years, or even to spend the rest of their lives following soaps on the television, sitting on their ever fattening arses, waiting for their lives to change or even waiting for someone to come along and change it for them. That's because they don't know how close they came. Isn't life just like that? That a millimetre here, or an extra trip to the shops, or even an extra drink at the pub before someone climbs into their car, can make all the difference. It can make all the difference in the world.

After planning it for so long and imagining of how it would happen, I was worried, I was unsure about my ability to see it through. But as soon as I stepped out of the bushes it all changed. Once I grabbed hold of her something else took control, something that had been buried deep inside of me. Ten months of anticipation was unleashed onto that concrete pathway where she walked. Sometimes events don't quite transpire into actions. But sometimes actions have the ability to surpass all expectations. It was like that for me. As soon as I touched her there was no turning back. As I gripped her body against mine there was no denying my purpose. Once I crossed that invisible line that states that one cannot get personal with another until such time that a friendship has allowed it, we both knew it. That's why I grabbed her in the way I did, I did it so that there would be no other way out for me. I couldn't lumber out of the bushes, grab her by her breast and then say 'sorry miss, my mistake'. No. I gripped her breast tightly and I squeezed extra hard to give myself no other course of action. Don't we all do stupid things? Don't we all do things that we know aren't right, but we do them anyway. Just to force ourselves into a corner and to make ourselves react. So I gripped her by her breast, her left breast to be exact, and I did it with such force that I knew I'd have to go on and kill her. Once I had hold of her it was easy, I'd committed myself.

When I touched her, I can't deny that something stirred inside my trousers. But that's not where my mind was. My mind was focused. On how I'd planned it. On how it would play out. On how it would conclude. I had stood in those bushes and I'd travelled that route so many times that there was almost a pathway cutting through those trees. On that day, it was easy. The girl was compliant. She was too scared to be anything else. As for me, well I was all sweaty palms, which were sticky and uncomfortable inside my PVC gloves, but I still managed to squeeze her tight. And my stomach had a vocabulary of its own, what with the way it was churning and the noises it was making. And it seemed like every pore in my body was leaking, I kept on having to wipe my face to keep the water out of my eyes. My body was gripped by fear. My arms and my legs felt like they'd metamorphosis into blocks of concrete, so much so that it was an effort just to grip the penknife. I didn't dare flick the blade as I didn't trust myself to handle it properly. I was determined though. When I spoke, my voice came out differently, it was deep and tight and had a growl to it that had never been present before. It surprised me. It surprised the girl even more.

The girl was different to how I'd imagined her to be, she was less curvaceous and somewhat plainer, she had dull hair instead of the honey blonde I'd imagined her to have. But she was a victim in every sense of the word. She moved easily. And she didn't make too much of a noise when she cried. She didn't struggle. And she died quickly.

The clothes that she wore were summery. A slip of a dress. Cream, if I remember correctly. With thin straps that crossed over her shoulders and tied behind her neck. It was made out of a fine material that my blades swept through easily. All she had on underneath was a pair of cotton knickers. Nothing else. Just a pair of white knickers. The sandals on her feet had fallen by the wayside as we moved. I left them where they dropped. It all happened really quickly. As if I was an expert and I'd done it a million times before. I suppose I had in a way, I had in my mind. Afterwards, I left a couple of cigarette butts beside her. Both of them Benson and Hedges. I even took the time to sprinkle some ash into a pile next to a nearby tree. I left the rosary beads too. The ones that I left were a white set, which was significant because they were the first string of beads which I collected. Despite the fact that I kill, I still have superstitions. It all was different to what I'd expected, but it all came together.

As I made my way back to my car, my head was light, my legs were shaky and my stomach still queasy. All I could think about was how much I hated Maureen. Of how she would be waiting at home. That's all. That was the only thing that was going through my mind. I wasn't worried about the enormity of what I'd done. It was only afterwards, long after I'd left the scene, when I had the chance to think about things; it was only then that the real meaning got to me and the full impact of what I'd done hit me. But at the time I could only think about Maureen.

Chapter 6

I collect. I've been collecting for a while. But I've only recently
started collecting corpses and even they cannot be considered
to be a collection because I don't get to keep them. Which I suppose,
if you look at it like that, also invalidates the rest of my items because
I don't intend to keep the rest of my collection either. You see my
collection is different to an average person's. I don't collect any
particular type of music, I don't collect antiques, I don't collect books
or magazines, or stamps, nor anything to do with cars, ornaments
don't interest me. Not autographs. Nor anything to do with television
programmes. Not bric-a-brac. I'm not into films. Not plants. Not
cards. Nor medals. I collect DNA. Isn't that what collecting is all
about, about gathering together something that interests you? DNA
interests me. As soon as I began to make my plans to kill, I had to take
onboard this issue. Imagine, had I been carrying out my deeds twenty
years ago, I would never have had the foresight to consider future
detective techniques. When you think about all those murderers who
killed and then went on to make new lives for themselves, spending
twenty years or so thinking they'd gotten away with it, becoming
grandfathers, or upstanding citizens in the community, growing
mature and respected, having children, making it up the career ladder
and settling down to quiet lifestyles, then some smart ass guy in a
laboratory develops a system like DNA. Who'd have thought that
minute speck no bigger than a pin prick could one day link some old
man to an event some decades before. That he'd have his past catch up
with him when he least expected it. All those sloppy men who went

and committed their deeds without proper preparation. The art of becoming a murderer is to not get caught. And the art of not getting caught is preparation. Which is why my plans have taken me so long. You can't begin to imagine where my DNA has come from. Over time I've managed to accumulate my collection from all sorts of sources, from hairbrushes and combs, to cigarette butts, from stopping in the street to pick up chewing gum wrappers, to scraping dandruff off a sofa. It's everywhere. Litter in the street, discarded waste, forgotten items, the list is endless. All my items have been carefully gathered and sealed into plastic bags then labelled to help me remember exactly where and when I found it. Dated and everything. All properly organised. The bit that excites me the most is of how I've managed to do this right under someone's nose without them suspecting a thing.

Take for instance last Friday after work. I clocked off half an hour early and decided to visit a garden centre to prepare for events the following day, all I was looking for was a few bits and pieces to help with my alibi, maybe some plant feed, or a packet of water gel, nothing too bulky, just something to add to my version of events when questioned by Maureen. Only some young guy walking ahead of me in one of the aisles, eating a chocolate bar, dropped the wrapper. What was I supposed to do? Say 'oy mate', and then risk a thumping by handing it back to him? No. Walk on by and miss my chance? No. What I did do was to wait until he had moved on to the next aisle and then I carefully bagged it. A Mars bar wrapper to be precise. I wrapped a plastic bag around my hand, and picked it up. I then reversed the bag over the wrapper and slipped it into my pocket. It was as simple as that.

My collection comes from various sources, which takes a lot of effort. I normally expand it when I'm on holiday with Maureen. Day trips are good fodder as well. I like to keep a distance between all the places where I lift my booty, the last thing I need is a group of DNA connecting together and of detectives coming to several points to which I am associated. I'm not that stupid. But I am that clever. Maureen is a people watcher, she notices all sorts of quirks and habits that people have and she's only too eager to point them out. Which is amusing. Maureen is my accomplice. Though she's unaware of it. She's too busy watching everyone else to notice me. It's only when we're back at home and she has nothing better to do, that she follows me around. Then it's endless. I'll do this, you do that, put your socks in the washing basket, close the door after you, don't you think you should… have a bath… put your slippers on… go to bed. All the time there's this shadow tracing my steps. There's this hand which reaches out whenever I do try to do anything. I sometimes wonder whether it would have been different if we'd had children, that if she'd had someone else to focus her attention on, her time might've been more stretched and I would've ended up less of a priority. That she'd have been less needy. Less demanding. I think not. For some people are born to be who they are. And Maureen was born to question, to suggest, and to take control. Only I didn't see it until after we got married. I didn't see it until it was too late.

In the heat of Mrs Gibson's shed, I spread the plastic bags across the wooden bench in front of me and consider which object to take next. I scrutinize each bag carefully, taking my time to observe all the groupings and weighing up their potential impact. There's the Spanish waiters notebook, with the numbers on the top sheet in a style which can only be foreign. The sevens, with a line across the body, and the artistic fours, a page of that slipped into a pocket would baffle mister plod. Then there's the book of matches, with several strands missing, which I lifted from a café in the Pantiles on a day trip to Tunbridge Wells. Or how about that German bitch, Frau Guttenburger, whose bed and breakfast was a hoard of material, with bins that overflowed with tissues and crumpled packets and empty bottles. It'd be nice to implicate her in some way. Some people don't even attempt to hide their thoughts, they wear their opinions blazoned straight across their faces. Like an open book. There for everybody to view. She was one of them. With her superior sneer and her impatience at even having to speak to me, even her stance was offensive, what with the way that she folded her arms every time I talked to her. If only she lived in England, I'd have some joy at squeezing the air out of her. Only sometimes I get to thinking that death is really not so bad, that it's like switching off a light, and that living is the real curse. Especially living with tragedy. What could be more tragic than having your husband arrested for murder? I pick up the bag at the back of the bench. Herr Guttenburger's pinky ring. I turn it in front of me. The gold band, with a ruby inset, looks dull in the half-light. I spotted it sitting next to the soap on the basin in the downstairs bathroom the day before we checked out. Now, every time I look at it, I imagine her face if the police were to show up. That would really be something.

After some thought, I abandon the idea. The thing with evidence is that I want to keep it twice removed, the tissues from the bed and breakfast are twice removed because they came from other guests staying in the house, therefore anyone trying to trace the person would have to link those guests to the bed and breakfast and then link the bed and breakfast to me, which is impossible. I'm only once removed from Herr Guttenburger. If he was on any database then he could be traced, the police would then use his records to trace anyone that had stayed at his inn, in particular they would look at English tourists, and my details would be amongst them. Twice removed is the key.

I put the bag down and begin to rethink.

My eyes wander over the other groups. Bank slips from cash points…, cigarette lighters… keys… used chewing gum… one group of bags draw my attention. The bags to the left of me. The top bag in particular. The day trip to London. The street vendor. The man with the clammy hands who worked at a greengrocers stall. The money, which is bound to have traces of fruit acid and dirt from his potatoes and maybe even traces of his sweat. Today he's probably sat with his family, or having lunch, or even down at the pub with his mates talking about football, or maybe he's even got a woman on the side and right now he's enjoying an afternoon with her. Then the police might trace him and suddenly he's a prime suspect and having to tell his wife and family where his Sunday afternoons are really taking place. All because of me. I cast my mind back to that day. I even struggled with my bags and got him to drop my change into my pocket so that I couldn't contaminate it. The man was ever so helpful and obliging.

My mind made up, I reach for the bag.

I open the seal and tip the coins onto a clean piece of paper. The coins which I select are a penny and a fifty pence piece. I use tweezers to pick them up and then transfer them into a new bag. I put the leftover coins into my pocket. I gather up the rest of the bags and put them back into their storage box, then replace the box onto the top shelf of the unit at the back of the shed and bring down a larger box next to it. I put the second box on the floor and empty the contents onto my workbench.

Jumpers. Trousers. Hats. Gloves. Jackets and boots. I've thought of it all. Eighteen months of shopping on the sly can add up to quite a collection. I started with a dozen sets of each item. And now I'm down to ten. So that's ten disguises left to do six murders. There's the hippy, the football fan, the golfer, the workman, the birdwatcher, the clubber, the dog owner, the beach bum, the tramp and the businessman. All of which are easily absorbed into everyday life. All of them barely noticeable in their right settings. Most of the clothes are from second hand shops and all of them are easy to get rid of afterwards. After each murder I dispose of my outfits in the Monday morning rubbish collection three streets away from my house, I pop them into a black bin liner with a whole load of other rubbish and then add it to the pile of other bags waiting there. Within half an hour the contents are mangled into the discarded waste of family life. My clothes, and the only thing that links me to any of the crimes, are shredded into an amalgamation of garbage from suburbia. A throw away society. Which includes my aliases. A fitting end to them, I tend to think.

I sit back in my chair.

I begin to sweat as ponder my next move. I pull out a tissue from my pocket and wipe my brow.

I think about location, I think about age group, I think about approach, I think about possible responses. I plan it all. What I'll say. How she'll react. Where we'll go. How it'll end.

Once I settle on a plausible scenario, I choose the appropriate items. The items I select are the thick brown woollen hat, a patterned jumper, some black cotton trousers, a long, dark overcoat, some brogues, some green gloves and a pair of socks.

I put the clothes into a plastic bag and then pack them into my holdall, along with the bag containing the coins. I take some scissors from the toolbox. I slip them out of their sheath and clean them with mentholated spirits and then pack them away again. Finally I check the blade of my penknife. I run my finger down the edge of the blade. The knife is as sharp as ever, having not been used. I give it a good hone anyway. Then put it into the holdall.

I'm all prepared for my next move.

"I've mowed the lawn and I've weeded the borders" I say to the figure in the high wing chair.

Mrs Gibson looks round, her stooped back straining to turn. As she twists, her blanket slips to her knees. Her fingers reach out and pull it up again. She tucks it back around her body and then looks at me again.

"You are good to me" she says.

I move round to the front of the chair, taking care to stand to the side of the fireplace so that I don't block the heat from the two electrical bars which are on full, even though it's a hot summer's day outside. "Someone has to look after you."

"I only wish I'd had a son like you," she whispers "the world needs more people like you."

"I'm flattered" I reply.

It's as I speak that Mrs Gibson's cat, Smoky, walks into the room. He slinks past me with his tail in the air and I bend to stroke him. Before my hand makes contact, he turns and hisses, arching his back and stretching his paw. His claws graze against my knuckles. I withdraw my hand quickly and stand up. I silently remind myself not to bother again. It's the same every time I get near him. I've long stopped wondering if Smoky has ESP, I don't think he can have otherwise he'd know that I'm not that bad really, that it's not all down to me.

"Ignore him" says Mrs Gibson, tapping her blanket to get his attention. "Naughty" she remonstrates, as he jumps onto her knee. But then she puts her hand down and strokes his back lovingly. He rolls over and exposes his belly. She rubs the tuft of fur below his chin and then rests her hand on his side. He curls up.

"Are there any more jobs that you want me to do?"

"No, you've done more than enough as it is" she replies, her dewy eyes watering as she looks up at me. "I was watching you as you mowed the lawn earlier, the garden looks much better now."

"I'm glad you think so."

"Have you locked everything up?" she asks.

"Yes" I say. "I've double locked the shed, no-ones going to get in there in a hurry."

"And the back door?"

"Yes, the back door too. I've put the chains on, I've locked the bolts and I've clicked the latch as well. You'd need a sledgehammer to get through that door."

"What about the side gate?"

"The side gate's secure."

"I worry" she says quietly.

I want to tell her that she needn't worry with me around because I've grown attached to her and if anyone tried to break into her home then they'd face the wrath of me. And I would truly make them suffer. I've come to enjoy my time with Mrs Gibson and its funny how you can make a connection with some people but not with others. I've made that connection with her. Although I don't know why, because when I think about it we're completely different, me being full of a hate which is so ingrained that it leads me to commit the most dreadful deeds, and her, well, the way I see it is that she's as pure and honest as a person can get. At other times I see it differently. Those times sadden me because I recognise myself in her. It's like looking at a mirror. And it's always the same thing that gets reflected back. Loneliness. I've got a wife, I've got a job, and I've got my time here, but deep down it doesn't sustain me, there's an eerie echo, a hollow, deep at the heart of me. Somehow nothing gives me satisfaction anymore. That's the truth of it.

"You shouldn't worry in a house like yours" I say, sitting down on the sofa and giving her the only thing I can; giving her my time, "I bet Colditz had less security than this place."

"You can't be too careful these days, the world isn't what it was" she responds, shaking her mop of hair and pulling her blue cardigan together, wrapping it around her chest, "I don't know what's become of the youth of today, they loiter in the street, they make a noise, they don't go out to work, and their families have no control over them. They intimidate me."

"Different times" I tell her.

"It's different alright" she replies dismally. "In my day these things wouldn't happen."

"Things?" I ask

"Terrible things" she says. "On the news and in the papers. Terrible."

Mrs Gibson slumps in her chair. Her hands drop and come to a rest on the arms of the seat. Her fingers, with their paper thin skin, tremor softly from the exertion of having closed her cardigan.

"I'm sure that they exaggerate these things when they report them."

"No" she counters "it's out there. It wouldn't have happened in my day, in my day people were more considerate, the children were chastised, they were brought up to behave themselves, it was the libertarians in the sixties that ruined it, they came along and convinced the parents to let their children do as they pleased and now look at what we've got."

"I agree."

"With each generation they get worse. I pity you for when you're my age." She coughs and then covers her mouth with her handkerchief as she splutters, it's a rickety feeble cough which rattles her frail body and seems to be bigger than her. The noise which fills the room is both pitiful and sad. Finally she dislodges the cause of her irritation. She spits into the cloth whilst pretending to blow her nose, and then dabs her mouth. "People have no sense of decency anymore," she says "no sense of right and wrong, not like us. The world is out of control."

"It's all changed."

"Everything changes, but that's no excuse for the bad things that happen, the people of my generation went through the war, through real hardship, many people died for this country, many more were injured, but it didn't turn us into criminals, it didn't stop us from being good citizens."

"You're right."

And when I say it, I mean it. Everything she says makes sense. Until I step out of the front door that is. It's only when I'm not in her company that I change and the other side takes me over. Away from her presence, that other side of me exposes my weaknesses, and then justifies my actions. It takes over and changes who I am, or who I think I am. It swamps my reason and possesses me. It tells me that I can't stop now. That it's too late. That if I were to stop now then the first two murders would've been in vain. It tells me that, unless I complete what I set out to do, then I shouldn't have started killing in the first place. That I have to see it out no matter what. That the woman before me won't be around forever. Nobody lives forever. All we can do is make the best of what we've got. Before it's too late.

"It makes me sad to see how everything has slipped away, our morals, our standards, even our neighbourhoods, hardly anyone attends church these days and family life is changing, the social fabric of society is crumbling away. These were the very things that kept us respectful and kept us righteous and they are the things that are being lost. I worry, I worry so much that I have trouble sleeping at night."

"Have you spoken to your doctor about it?"

"There's nothing my doctor can do," she responds solemnly "I can't sleep through fear. I lie awake in bed at night worrying about whether I'm safe or whether someone's going to break in."

"The doctor might be able to give you some sleeping pills."

"I don't want to take any more tablets, I take so many that I rattle, and anyway sleeping tablets are no use, if I were to take them and someone did break in, then I might not hear them until it's too late."

"But, if it were to happen, you might be better off sleeping through."

"At one point that might have been true," she says, "but not any more. They don't just come to take what they can carry anymore. The nights are bad when you get to my age." Smoky stirs on her lap. She puts her hand on his back and gently massages him back to sleep.

"I could put some more locks on the doors, if it helps."

"No. Any more and I'll be trapped. I have enough trouble trying to open the ones that are already there. It's a fine balance between security and prison."

She smiles at the thought of it. We both smile.

"Probably not one of my better ideas."

"No" she agrees.

"It can't be easy though."

"It's not."

I lean across but Smoky opens his eyes and looks up. I stop myself from patting her hand and move back again.

"You know that you can always phone me, day or night, it doesn't matter what time. I'm always at the end of the phone if you have any worries" I tell her.

"That's good of you to say, because I have a favour to ask" she says, leaning across to her side table and shuffling through the papers until she finds what she is looking for. She pulls it out. "I've been given a lifeline" she explains, showing me a small box which is connected to a loop of string. I take a look at it; on one side is a red button.

"What's that then?" I query.

"It's an operator service for old people like me, in case I can't get to the phone" she says, as she turns it around and points to the button. "If I press this button, it connects to an operator and I'm able to talk to them, it's a bit like a walkie-talkie. Then, if I need help, they'll either send someone round to check on me or contact someone I know. Mike and Tracy next door hold a key and they've said that they don't mind being contacted but I need to give them another number in case they're away on holiday. And as you hold a key…"

"Sure" I say, "put me down."

"Thank you."

"Don't be silly, you don't have to thank me" I say, reaching over and taking the box. I take a good look at it. "When did you get it?"

"Last week. Anne, my home help, arranged it for me because she's worried about my arthritis. It's been getting worse, especially in my left hand as that was my pearl hand. She said that I should have something in case I have an accident and I'm not able to make it to the phone."

"Well then" I say, "what are you worrying for?"

"I'm supposed to wear it around my neck but I don't like to because I'm scared of knocking it. I've already hit the button twice accidentally."

Mrs Gibson laughs. And I do too. But all the while my eyes are drawn to the button. It reminds me of how fragile she is. And how little time I have. Of how little time we all have.

"The operator probably thinks I'm senile" she chuckles.

I continue to laugh. But behind my laughter there's concern. I only ever have one worry. That is if Mrs Gibson was to die. I don't worry that someone might come along to clear out her shed, the items have no true meaning to anyone else, they're just the type of strange hoardings that most old people have, especially Mrs Gibson. Nor do I worry that I'd lose my collections, I'd just start again. What really worries me is that Mrs Gibson thinks I'm a nice person. She thinks I've got a good heart. If she were to die, then she might end up out there, somewhere, and able to look down on me. Then she'd know that I'm not the person she thought I was. And even if I were to stop my murders, if she did die, it'd be no good, she might be upstairs in the clouds and be able to read my mind. I can escape the murders, but I cannot stop my thoughts. Mrs Gibson's mortality concerns me and for a murderer that's not a good thing.

"Put it on" I insist, holding it out to her.

"But…"

"I'm sure the operator is used to accidents and you'll have to get used to wearing it."

"It's reassuring to have" she says, slipping the string over her head, "even if it's a bit cumbersome."

"Still, if it's there to protect you."

"Precisely."

The room falls silent. It's a comfortable silence, there's no strained atmosphere here, there's no tension and no pressure to be polite. I can either speak. Or not. I'm not expected to put on a performance at this address. She fiddles with the string around her neck, adjusting the line of the box. My eyes flick over to the television, even though it's switched off. Smoky purrs softly. The bars of the electric heater turn deep orange again.

"I'm going to have to go soon" I say reluctantly.

"Maureen?" she queries with understanding.

"She'll be expecting me."

"Of course."

I stand and stretch. "I don't want to leave."

"Nonsense" she replies.

"I really mean it" I say.

"I know."

But she has no idea.

"Right then" I mutter, spurring myself on. I walk to the door, reach for the handle, and then hesitate. "I might pop in after work one night next week if that's alright with you, the apple tree needs trimming and I didn't get round to it today."

"You've got the key."

I pat my pocket. "Yes."

"Well then…"

I open the door and walk into the hall. I pick up my jacket from the coat rack. Once I've slipped it on, I pop my head back round the door.

"I'm going now. Take it easy and don't go worrying about anything, you've got your lifeline, focus on that, at least help is at hand if you need it so don't be afraid to use it. You can always phone me if you're worried about anything."

"Thank you."

"Bye then."

"See you soon" she replies.

I swing the door to, to keep her heat in and turn to leave. It's as I pick up my holdall, which is waiting at the bottom of the stairs, that I hear her speak.

"I don't know what I'd do without you" says the voice from the lounge, all quiet and lonely.

I walk to the door, slip the lock and swing the door open. "Me too" I say, as I step out into the bright afternoon sunshine.

Chapter 7

I flip the newspaper open and move from page to page until I find what I've been looking for, the article is on the sixth page and I feel disappointed. It is tucked under an item about the state of the stock market and the need for workers to make extra provisions for their old age, the latter article taking up double the space of the former.

The photograph of her was obviously taken years before and in it she looks youthful and slimmer, her hair is darker, and her face heavily made up. Her head is tilted in the style of pose which you'd get at a photographic studio. The headline states, WOMAN STRANGLED. The report underneath goes on to say that a murder hunt has begun, that her body was found hidden in undergrowth one day after her husband reported her missing, that her name was Nancy Miller, she was 36, she was the mother of two children, a girl of eight and a boy of fourteen, and that she was strangled. It goes on to report that she went missing whilst taking a short cut home after visiting her parents and that her body was found shortly before police planned to make a major missing persons appeal. It concludes that the police are appealing for anybody in the vicinity of Dinton Pastures near Hurst on the 26th July to get in touch.

I close the paper and drop it onto the coffee stained table in front.

"Anything interesting?" asks my workmate Harry.

"Nothing much" I reply, pushing it towards him, "just an article about pensions."

"Don't speak to me about bloody pensions, that's all I need at the moment" he snaps. He scratches his head and yawns, which is what he always does when he's stressed. He seems to get a restriction of oxygen that leads him to yawn. Working alongside him for the past sixteen years is similar to my marriage. I know him like a wife. I know all his habits. And all his quirks. And I know what's sucking the air out of him at the moment. His divorce. It's draining him. Which in turn is making him yawn far more frequently. Anyone around him can see the impact it's had. The man in front of me has turned from an arrogant, self-assured, bloke to a bitter grey, overnight. I reckon that it's down to the bloody solicitor's taking their time and taking their whack to boot. I've a good mind to make his solicitor my next victim. Or his wife for that matter. But Harry wouldn't thank me for it. Because deep down he doesn't want the divorce. Yet all the time he's going along with it just to keep Sheila happy. He's giving her the house and a chunk of his salary. But her lawyers aren't content to leave it at that. They want to rake over his pension. They want to get each and every penny they can and they want to play it out for as long as possible. For as long as their hourly rate stays up in the clouds, they're prepared to convince Sheila that she's entitled to far more than she was ever worth. All because she had children. She gets the lot, whilst Harry, who's worked the long hours, Harry, who's done the overtime, and Harry, who's grafted like a dog, stands to lose it all. You can guarantee that if the lawyers weren't on such a high rate, if they worked for a fixed fee, then they wouldn't behave the way they do.

Harry picks up the lid to his lunchbox, seals his sandwiches back into their container, and then bashes down the lid.

Bob looks up from his Pot Noodle.

"I've heard rumours that our pension fund is being closed" he says.

"What does that mean?" asks Harry anxiously.

Bob smiles in a way that only he can, he's a regular wind up merchant and everybody knows it, but poor old Harry falls for it every time.

"It means that anyone who joins the company in future won't be able to join the pension scheme" he says, with a satisfied smirk, "but it won't affect us."

Harry sighs with relief. He pushes his box of sandwiches towards the centre of the table.

"No, it won't affect us" says Keith the union rep sarcastically, walking across and sitting down next to Harry, "but the way that the government have raped our pension funds with their tax raids means that they'll be worth fuck all anyway."

"Fuck off, Keith" says Bob.

Keith smiles smarmily. "There's no need for it, Bob" he replies smugly.

Bob scowls but says no more, he knows when he's beat, he's the master of the pecking order. He gets up from his seat, leans over the table, grabs the newspaper, and then heads off to the toilet block.

Keith picks up the sandwich box from the middle of the table, which is the only reason for his presence anyway, and lifts the lid. "These going?" he asks.

Harry nods and he claims ownership by prodding every sandwich with his dirty oversized fingers before settling for the top one.

"I've heard that if the company goes bust, there's a real chance the pension fund will only pay out to the people who've already retired" says Mick.

"Bollocks" retorts Jeff angrily.

"No, it's true," Mick insists "that's the way it works. There was that steel company which folded over in Wales, the ones that were still working when it went under ended up losing their pensions but the ones who'd already retired got to keep theirs."

"Are you sure?" asks Harry.

"Yeah, of course I'm sure" says Mick "my brother-in-law in Port Talbot knows one of the guys who used to work there, he plays five-a-side with him twice a week. He said that some of them were left with fuck all because their fund had a black hole in its finances, it only had enough money to pay for the people that had already retired and the rest never got a thing. They lost out completely. Imagine that?"

"Surely they can't do that if a person's paid into it, surely everyone would get a proper cut?" says Jeff

"They can't if there's no money left to pay them with" Mick replies.

"That can't be right" retorts Harry, his brow furrowing "they'd have to divvy out what's left in the fund to everyone equally, wouldn't they?"

"No" says Mick, opening some crisps and spilling them across the table, "it doesn't work like that, most of the ones that had already retired were guaranteed their money because they'd already transferred their pension into an annuity and so their money was ring fenced. Then there were the ones that took a lump sum when they retired, you can't claw that back. It's the ones that were still working that have lost out. Some of those blokes paid in for twenty odd years and ended up with peanuts. I wouldn't be happy if that happened to me."

"Me neither."

"The government have got a compensation scheme, haven't they?" asks Jeff, turning to Keith.

"Not really" Keith replies. "The government have said that they're going to do something, but they won't say anymore than that. It's just talk"

"What d'ya mean?" asks Harry.

"I mean that the compensation scheme would be alright if it was just one or two companies going bust, but the way our country's going, these companies are falling like flies. They just don't have the money to compensate them all. Even if they were to take the issue seriously, they know that if they start to pay out properly, it'll only encourage more companies to take that route and fold. The government won't do anything about it because they can't afford to."

"But they are doing something? They are addressing the situation, aren't they?"

"Not really. I personally don't think that it'll add up to anything. It's alright as a piece of political rhetoric but it isn't much more than that."

"How's this pension problem come about then, Keith?"

"Economics mate, simple as that" says Keith, picking up another sandwich "it's because people are retiring early and living longer, these schemes weren't devised to pay for people to take retirement at fifty and then live another thirty years, the funds can't cope with it, not now there's less workers putting in. The global economy isn't helping much either, not with all the jobs going abroad. Even the common market isn't going to get us out of that" he mumbles, stuffing the sandwich into his mouth.

"Thatcher signed us up to the common market" says Jeff bitterly.

"Actually it was Heath" says Keith, through a mouthful of crust, "and if you're gonna blame him, you might as well blame the Wright brothers."

"How do you work that one out?" asks Harry.

"Simple" says Keith, "they're the ones that invented flying, aren't they? The global economy is all about transport, the world's a smaller place now. Why have some tosser in a factory in England handcraft a table when you can get the same thing for a tenth of the price from someone in Thailand and you can get it shipped over in a day with international post. That international parcel takes some beating, they can deliver quicker than the Royal Mail these days, ask my missus she does Ebay."

Mick burps loudly to register his opinion. Everyone ignores him.

"I've heard they're closing Ayrshire at the end of the month" says Pete, grabbing a vacant seat and then leaning over to take a crisp.

"Ayrshire is unproductive" says Mick, slapping his hand away.

"No more than here" says Pete, managing to palm a few.

"Of course it is!" Mick snaps back. "It's all about communications. The communication network up that way is poor, it adds on extra charges to the cost of transport. That's what makes it unproductive. We're bang on the M40 which makes us accessible. It was bound to happen sooner or later."

"Location makes no difference anymore" says Keith, pushing the empty sandwich box back to Harry, "we're competing against third world countries like Romania and all the other former eastern block countries now that they've been let into the E.U. The next thing you know the bastards at the top will be moving the plant to a country with less regulations and smaller wage bills to ours. I tell you, Ayrshire's just the start."

Harry scratches the bald spot on his head and then yawns again.

"You're the union rep" says Mick snapping at Keith "can't you do something about it?"

"There's fuck all the unions can do," Keith replies "we just don't have any clout any more. We can represent the workers at tribunals and sort out maternity pay, but we can't stop the management from destroying the company. There's nowt we can do if they want to move the company abroad."

"It's not right" says Jeff.

"No it's not," Keith agrees "but that's just the way it is."

"It's not ethical" says Mick.

"No, its not," Keith replies, "but what's ethical about third world countries? What's ethical about the kids out there, them ones that are starving?"

"What's ethical about my kids starving?" Mick retorts.

Keith doesn't reply. Although he could, Keith could have an answer for everything if he wanted. Instead he gets up, pats the mug in his hand and walks off to the coffee machine.

"Look" I say, to the group around the table "there's no point in worrying about it until it happens."

"It's alright for you" Mike snaps, turning on me angrily "you get on with your wife, you've got a nice house and you've got no kids to pay for. The fucking kids these days cost an arm and a leg," he says bitterly "you don't know the half of it."

But I understand only too well. Job insecurity. Bills to pay. House with a mortgage. Wife with a tendency to stifle. Only it's not the type of details I want to share with my work colleagues. I get up and join Keith at the coffee machine. While behind me the conversation continues. And has done for the past two years when an American company took us over and handed out redundancy notices to one third of the workforce. Within weeks of them taking over, our engineering firm, John Cooper & Sons, was melted into a mini version of the previous company. More productive, said the management, when what they really meant was more work for the same pay. And instead of assembling fifty components a day they required seventy. Now the fear of unemployment is the only topic of conversation in these walls. And at forty three I wonder where my future holds. Back at the table, Harry has the look of a man that hasn't slept in a year. He wears the look of defeat as if he were born with it. Right now I could pat him on the back and move him to the side, well away from all the others, and let him in on my secret. I could tell him that he needn't settle for a divorce, that I could take care of things and make it look like an accident even, I needn't even connect it to the other women, I could make it look like another random killing, because it really wouldn't bother me if I added Sheila to my list, in fact in some ways I'd be happy to do it. Only I know Harry and there's no way he'd take up my offer, he'd rather hang on in to the bitter end. He'll hang on in there waiting for Sheila to change her mind because he can't see it. Sheila won't have him back. Not in a million years. Why should she when she'll end up with the lions share? She'll be a damn sight more comfortable than him in old age, that's for sure.

Harry gets up and walks across to me. "Are you coming back?" he asks.

"In a minute."

"Suit yourself" he shrugs. He turns and walks back to the shop floor alone.

I hold the chipped cup with the dirty brown liquid for a few seconds longer but the atmosphere in the canteen is stifling. The temporary employees all sit around dolefully, checking their watches with miserable consistency, all wanting to get back to work to show how efficient they are so that when any vacancies do arise they'll be first in line to fill them. The long term employees are even more morose, each wanting to slip on the floor and hurt their back, or get slandered by the management and be able to sue for compensation, anything, any excuse to get them out of these walls without having to worry about the bills for a while. A job for life that's what a lot of us believed in when we joined the company. That's what we'd been brought up to believe. It's what our parents had so why should we have thought it would be any different. I went to work thinking that that's where I'd stay for my working lifetime. That I'd work until retirement and collect a gold watch in the process. I thought I'd see my days out in a house without a mortgage, with the addition of a lump sum bonus left over after my endowment matured. My private and state pension would fund a nice and cosy lifestyle and I would lead a stress free enjoyable twilight. I joined the company as an apprentice at the age of sixteen and worked alongside Albert Finnegan who'd been at the company for over forty years. I aspired to be no more than the gammy-toothed, wily old man who gave me my grounding. The eighties came and changed it all. Now each decade erodes the history of the company and replaces it with what the management is prone to calling modernisation. Now nothing is safe anymore. And no one is secure. And for all that grafting, I'm left in a hole. The endowment with a shortfall. The house which has been repeatedly re-mortgaged to keep the bills paid, and the pension which is looking increasingly vulnerable as each year passes. To cap it all there's talk of redundancies again. And that the pension pot might not have enough funds to support us. Just when you think that it can't get any worse they mention that the age of retirement will have to increase and that men in my age bracket are going to be working until we're seventy. Well thanks for that Mister Prime Minister but I might have to make my own arrangements.

Mick and Jeff continue to argue their point about the role of the unions but I've stopped listening. I've got other things to think about. Other things such as my outfit which is sitting in the boot of my car in the car park outside waiting to be used. I'm pretty sure that I wouldn't have turned into the person I am today if the financial net wasn't closing in. I'm sure that if I had more to lose then I wouldn't risk it. But I've done my calculations and no matter which way I look at it, it all adds up to nothing. I've got nothing to lose and everything to gain from doing what I'm doing. Death equals a life for me. Simple isn't it.

I take a few sips of the murky coffee but it tastes unappealing. The time on the clock above the coffee machine signals that our lunch hour is nearly over. Several people stand up together.

"Can't wait for the football season to start again" says Keith.

"I know what you mean mate" I mutter.

"At least it'll give those fuckers something better to talk about" he says, nodding towards the table.

"Argue about, more likely."

"Yeah."

I put my cup down onto the side. "Coming?" I ask.

"Yeah."

We make our way back to the shop floor. As we do, we pass the table where Mick and Jeff continue to debate with increasing animosity. On the next table, we past two young contractors, one is offering his open cigarette packet to the other. As I walk by, I can't help but stare at them. There they are, two spotty teenagers slouching around without a care in the world, lighting cigarettes as if they've got all the time going. Two lads, who probably live at home and who haven't taken on any financial responsibilities yet. Two lads, who don't want to work and who live each day as it comes. A tinge of bitterness creeps in as I pass by.

I enter the shop floor with predictability.

And take my place alongside Harry.

Chapter 8

Killing is a funny thing. Like when someone is dead, then they are dead. But it's never as simple as that. It seems that there are different levels of murder. There's gory murder, there's mass murder, there's crimes of passion and there's gangland reprisals. All different. Then there's murder on a particular day, like Christmas Day or New Year's Day or an anniversary or a birthday, which makes it less tolerable. Different circumstances all go to add a different emphasis to each killing. Some are more acceptable, some are less. Some happen with the minimum of attention, without people being aware of it, whilst some draw huge publicity, usually because the victim is less acceptable, like a child, or someone famous. Then there's another interesting category. There's daytime murder and night-time murder. Different.

My first two victims were struck in broad daylight making it easy. People feel safer during the day and they're less guarded. They expect the light sky to protect them and the last thing they expect is for me to be waiting for them. Which is fine by me. People are seldom noticed missing during the day, which gives me extra time too. It's only when darkness falls that people become guarded and they notice more. It's only then that they expect the bogey man to strike. Newspapers place less significance on daytime murders too, as if daytime murders are less gruesome. Unless it's a really brutal killing, of course. People assume that a murder during the day is connected to someone the victim knows, like a husband or a lover, a loss of control rather than an indiscriminate attack by a stranger. And so the myth continues. While it helped with my first two crimes, I've recently begun to rethink my plans. This time I want it to be different, I've become impatient, I've decided that it's time to let them know that I'm out there, and for the game to begin. In future, I don't want buried news, I want front page. This time I want their attention.

One hundred yards in front, on the opposite side of the road, the girl steps out into the night. She exit's the neon lit building, turns right, and then gets quickly into her stride. Behind her, the foyer lights dim. She is short and petite with mousy brown hair. The clothes that she wears are a uniform, which consist of a white blouse with a navy blue waistcoat and a navy blue skirt to match. Her tights are the colour of American tan and her shoes are open toed sandals with a small heel. Age? I'd guess at early twenties but who knows with women these days, some look older, and some younger, what with make up and clothes and even cosmetic surgery, it all goes to confuse me. I'd put her at early twenties anyway. I watch her leave the bingo hall alone, and then take the first turning on the left, Willows Avenue, just as she has done on the previous three weeks.

When she's out of sight, I reach for the ignition.

The engine purrs into life.

I steer my car out into road. And then drive to Millbrook Avenue.

I have pre-planned my actions, I know all the CCTV cameras in the area, on the streets, in the shops, at the petrol station. Modern technology throws up a minefield of issues, but none which can't be worked around. An extra two minute journey is all it takes to remain concealed.

Millbrook Avenue is one block away from the local theatre, at this time of night the local performance has yet to conclude, and is used to having non-residents cars parked along it, which is why I picked it. To the left, a brick wall runs the length of the street; it is ten feet high and surrounds the local cricket club. To the right, several blocks of purpose built flats stand away from the road. I look for a place to park on the left hand side so that my car won't be overlooked.

Halfway down the street, in the shadow of an old oak tree, I find the perfect spot.

I park. And glance at my watch. The time is exactly as it should be.

I pull on my gloves and slip on my hat. My finishing touch is to wipe some dust off the dashboard and smear it across my face.

I climb out of the car and begin to walk.

I walk the next three blocks, staying in residential areas.

I reach my destination with twenty seconds to spare.

I loiter in the doorway of a small lock-up garage, being careful to stay in the shadows. Then wait. The night is quiet, apart from some thin music coming from a house down the street. Other than that there is nothing else to be heard. Nothing, but the sound of my breathing. Soft and misty. Measured. And paced. As I hold myself in check. Counting off the seconds.

The girl's shoes announce her impending arrival. Clipping along the pavement. Striding quickly through the darkening night. One heel slightly louder than the other. The noise rushing along to greet me. The girl hastily eager to get to where she is going.

I peer round the edge of the brickwork. And watch as she comes into view.

Her brown hair bounces in time to her step as her arms swing loosely. Her face is brave and unperturbed by the darkening sky. She walks along the opposite side of the pavement. Her destination, ten feet and closing.

She focuses ahead, watching the route she intends to take. Unaware that I'm in the shadows. Expecting her.

I wait until she passes. And then quickly skip across the road. She turns as she hears me coming. I am upon her before she can react.

"This is a robbery…" I say, grabbing hold of her arm, "…I'm tooled up, so just keep walking. Keep your eyes looking ahead and don't, whatever you do, look at me."

The girl's shoes lose their rhythm for a couple of steps. Her heels scrape along the pavement as she adjusts to the shock of what has happened. A gasp escapes from her lips.

"What…?" she questions.

"Keep walking" I hiss.

But she hesitates.

"Keep walking" I repeat menacingly, my voice ever more threatening.

The girl falls back into pattern and into step alongside me.

"Where are we going?"

"Down the road."

"What do you want?"

"Money."

"I haven't got any."

"I'd like to check for myself, if you don't mind."

A few metres down the road, she instinctively turns to look.

"Look ahead" I growl.

She does as she is told.

My eyes leave the road for a couple of seconds as I turn and take a good look at her. Her face in shock and has drained of colour, it has turned to a white so pale it is almost ghostlike in the moonlit night. She stares ahead, blinking rapidly as she tries to control the tears which threaten to build in her eyes. Her nostrils flare. Her jaw is locked tight.

I hazard a guess at what she's thinking now. Maybe she got a good look at me and is trying to remember every detail for when she intends to relay the events to others later on. Or maybe she's wondering what's in store for her and what I'm going to do to her. Maybe she's forming a plan of how to react. But before I can get right into her mind to gauge her properly, which is what I like to do in order to keep control of events, she makes her move.

"Here, take my bag" she says, shrugging the strap off her shoulder and thrusting it towards me. It hits me in the stomach before I can stop her but I don't let it distract me. I keep a firm grip on her arm. As long as I've got hold of her, she's not going anywhere.

"Not here" I snarl, pushing the bag back, "let's go down to the viaduct and you can give it me there."

The girls face twists into dismay as she realises she's not getting away that easily.

"I don't live that way" she says.

"Think of it as a detour" I retort.

I keep her moving, walking by wrought iron gates and pathways

57

that break the distance to doors that block, within yards of people's living rooms.

"Just take it" she pleads, holding out the bag.

We're both aware of the point which we're reaching; the row of houses which we're walking past is the last one before the junction ahead. Beyond that, the road begins its descent down towards the common and the viaduct at the bottom. All that lies ahead are fields and a rusty old fence which barely keeps the nettles at bay. I know that after this point I'm safe. She knows that she's not. She slows down.

"Please" she begs. I ignore her cheap plastic offering and drag her forward.

"Wait until we get out of view."

"No one can see us."

"You don't know that."

"But I do" she says, looking around.

"You didn't see me earlier on, did you?"

We cross the last junction and start our descent. My hand still gripping her arm, I start to feel her tense. The muscles in her upper arm begin to swell and I know exactly what she's about to do before she does it.

When she starts to move, I'm ready for her. She is barely one pace in front before I dig my fingers into her arm, squeezing real tight, twisting her shoulder forward and stopping her in her tracks. I swing my other hand across my body, bringing with it the contents of my pocket. I push the lining into the side of her stomach just below her ribs. And there can be no doubt. The gun in my pocket is loaded with pellets. But it looks and feels like the real thing. And it can do as much damage on a soft target. Like flesh.

"Don't be silly" I say "it isn't worth it."

She recoils from the barrels in horror and looks up at me with her eyes wide with terror as she realises what it is.

"Why?" she asks, her voice wavering.

"We're nearly there" I respond coolly.

I let go of her and push her in front, feeling confident enough to know that she won't make a run for it now.

She looks back at me, the agony of her expression caught in the amber haze of a streetlight.

"I've got a credit card on me, I'm happy to give you my pin number" she cries. "If you take me to the cash point…"

"You're not going to stop, are you?" I snap.

"Stop?" she cries.

"Stop talking" I shout meanly. "You're not going to stop talking, are you?"

She shudders.

"Sorry" she says her voice barely a whisper. I walk forward.

"Are all you women born with a talking gene?" I ask bitterly.

Her face crumples. A tear escapes and slips down her face. She wipes it away, only for another one to appear.

"Don't start that" I moan "don't even think about crying. I can't stand it when women cry."

"Sorry" she repeats.

I walk up to her and grab her arm.

"We're nearly there" I say, cooling down and realising that I'm taking my frustrations with Maureen out on her. Her talking was reminding me of being at home. She was starting to grate though. "All I want is for us to walk down to the bottom so that we can find somewhere where we can't be seen, I want some time to look through your bag and then I want time to get away. I'll make it quick, and then all this'll be forgotten about in the morning."

"There's nobody here" she says.

She's right of course, there isn't anyone around, we've nearly reached the bottom of the hill and the surrounding area is quiet. The common is a barren intersection between a council estate and the private houses that we passed a few moments ago. The viaduct cuts through the middle, separating the rich from the poor. It's a place where few people bother to cross the divide. But this is the route she'd be taking anyway. I know because, unbeknown to her, I've followed her home on several occasions.

"Look" I say, switching up a gear, "I wouldn't do this if I wasn't desperate, I'm on the streets, I've got no money and no job, I've got nowhere to live and nothing to eat. I'm genuinely sorry to do this to you but I've got no choice."

The girl dares to look at me and notices the pieces of green cord that hold my shoes together. She sees my polyester trousers, which are in need of a good iron, and my chunky knitted jumper with the snags on the front. She stares at the stains on the front of my coat.

"You could find yourself a job," she says, daring to challenge me.

"It's not that simple."

"Is it easier to rob someone then?"

"Not at all" I reply. "This is the last thing I want."

"Then why don't you go out to work like normal people?"

I sigh ruefully, as if I've heard this a thousand times before.

"I need somewhere to live in order to get a job and I need to get a job in order to pay for somewhere to live... my life isn't easy... and doing this isn't easy... do you think I'd live like this if I had a choice?"

"Everyone has a choice" she replies.

I hear her words. They impact on me.

"You've no idea what my life is like" I say, in a moment of brutal honestly, "you haven't got a clue of what it's like for me, you're young and you don't understand how hard life can be. The older you get, the harder it is..."

My words silence her. Or maybe it's the viaduct directly in front of us. She stares up at it, taking in the expanse of the structure. Only, the expression of her face has changed. It's become hard and bitter and angry.

I stop myself from feeling provoked at her attitude, I'm too big a person to let her upset me, but the sympathy I had for her only a few seconds ago has dissipated into the most awful thoughts. Now I know that she's dead. Not that there was any other outcome, it's just that now my incentive is there, brewing beneath the surface, ready to do what I've brought her here for.

I revert to lying. It's her fault that I do. "You don't know what it's like out there... its hard... life is hard... being on the streets is bloody difficult, I can tell you..."

All the while we're having this conversation, we walk on.

"...I'm in a catch 22 situation, it's as simple as that, no job means no house, and no house and no fixed address means no job… that's what my life is all about… you'll go on to the comfort of your home tonight… but me…"

The girl accepts what I tell her without further comment. But there's still the lingering indignation in her eyes. And there's still the rumble under my skin where she's irritated me. We reach the viaduct without anyone, or any cars, passing us by.

I move her towards a wire mesh fence which cordons off the grassy verge and leads up to the railway line and then point to the hole that I cut into it the day before. "Look, here's a gap in the fence, we'll just go inside here so that no one will see us"

"But…"

"You go first."

She pauses long enough to consider the gun thrust towards her, and then climbs through. I follow. Once through, the area is overgrown with bushes and shrubs, between them a dirt track snakes upwards. I steer her up the pathway to the side of one of the tall supports. I pick my spot carefully and then bring her to a halt. "This'll do," I say "give me your phone and your purse and I'll let you go."

Her reaction is one of surprise and she quickly opens her bag. It's as she bends her head that I strike. When she least expects it. I circle my hands around her neck. And squeeze. Her bag drops to the floor, sending the contents scattering, as she looks up at me in horror. It's all there to see, it's painted onto her youthful face, the expression which speaks for itself, she realises that I've lied, that she's not here to give me some bits from her bag. The look that conveys how young, and naïve, and gullible she is. The look that says she would've stood a better chance against the gun earlier on. And why, oh why, didn't she just take the chance, why didn't she make a run for it when she had the opportunity. She's so scared that she doesn't resist. Gone are her sarcastic responses, gone is her voice and her questions and her opinions, she is mute now, mute apart from the gurgling noises. I grip her neck so forcefully that it lifts her clean off the floor.

It's then that I'm aware of the trickling noise.

The water splatters gently onto the ground. And then begins to flow more fully. A sweet smell rises to my nostrils. I recognise it, it's the combination of the mildest scent of coffee mixed with a sweetly sugary aroma. The smell of urine. It splashes beneath us. Droplets bounce against my trousers and shoes. I don't let it distract me.

She starts to struggle. It's all a bit pointless. I tell her so.

"It's pointless you struggling darling" I say.

Eventually the energy drains from her body, the gurgling recedes, and she becomes heavy.

I drop her onto the floor and lean over her and continue to squeeze until I am sure. When she is dead, I reach into the inside pocket of my coat for my scissors and take them out, then start to cut. Her cotton work blouse, with the full house motif on her breast pocket, cuts easily. A cream padded bra waits underneath. I snip through the centre. Her bra falls aside, exposing her underdeveloped chest with her pimply nipples. I move on. I pull her skirt over her waist and then pull her tights down, avoiding the sodden patch in the middle. Her knickers remain in place. They are cumbersome cotton floral knickers, the sort that anyone with a boyfriend would be disinclined to wear. I cut either side of them at the hips and flap the material over her thighs. Her pubic hair is thin and downy, a lighter ginger colour to the auburn hair of her head. I bet myself that she's still a virgin. But I don't have the time, or the inclination, to check. The clock is ticking.

I check my watch. Maureen always gets home from visiting her sister at ten forty-five promptly. It leaves me with half an hour to finish off, get changed and get home before her.

I reach into my pocket and pull out the bag of DNA.

I tip the bag to the side of her. Two coins drop and roll off before landing nearby. Finally, I put the rosary beads in place.

I leave the scene less than five minutes after entering it.

And melt into the shadows.

Chapter 9

'Good evening and welcome to the main news this evening' says the newscaster. 'The body of a woman, thought to be that of the missing teenager Shania Jones, has been found less than one mile from where she was last seen alive. Shania went missing two days ago shortly after finishing work at the Full House bingo hall in High Wycombe and since then there have been emotional requests from her parents for Shania to get in touch, but early this morning brought the grim news that a body has been discovered nearby the route she would have taken home on the night she went missing. For the latest report we go to Gareth Edwards who is at the scene.'

'Thank you Hugh,' says the second reporter, holding up his microphone and looking directly into the camera, 'I'm at the scene in High Wycombe, less than two miles from the bingo hall where Shania worked and from where she was last sighted two days ago as she left work for her two mile journey home. I can tell you that the body of a woman was found early this morning on the embankment to the left of me. It was spotted by a man who formed part of a railway inspection team who were carrying out routine maintenance work up on the bridge behind me. As yet the body has not been identified and police are stressing to us that they are at a preliminary stage of their investigation but since the news of the discovery this morning, several developments have taken place.

It was just before seven o'clock this morning when the alarm was raised, shortly after that the police arrived and sealed off the area. At around 8am, a forensic team entered the scene to assist in a detailed search of the spot where the body was found, this has continued throughout the day. At the moment I can tell you that the body is still in place as scene of crime officers comb the nearby area to search the area and it won't be until these are completed that the body will be removed. A post mortem examination will take place after that to determine the identity of the body and establish the cause of death.

In a separate development, Detective Chief Inspector Wilson, who is the officer who has been liaising with Shania Jones's family, also paid a visit to the site earlier on today. He arrived at the scene at eleven o'clock this morning and stayed for approximately one hour. At the moment it is too soon to say whether the body discovered is that of Shania Jones but at the moment one can only feel that the omens are not looking good.'

'Thank you Gareth' says the newscaster at his desk, 'we are expecting a further update from the police within the next hour and if we get any more news during the programme we'll go back to it.'

"Terrible isn't it" sighs Maureen grimly, flicking the channel to another station to see if she can catch anymore news about the murder, "her poor family must be going through agony."

"She shouldn't have been walking home alone," I reply "a young girl like that, its asking for trouble being out that late at night all by herself."

Maureen bristles visibly at my comment. "It wasn't that late" she says indignantly "it was only after ten o'clock. Anyway, you shouldn't say things like that, it's bad luck to speak ill of the dead."

"If it is her" I say.

But I know that it is. I've followed the news since she disappeared and there's never been any doubt for me, she has been constantly in the news.

"If it was my daughter I wouldn't be letting her walk home at that time of night" I add.

"We don't have a daughter…" says Maureen, tossing an invisible grenade into the conversation, "…or a son."

"No, but if we had" I bat back, reminding her that it takes two to reproduce.

It's my turn to feel agitated now, I don't know how the woman opposite can blame me for our lack of offspring when she only ever let me touch her reluctantly, not that I want to do anything like that anymore. I'm long past finding Maureen desirable. No, the woman opposite me is the biggest dose of bromide I've ever seen. She's enough to turn any man impotent.

"We don't" she barks, getting the last word in on the subject.

I let her words linger in the air in silent protest.

Maureen flicks the channels aggressively. Brief pictures light up the screen and then disappear just as quickly. The Simpsons tune hits two notes before it is replaced. A quiz on BBC 2 vanishes in one syllable. ITV is into the adverts and back on BBC1 the newsreader is onto a story about the European Union. She settles on it just in case they go back to the main story. "It doesn't look too promising, judging from where the body's been found" she says.

"No."

"It was less than five miles away as well" she continues, wiping a piece of errant lint off her chair, "practically on our doorstep. It's frightening to think that there's been another murder so close to us. I've walked under that bridge many times." She puts the piece of lint into her pocket, and then places the remote control onto its designated shelf. "In fact, if you remember, that was the route we used to take when we were dating."

"I don't remember…"

"Sure you do" she interrupts, cutting me short, "we used to walk through there when we went to visit the social club in Finsbury Road."

"No, I still don't…"

"You do. It's at the bottom of the road we took on the way to the conservative club where my father was a member. He used to sign us in on a Friday night."

"I remember going to the conservative club, but I don't remember… wait a minute… it's coming back to me now, I'm starting to remember it, wasn't it off Willows Lane?"

"That's right," she says, clipping her tongue to accentuate the 'T' at the end of the word, "it was when we were first dating, before your family moved over to my side of town."

I look across at Maureen and despise her. Her predictability is flawless. I wondered when she'd have to bring that bit up. As soon as this conversation started, I mentally bet myself that she'd have to mention it somewhere. It, being the fact that I was born and brought up on a council estate. That I was the boy from the wrong side of town. Even now it remains part of her conversation. It's as if it's a part of her thoughts, as if I never quite made the grade. I've kept a roof over our heads, our fridge is always full and I've paid the bills on time. I've taken her out, she's had her holidays, and her jewellery box is adequately stocked. She's got a full wardrobe (of several sizes of clothes). And I've paid for all the things she desires. But I'm still the boy from the wrong side of town. "Of course it was" I seethe, through gritted teeth.

But she has lost interest. She's got her jibe in and is content to leave it at that. She looks at her watch. "Dinner is almost ready" she chimes.

On Maureen's orders the conversation ends. She walks into the kitchen, as regular as clockwork, at precisely twenty past six.

Her superiority at being born on the better part of town depresses me. When I first met her, I thought that I'd done well, that I'd met a woman of good standing and I could show my family and friends just how well I'd done. But it came at a price. It's a price which I've paid for the best part of my marriage. It leads me into a craziness that makes me kill. But Maureen is the real killer in this house. She suffocates. She spreads her control over everything. Even the oxygen in the air seems thin when she's around. The worse thing is that there's no decent escape. Not without penalties. Not without splitting the pension, and then dividing the house, not without giving, giving, and giving. I work and she doesn't, not really. Two half days a week in the local bakery is hardly a contribution to our finances. It's pocket money for her and nothing more. No. There's only one person in this household who keeps it all going. Me. I pay and I pay and I pay. And for that I have paid. All because I wanted to impress people. That's the price of self importance. It's the price of moving up in life. I know I'm being harsh as it was more than that at the beginning. Only, if I'm honest, it did play a significant role.

The serving hatch opens and Maureen leans through. "Switch it over to ITV," she requests loudly, "I want to see if anything else has been reported about the girl on the news."

I pick up the Clingfilm wrapped remote control and turn the channel over.

"And turn it up" she shouts.

I oblige.

When I first met Maureen she was without doubt, the most attractive woman that a man such as me could wish to meet, her hair was long and blonde, her body petite, her clothes were always neat and tidy, and she had a smile which could move me in a way that I'd never experienced before. But that was then, and this is now. And she has changed. And so have I. I share my house with a colostomy bag, which is an unfair thing to think, I know, because she doesn't look like a colostomy bag. But there's something about her which reminds me of one. For a long time now I've had these thoughts. For a long time I've been incapable of being in the company of Maureen and not making the connection. It lingers in the recesses of my mind whenever she's near. It eats away at my thoughts. I always thought that having a colostomy bag fitted is one of the saddest things that could happen to a person, but that was before I spent so long with Maureen. Now I can honestly say that I know what sadness really is.

AND she smells. No, she hasn't got a hygiene problem and there's no unpleasant aroma when I'm near her. But she radiates a disagreeable quality which I can only equate to the discomfort that you get when you smell something bad. I hate. That's why I kill. I kill because of Maureen.

"Dinners ready," she chirps, in a singsong voice from the kitchen, "sit at the table."

I stand up, switch the T.V. off, and then walk through the archway to take my place in the dining area. I've learnt to never pick up my plate from the serving hatch. I've learnt to let Maureen walk through from the kitchen and then pass the plates across. I suppose she has to do it to have a role in life, to justify all the money, MY money, which she frequently spends.

It's Thursday, which means steak and kidney pudding with chips and mushy peas for dinner. Maureen's menu is like everything else about her, it is organised. Organised to the point where she has a set dinner for every day of the week. Monday is lamb stew with dumpling, Tuesday is gammon with new potatoes, Wednesday's are set by for shepherds pie, Thursday is steak and kidney pudding, Friday is fish, of course, on Saturday we have lasagne and Sunday is roast beef. Save for our trips away, this is my life.

"The plate is hot" says Maureen, in a monotonous tone which has become bored from the years of repetition.

I sometimes think that Maureen lives like this on purpose so that I take her away more often. But that's wrong. She does it because it's her way of keeping everything neat. She likes to tie her life into structure. Her life is one of routine and organisation. Now boredom is feeding inside me like a parasite. Always there. Leeching. Sucking at my insides. An itch that wants to be scratched. A scream in the back of my throat that's waiting to be released. I want more out of life than I'm getting. And it's been like this for years. Only I didn't have a clue how to change things. Then one day I could stand it no more. That was it. I'd taken more than a man can handle. The barriers of self control began to slip. It was then that I began to think. The idea came to me shortly afterwards.

"Has there been any more about that girl who's been missing?" she asks, taking her place opposite me.

"No."

"Well, we can watch the news together later on" she says firmly.

I look across the table. Maureen cuts a small slice of the steak pudding and adds some chips onto her fork, finally she dunks the pudding and chips into the peas and slips it all into her mouth. The silence is taken up by the sound of her chewing. It's a sloppy, squelching sound which grates against the airwaves and scratches at my nervous system. I tense up.

She notices my reaction and stops eating. She covers her mouth with her hand, which allows her middle class manners to talk even when she has food in her mouth. "Aren't you hungry?" she asks.

I look at her. And hate.

"I was just thinking that we could do with a trip away" I hear myself say.

Her hand drops to reveal her face which has broken out into a large smile. Her eyes widen eagerly as she quickly chomps at the mouthful she's so desperate to ingest. Maureen's mind is already made up. She knows where we're off to next. Only, I have to wait, I have to suffer that intolerable squelching sound before I'm let in on the details.

She swallows greedily, freeing herself to speak. "How about France?" she says excitedly, through a small globule of massacred food which is sat in the corner of her lip, "we haven't been there for a while." She puts her knife and fork down to form a cross over her plate. And then rests her hands in her lap. All prim and proper. Her face beams in delight, whilst the food stays embedded into a fold of her cheek. "Why if I think about it we haven't been there in over a year."

"Is it that long?" I ask, with little real interest.

"Yes. It was in the beginning of May last year. I remember because it was shortly before my birthday and you got me a present while we were there."

"That's right."

We lapse into silence. The faint hum of the fan assisted oven can be heard in the background. Rice pudding for dessert. Maureen picks up her knife and fork.

"We could do with getting some wine in" I muster, struggling to be sociable.

"That would be nice."

She punctures the Steak and Kidney pudding with her fork and the gravy oozes across the plate. "I know" she says, cutting into the suet, "we can go in two weeks time. I've got the Saturday off work then and I'm having my hair done on the Friday instead of the Saturday because my stylist couldn't book me in as she's going to a wedding, so I'm free on that day. I can phone the ferry company tomorrow to book the tickets."

I nod in agreement. Maureen dunks her piece of suet into the peas and then adds a chip. "That's settled then" she says "a day trip to France."

What do you do when the conversation has run dry?

I've been with Maureen for over twenty years now and there's nothing I don't know about her. Or her family. Her childhood, her work life, her qualifications, her interests, her petty irritations, her cellulite, her trouble with clothes, her dislike of the woman next door but one, everything's been covered, some of it on many occasions. Living with the same person for twenty years might be comforting for some people but I tire of hearing her recant her story about her trip to Rhyl when she was fourteen and of how she ended up in hospital with appendicitis. Or of how her father caught her smoking outside the local youth club at the age of fifteen and grounded her for a month.

What are we left with? We're left to fill the gaps. We're left to make arrangements to do something, because if we didn't then we'd sit at home in silence. Now I silently scream. I scream on the inside. Every pore in my body wants to let out a raging noise. Every cell wants to expel a mighty roar. I urge for something else. I want to implode. Or explode. I want to do something drastic to change my life. I want to swing a bloody great big axe which will cut through everything I know. I want to hack at it. And smash and smash until it all goes away. I want to screw my life into a ball and crunch it up, until it no longer exists, until I have to find something else to replace it. Until there's no choice left but to move on. The process of elimination, that's how I see it. Which is why I've thrown the dice into the air. It's this that has driven me to become a killer. I've simmered, and I've kept quiet. I've done as I'm told for far too long. And you can't believe how difficult that is for a guy like me. Now, whatever happens, I know that change will come and this new future is so damn close that I can smell it, I can feel it too, like it's waiting around the corner, and that corner is within reach, like a finishing post, or a piece of ticker tape at the end of a lap. I can't begin to describe what it feels like, I only know that as I sit here and pick up my cutlery, ready to eat my Thursday night steak and kidney pudding, that I'm well aware that my new life is beckoning and that there's a new birth on the horizon. I also know that whichever fate is waiting out there for me, one thing is for sure, my Thursday night pudding will be relegated to place that it deserves. To history.

Chapter 10

Sometimes I catch myself, I'm sitting in a chair or lying in bed, I'm with Maureen or at work, I'm driving down the road or standing in a queue, and I catch myself. Everything is going on around me, Maureen is talking, the television is blaring, the production line is moving, only I don't seem to connect with it, its all just a hum in the background, but I have no place in there. It's as if I'm separated from it all, I'm separated by my thoughts. The craziest of thoughts. The craziest and wildest of thoughts. Thoughts about Maureen. And thoughts about life. Big thoughts about all sorts of issues, like the world and religion and shit like that. Bizarre thoughts, about suicide and death and destruction. Insane thoughts, of how I can offend the worlds population in as many different ways as possible, (and believe me, I've just about thought of every conceivable notion going), they all tumble through my head until I can't work any of it out. It's when I get to this stage that I start asking myself some really serious questions, questions like, why am I on this planet? And, what's it all about? Questions which have no real answers really. And it only goes to confuse me even more. It only goes to add to my issues. It's at these moments that I feel at my most disturbed, and I wish I didn't feel this way, I really do. I wish I could stop myself from thinking at all, but the thoughts don't stop, they just keep popping into my brain. Today I feel like I have more questions than answers, today I don't like what's happening to me at all, it's at this very minute that I pray for the years that have passed me by. I ask for those days to be given back to me so that I can use them again, and I can make them different. And by different I mean that if I could start again I'd make different choices, I know I would, if I could start again, then I'd make my life simpler. I could become another person, or be born a different character, or even be born under a different star sign, if that helps. I wish I was kinder or had some kind of consideration for everyone else, that I could have it in me to be a missionary, or a priest, or an aid worker. That I could get satisfaction from giving, instead of taking. Deep down, I know that it's too late, and that if I was meant to be that other person then I should've set out my stall years ago. But I didn't. Now, all the things around me only add to the life I have. Like being trapped into a web, or stepping into quicksand, it seems like the more I struggle against myself, the deeper I sink. Then there are other days. And those other days are just as complex but they seem to be less confusing, I get to thinking that life isn't about good and bad. It isn't about right and wrong. Or about doing godly things. It's all about power. And energy. And by taking I absorb. That's what I think. I think that it's all about survival of the fittest, and by bending the rules I'm actually becoming a stronger person. When my hands are around a woman's neck, and when I'm squeezing real tight, well it only confirms what I believe. Because when I'm killing I get sensations which never visit me at other times. I can actually feel my body grow and my muscles expand, my whole torso strengthens, it's not just my body that it affects either, it's my whole being, as if I'm more focused and cunning and steely. Like a super being, I feel invincible. The energy of my victim seems to transfer into me, rushing into my veins and hitting them with force, like a potent drug intravenously injected into my system. And, oh, the rush I get. There's nothing that compares. It's in those moments I believe that no one can stop me and that my life will only get better because of the things I've done, that there's no one out there who'll ever be big enough to even come close to the guy I am. It's in those moments that I believe the ones who conquer this world are the ones who are big enough to take it on. That the world is made up of Chiefs and Indians, there are those who make up the rules and there are those who follow the orders. Well I'm done with being told what to do, and I'm done with only doing what is expected of me. From now on I'm playing with my own rules, and as no one else knows my rules, I'm at an advantage. Then sometimes I think that even this is bullshit. That it's all just a whole load of crap to confuse me even more. So it goes on. My brain ticking over and over. With one Technicolor drama after another. Sometimes I just want to get away from it all. But how can you? How do you walk away? How do you escape from yourself? And this is it, I can't. There is no escape. So maybe, I ask myself, that all this killing is just a distraction, that all of this is a way to escape from my thoughts. To switch off. To tune into another frequency. Crazy isn't it. But there is more to my crimes than this, I know there is. Only sometimes I really have my doubts. Because suddenly I realise that I've been staring at a wall for maybe half an hour or more. And if anyone were to see me...... then! And if I were to witness anyone staring at a wall........well! But I'm not just staring. Oh no. I'm not. It's all going on inside me. Big thoughts. Life changing thoughts. Thoughts of murder. Thoughts about the future. Thoughts about where I'm from, and thoughts about where I'll be when all of this is over and done with. It's here where my brain is at, at the moment. I'm thinking about what's ahead of me. I'm thinking about the way she walks, and what her neck will feel like. I'm thinking about the type of underwear she'll be wearing, and the way her knickers will fall away, and the colour of her hair beneath. That's what I'm thinking. And there's nothing to stop me, and there's no one to stop me from having these thoughts. I can't even stop myself. It's that powerful. The bottom line is that I know it'll happen real soon. I don't know why. I just know.

Chapter 11

I stop the car at the end of the darkly lit alley, wind the passenger window part way down, and then wait. Two women loitering in a doorway glance over. One makes her move. I take a look at her in my rear view mirror as she walks towards the car. She is in her mid thirties with a ruddy face which is worn from the elements. Her hair is long and dark and straggly with curls that are matted and unkempt, they fall loosely around her shoulders. Her body is thin and gaunt. Her chest protrudes from the V of her low cut top and her arms are waiflike. Her legs are equally thin, they're long and scrawny and seem underdeveloped compared to her age, they stick out from her short skirt and are clad in high heels boots which she struggles to walk in.

I look away. My eyes skirt the surrounding area, checking the doorways, checking the bushes and keeping watch of the street corners. All is still; apart from one beer can which tinkles lightly as it is pushed along by the wind. Satisfied, I turn and wait for her to appear in the passenger window. She stops next to it and then peers in.

On closer inspection, the woman is heavily made up. Thick congealing make up clings to her face. Open pores bridge her nose and cheeks and are smudged with harsh red blusher. Deep lines furrow her forehead. Lesser ones surround her mouth. Her eyes are dull and heavy, her manner uncouth. She shivers slightly against the wind, her clothes being totally unsuitable for a night like this. I transfer my gaze to her bright pink top and wait for her to open up the conversation.

"Are you lost, love?" she asks, her Scottish accent burring gently.

"I'm not sure" I reply casually, ogling at her chest which is framed into the bottom half of the window. I conclude that she's not wearing a bra. But I suppose that in her line of business a woman like this hardly has the need for underwear. Then I get to wondering what else might be waiting underneath her clothes. Or not under there, more likely. I look up.

"Are you looking for business?" she asks, cutting to the chase.

"It depends on how much."

"It depends what you're after" the woman teases, giving me a jaded smile.

I take in her nicotine stained teeth, then the lines above her top lip which become more pronounced when she speaks. I note the dry skin on her bottom lip. And the cold sore at the corner of her mouth which oozes clear liquid.

"What do you charge for full sex?" I ask dispassionately.

The woman takes a deep drag of her cigarette and then tosses it into the gutter. A red ember flickers up into the air then disappears. "Forty quid," she states miserably. "Anything else is negotiable" she adds, trying to keep the smile going. But the creases around her eyes end up losing the battle, they sink into blandness. As do her eyes which are remote and dull.

"Okay, that's fine. Get in" I order.

The woman stands and reaches for the handle. Then hesitates.

I take a look in the mirror to see if there's any particular reason for her reluctance. The road is quiet. Everything is still. The woman whom she was talking to when I pulled up has drifted into the night. There is nothing to concern me. Satisfied, I lean across the passenger seat and look up at her. "You ok?" I ask.

"Yeah" she replies, but as she speaks she is looking to where she had stood earlier, as if she's expecting to see someone. The patch she works is empty. The street is dark and shadowy. For a second she is unsure. As if she senses all is not right.

I glance at the clock on the dashboard. It's just past three thirty in the morning. I've got the time to wait. Maureen is sleeping soundly, mainly thanks to the large dose of sleeping tablets which I ground into her cocoa earlier on. Nothing is going to wake her in a hurry. I've got time to wait, but I say it anyway. "Come on love."

A blast of wind rattles down the road, ruffling her hair and making her underfed body tense. She shivers against the night. And then reaches out. The handle clicks and she slides into the seat beside me.

I press the control button to wind the passenger window up. Immediately the air is taken up by the smell of stale clothes. It's a musty smoky odour which hums in the confinement of a car. I switch the air con up and put the car into gear.

"What's your name love?" I ask, as I pull away from the kerb.

"Chrissie" comes the reply.

"Chrissie" I repeat, turning to give her a weak smile.

I look back to the road. As I do, I catch sight of myself in the rear view mirror. My hair is combed back and heavily greased, giving it a darker appearance. My eyebrows are equally dark to match. My contacts are in place. My cheeks are smeared with the faintest hint of blusher. My blue pinstriped suit speaks corporate. My expression says nonchalant.

I look away.

"Well, hello there Chrissie" I say, moving the gear into second. I keep my eyes on the road, I keep my speech to the script, I am in control and I'm already guiding her. Only now it's easier than ever. My penknife in the glove compartment is merely a reach away, but I'm not inclined to use it. There will be no need for it tonight, I'm sure of that. "It's nice to meet with you." I turn out of the road where I met her and then switch into operation. "Look Chrissie," I stutter nervously "I don't know this area well, is there anywhere in particular that you go?"

"I know lots of places," she says, hitching her up her skirt to reveal her thighs, "but it'll cost you."

It's as I expect, the woman beside me has got her foot in the door and is now ready to juggle the price around. But price isn't something that worries me. It's location that counts. It's the only thing that matters in these situations. I probe a little further. "Like where?" I ask.

"I rent a flat a couple of blocks away from here. It's a maisonette down in Edgbaston."

"Does anyone else use it?"

"Two other girls work it as well," she says "but don't worry they're in the same line of employment as me, if you know what I mean."

I hesitate, as if contemplating her suggestion, and then shake my head slowly. "I'm not sure about that" I say doubtfully, flicking the indicator on. I take a left into another back road. "I'm not from around here and I don't want to take any risks, how about somewhere quick and quiet, maybe somewhere outside?"

She sniffs loudly. "There's an alleyway up that way, if that's what you want" she replies gruffly, her seductive voice a thing of the past, "or there's round the back of the local supermarket, but you'll have to park in the far corner away from loading bays because they've got surveillance cameras trained around the building." She turns to me, folding her arms abruptly. "You won't be getting it any cheaper if that's what you think!"

"Look love," I interrupt her gently "money's not an issue for me, I'm not concerned about the cost, I'm in town on business and I want to do business with you. I'm high up the corporate ladder, one step from becoming a partner in a firm of solicitors, if you get my meaning, the last thing I need is to be spotted in some supermarket car park in any circumstances that could get reflected back onto me. And I can't risk being caught in a house that's being worked either. You do understand, don't you?"

She nods knowingly, her expression softening. She unfolds her arms and begins to relax. "I've seen it all before love," she replies candidly, "dealt with them all I have, the policemen, the lawyers, the teachers, the court judges, you name it, I've seen them. In fact one of them recently fined me for soliciting, although he did visit me afterwards to pay for my fine, if you know what I mean…"

"All I'm saying," I cut in, "is that it's better for me if we can find somewhere discreet."

I weave the car through a series of side streets, taking a rat run to the edge of town.

She stares out of the window, looking out for possible places to earn her money. All the while, she doesn't sit still, her foot taps against the floor, her body twitches, she fidgets and jerks. She is constantly on the move as if in perpetual motion.

"What about there?" she asks, pointing out to an old mill.

"No."

"What about a park?"

"No."

"I could phone a friend that owes me a favour" she says. "But, like I say, it'll cost you."

I shake my head. "I can't do that. It's too risky. We have to find somewhere discreet, maybe somewhere out of town, somewhere that you've not used before, where there are bushes and a drive into it, so we can spot if anyone comes along. It'll be less risky that way."

She looks at the time on the dashboard and then huffs audibly. "I'll have to charge you extra at this rate, I'll have to start charging by the hour" she moans. She slumps into her chair and starts to pick at her nail varnish. The atmosphere in the car starts to change. It's not the way I want it to be. She becomes restless and shuffles constantly. Scratching and picking. Coughing and spluttering. I notice some angry red scars on her arm.

I drive out onto a bypass. "Don't you worry about it, I'll make it worth your while and if it's more money that you want, then I'll pay."

"Yeah?" she asks.

"Yeah" I reply. "I can pay you a whole lot more, if you're interested" I say, suddenly realising what the marks are.

A chip of red nail varnish falls onto her leg. She flicks it away.

"How much?" she asks desperately.

"How much does it take?" I respond, trying to engage her into conversation.

She flicks repetitively at her thigh, even though the nail varnish has gone, as she considers how much to go for. Too much and she loses the deal, too little and she feels cheated. But she figures that as she's in my car anyway, I'm more inclined to agree with whatever she asks. So she settles on a figure which she knows she'll never get but she thinks she's worth anyway.

"A hundred" she blurts out.

I eye her. Not unappreciatively. But with a little bit of doubt. Just to get her feeling less sure of herself. Just to string her out and to play the game a little longer. Then I gaze out of the windscreen whilst tapping my steering wheel, as if considering her request.

Chrissie bounces up and down, unable to take the tension of the situation. She switches the stereo on, and then turns the volume up. She turns it down, then up again and fiddles with the bass.

I give it to her straight. "A bit much for me love" I say.

Chrissie shrugs as if she couldn't care. But beyond her nonchalance, two deep creases at the top of her nose become more prominent. Now she's silently cursing herself and wondering just how much I would've agreed to.

I keep silent. Letting the silence speak for me.

She glances at the clock on the dashboard. No doubt counting all the time which she's wasted with me so far. Counting how many clients she could've had in the minutes that she's been with me. In her heyday that is.

She scratches meanly at the scabs on her arm.

I let her stew for a little while longer.

Then speak. "Seventy-five" I say coolly. "You look like you're worth that."

She turns and looks at me in surprise, flattered by my comment. And relieved that the meter is ticking once again. All the while she barely notices which way I'm driving. Because despite what I've told her I know this area very well.

"Look," I say to her gently, "I know I've cut the price, and its not that you don't merit a hundred pounds, it's just that I would only pay out that kind of money for something extra special, if you know what I mean." I take my eyes off the road and look deep into her eyes. I raise my eyebrows purposely, letting them do the talking for me.

Her cynical face, having seen and heard it all before, hardens in response. She wonders what perversions are lurking beneath my pin-stripped suit. She's probably heard them all in her day. But it still dismays her. It still reminds her of what she is and the lengths she has to go to make some money. Now she's cursing herself and her judgement because for a second she really thought I was sincere when I said that she was worth it. She thought I was different.

"I'm willing to pay you more" I state calmly "if that's what you want, only it's a lot of money and I have to warn you that, if you want to name your price, you'll have to earn it properly."

Chrissie cringes. Her teeth grind loudly. She stares ahead as she digests my words.

"It's not that bad" I say sadly, looking back out into the dark country road that we're now travelling down, "not really, it's just that I've always had a thing about nature and I don't know why, I suppose I shouldn't be telling you this" I say "but I've always had this fantasy about having sex up against a tree." Chrissie heaves a sigh of relief. For a minute she was thinking the worst. And she isn't in the mood to face that tonight. But she knows and I know that even my worse of suggestions would've been palatable. Poor old Chrissie looks like she hasn't earned that type of money for a good ten years. If ever. She relaxes. In her mind the till is clinking. And the money talks.

"Al fresco" she says.

"Stupid isn't it" I reply sadly.

"No" she says quietly to herself, her voice barely a whisper. "One hundred, you say?"

"That's what you wanted, isn't it?"

"One hundred?" she checks again, wanting to hear me say the words.

"Yes" I reply. "One hundred. But only if we have sex up against a tree."

With accurate timing I pull into the lane on the left side of the road. From the left I swing a sharp right and two hundred metres down a dirt track I pull into a lay-by.

"Is it a deal?" I ask.

Chrissie doesn't even have to think about it. She reckons that she can bring me off in seconds and then head back into town, back to all her smack head mates and back to a night free from punters, free from standing on corners and free from the risk of being arrested and spending the night in a cell. Back to a night where she can get well and truly out of it, where she can forget about all the men who've touched her over the years, where she can forget about the drunks and the pervs and forget the humiliation which lingers beneath her cheap polyester clothes.

"Ok. But you have to pay me upfront first."

"No problem Chrissie" I reply.

I pull a bundle of twenties from my trouser pocket, count off some notes from the top and then hand them to her. Her greedy hand snatches them and then she turns and tucks the money into her boot. She opens the door. Now that the deal has been struck she's not waiting around.

"We won't go far" I say, "just inside the bushes so that we can move back if we hear any cars approaching." It's as I'm stepping out of the car that I reach for the gloves in the hollow of the door. "What about over that way?" I suggest, pointing towards the footpath.

Chrissie doesn't speak but just stares blankly into the darkness. She marches ahead, and then curses as one heel sinks into some mud. "Bloody hell" she snaps.

As she checks her boot, I slip on my gloves. It goes unnoticed.

I walk up to her, cup her arm and steer her into the forest.

"Here" she says, just inside the bushes.

"A little further."

"Here" she says, pointing to the next tree we come to.

"That one over there" I tell her, nodding to a large tree ahead of us. "It's got to be an acorn tree, I've got this fantasy that we fuck so hard that we shake the acorns off the branches." Chrissie doesn't respond, she just continues to stare as she walks further into my trap. The tree we reach is only metres away from the car but it is far enough. It is safely tucked into the bushes. And the bushes are safely in the middle of nowhere.

She shrugs my arm away, walks up to the tree, turns, and then lifts her skirt up. Three metres to the left of her is a shallow ditch. Newly dug. She doesn't notice it.

She opens her legs, exposing her nakedness and I move in.

In a way I think she's relieved. In a way I sense that it's the answer to all her problems, when I grip her neck in my hands I truly believe that it's welcome. That she's finally found a way out. She didn't grow up wanting to be a hooker, nobody does, but she sold herself once and got used to the money. Used to the money but not at ease with the way that she earns it. And everyday she must consider how to escape from the cycle. And everyday her answer is the same. She puts on her make-up and strides out into the night. Now I'm here to give her a solution. To stop her habit. To fix her world. To make things right.

She tilts her head backwards, as if offering her neck. I can only oblige. I do the one thing that I'm capable of doing, I squeeze extra tight. And in that shadowy night, I believe that what I'm doing is best for her and I'm sure that if anyone were with me now, if they were to witness her face, and her lack of resistance, they'd have to agree.

Her eyes close and her body stiffens as it absorbs the last particles of oxygen which are ending their flow around her abused veins. Suddenly she shudders. A violent convulsion overtakes her body as it battles against her wishes. My wishes are stronger. My wishes lay firmly grounded, rooted in their inception. I force one final thrust of power through my fingers. And she slips to her death.

Her body slumps as gravity takes hold. I push her back and then scoop her into my arms. It's not far to carry her to the grave. She is light anyway. No heavier than a small child. Her emaciated body is so thin that I can feel her skeleton against my arms. I lay her into the pit.

Standing above it, I take one last look. One last look before the animals come. One last look before the insects do their thing. She is at peace. Her body is relaxed. The withdrawal spasms from her addiction are gone. The tension she was carrying has been released.

I don't cut her clothes, I figure that nature will take care of it, but more than that I want her to have the dignity in death that wasn't there for her when she was alive. I feel akin to the woman beneath me, that she is just like me, just a victim of her circumstances.

I slip my hand into her boot and empty the contents. Her nightly takings don't amount to much more than I'd given her. I put the money back into my pocket.

I have one more thing to take care of before she is buried. I slip my hand into the inside pocket of my jacket and pull out a bag. I tuck the beads into her waistband and then begin to bury her. I get down onto my hands and knees and push the dirt with my gloved hands, filling the uneven gaps. Not worrying about getting dirty. Slowly but surely the mound of earth moves. Her face disappears first. Then her torso. Finally her legs and feet.

When out of sight, I take a minute to say a silent prayer. I pray for Chrissie's soul.

I get up and walk over to a pile of twigs and leaves, which I'd collected two nights before. I move them onto her grave and mix them together, arranging them carefully until the patch is completely hidden and the ground looks undisturbed. As a final gesture, I push an upright stick into the soil. It is less than a tombstone but a mark nevertheless.

Once satisfied that all is as it should be, I walk back to the car.

Chapter 12

I spend the next two hours meticulously cleaning the car, going through it inch by inch, vacuuming and polishing, wiping all the surfaces down with a disinfectant cloth, picking up errant bits of finger polish, cleaning the windows, rubbing the door handles, and then airing out the pong. When I'm finished, I drive it back to the car hire place.

It is half past five in the morning and I take the quickest route back into town. I'm beyond worrying if anyone sees me now, I feel far removed from what happened earlier, as if leaving the scene was all that it took to distance myself from what went on. My reflection in the mirror is back to normal, my clothes have changed, my lenses have been discarded and my make-up has been stripped. I drive down a dual carriageway, passing a couple of taxis and a few cars on the way. The occupants, early risers with sand still in their eyes, late night clubbers exhausted and ready for bed, and taxi drivers eking out their last fares before dawn, drive past in their own blurry worlds, taking no notice of me. I drive on.

The forecourt of the hire shop is stagnant, the cars are glazed with dew and the building is dark and vacant. I drive round to the side entrance and park up. I slip on a baseball cap, adjust it in the mirror, and then step out of the car. I empty the contents, a black bin liner and my holdall, from the boot, lock the car and walk around the building. I deposit the keys into a chrome letterbox and then walk away.

Two blocks down, I slip into an alley. At the end of the alley, I take a left. One block on, I cross the road and do a right. I pass the park and as I'm doing so I peel off a pair of thin latex gloves, which I took from one of Maureen's hair dye kit, and put them in the bin liner. One block further and my car is waiting. I flick the alarm off as I approach, slip my bags into the boot, open the driver's door and climb in.

On the drive home I think through the events of the night before.

I had it figured. Six months ago I came up with this part of the plan. And it was simple. All it was was that I'd kill three times and leave each victim in locations that were easy to find and then victim number four would be hidden, like a wild card, if you like. The reasoning behind it was easy; all I really wanted was a death which can raise its head over the parapet at any given point. In doing so I believe that it gives me an advantage, she could stay hidden for a long time, for months, or for years, or she could be found at any given moment, either during, or after I've finished my killing spree. Space. That's what it's about. Space between my crimes without having to stop my killings. Space from the grind of detective work, so that as far as the police are concerned I've only committed three murders. And they'll go on thinking that until she's found. Which also means that they'll only have three crime scenes to work from. In the meantime, I can move on to number five. Then, when she is eventually found, the police will have many questions to ask, they'll have to work out why Chrissie's murder is different from the others, and why I chose to bury her and no one else, why I didn't cut her clothes, and crucially, at what stage was she killed, and where does she fit into the pattern. The longer she stays in the ground, the more it'll put the detective process back when she's unearthed. I even took time to consider my victim, that's why it had to be her, not that Chrissie was THE one. It could've been any of the women that hang around the street corners late at night. All I was looking for was a prostitute. A person who could vanish without much of a hoo-ha, and I'm sure that poor old Chrissie won't be missed. Not really. Maybe her pimp might notice her gone, but he'll only notice that the money's missing and he'll only notice that until he finds another girl to work her spot. Maybe her pusher might notice that he's got one less client, but he'll find more clients, you can be sure of that, and you can guarantee that they'll be clients that look for him rather than him looking for them. He's not likely to report it, is he? Her junkie friends might notice her missing, but they'll be too busy jacking up to care. I doubt that there's anyone out there who cares for Chrissie enough to make anything of it. Even if that someone is out there, what are they going to do about it? Report it? Another missing person. Another statistic. With her being a hooker, she could've moved anywhere; she's not exactly in a fixed line of business. The police might look into it briefly but once they uncover her record for soliciting they're not going to bother. Not until they find her that is. I spent a lot of time considering number four and she wasn't as random as the others. Having met with her though, I guess Chrissie's number was up a good few years ago. If the truth be known, it was up as soon as she got her first payoff.

In front of me, the roads are starting to fill. The mothers coming out, rushing their children to child minders. The employed on the road trying to beat the clock to work. The bin men starting their shift. The world turning on.

I turn left at Princess Lane and enter the road which leads to my side of town. Ahead of me the early morning sunshine is bright. I pull the sun visor down and squint out of the window.

I drive past weary people treading a path, leaving their houses for a spot of respite, away from the dowdiness of family life. I notice the children walking down the road in their school uniforms, comforted by expectations of what life is all about. Leave school, get a job, earn money, find a partner, settle down, and marry. Live happily ever after. Only the real world isn't like that.

So that's four down and four to go. Which means that I'm half finished. I calculate it now. It hasn't taken me long at all, as I've killed four times within a ten week time frame. If I keep it up I could be finished before Christmas. Wouldn't that be nice?

I swing the steering wheel to the left and turn down Abbey Road. Straight into the congestion of the morning rush hour. Oh how I long to put this all behind me, how I long to switch off, and to relax, but I know that these things cannot be rushed. And having taken my time planning it, it'd be silly to rush and spoil it now. The cars tailgate forward. Inching along. My foot moves from accelerator to brake in quick succession. I stare out of the window and find myself drifting off. I imagine that I am hovering above the earth, way up high, and distancing myself from it all. Down beneath me on the ground everyone is struggling, everyone, with their poxy lives, and their sad expressions, with their bitterness and bile. The strange thing is that I don't feel bitter any more, I've enacted some heinous deeds, some terrible crimes, but I don't feel bitter, all I feel is that I'm being given my life back, that with every death I'm closer to living. I can't explain it, not even to myself, all I can do is feel it, and live it, and sense it. That's all. And with each death I float even higher and feel more at ease, I feel happier in myself. With each death I'm able to tick that invisible abacus which is etched into my brain, and move closer to my goal. I take a deep intake of air and feel my whole body expand. Then she pops into my brain.

My mood shifts.

I imagine Maureen now, still comatose by those pills, no doubt lying in bed, in our bed, making snuffling noises. I think about the way her face distorts with the angle that she lies on the pillow and the way that there's always dribble coming from her mouth when she's asleep. Suddenly I feel morose. And sad. Sad that whenever I feel a bit of liberation she's there to hold me back. Sad that I have to drive back home to face her. Sad that I made one small mistake. And now I'm living it. Now, there's not a day that goes by when I don't have more than my fair share of regret.

The car behind me honks. It jolts me back to life. I push the gear stick into first, step on the gas and check myself in the mirror. At the same time I'm already planning number five.

Chapter 13

"Bonjour" says Maureen, in a mock French accent which sounds as if it has come straight out of a scene from a bad comedy skit, "je voudrais deux of those, s'il vous plait" she drawls hesitantly, holding two fingers up on one hand and pointing to the plate of savoury pastries at the front of the display cabinet with the other.

"Oui madame," replies the woman behind the counter, picking up some silver tongs and then leaning into the glass cabinet. I watch from the back of the shop as she extracts the driest and stalest pastries from the rear of the tray and slips them into a box. She shows no embarrassment by her actions, only relief for having someone to offload them onto.

Maureen notices too. "Non!" she cries in alarm, as she witnesses what is happening.

"Non?" questions the assistant.

"Oui!" she squeals.

"Oui madame?"

"Non those," says Maureen, wagging her finger and desperately pointing to front of the tray, "oui those."

The woman shrugs vacantly. "Non au oui?" she asks.

"Oui" replies Maureen in defeat as her poor command of French leaves her with no alternative but to accept the dry tarts.

The woman turns to the back counter, closes the box and snaps some tape around it, then turns and slides it onto the marble top.

"Con bi an?" asks Maureen in dismay.

"Combien" the woman corrects her. "Trois euros, s'il vous plaît."

Maureen opens her purse and does the only thing I expect of her, she pulls out the largest note she possesses and waves it at her.

The woman, upon seeing the one hundred Euro bill, pulls her face. But says nothing. She walks across to the till and scowls angrily as she uses up all her change.

This scene is replayed everywhere we go. In the Hypermarket. In the boutiques. And in the grocers. Finally it replays at the café.

"Bonjour," says Maureen to the middle aged waiter. "Je voudrais un hot chocolate and un cheese sandwich, s'il vous plaît."

"Oui madam" replies the waiter in a bored tone, as he leans over and gives the table a quick wipe with a damp cloth. He brushes some crumbs onto his empty tray and looks at me. "And for sir?" he asks.

"I'd like the same please."

"Very well" he replies turning and collecting an empty cup from the next table before walking back to a group of men sat around the bar.

"You should try speaking a little French" hisses Maureen. But she isn't interested in whether I speak French or not, she's just making conversation. And at the moment she's too busy looking over my shoulder giving all the other people in the café the once over to notice me anyway.

"I'm not comfortable with it."

"How do you know until you've tried it properly?" she moans, suddenly taking the time to look across the table. She glowers at me in a way that only she can, and then realises where she is and composes herself. She returns to her fixed smile, which sometimes can be scarier than her scowl. Her public smile, as I choose to think of it. It's a toothy grin which never quite reaches her eyes. Once her face is fixed into place she goes back to scanning. "It's not difficult once you've mastered the basics."

I sit in silence, refusing to argue the point. Instead I glance over to the men at the bar in envy. When she realises that I don't intend to respond, she changes the subject. "Anyway, it's a lovely day," she says, shifting her sunglasses to the top of her head and tilting her face upwards to catch some rays, "it's better than being at work..." she pauses briefly, closing her eyes, and then flicks them open again and looks at her watch "…though I wonder what they're all doing now."

I hold my breath and silently start counting to ten. One.

"Business wasn't very good yesterday…"

Two. Three. Four. Five.

"…the takings were down…"

Six. Seven. Eight. Nine.

"…I think that it's since the new girl started…"

I hit ten and release the air bubble trapped in my throat. But the strain inside me doesn't subside. Whenever we sit at a table in a café or at a restaurant, it's always the same, Maureen starts to waffle. As if we're on show to the public. Like her talking is designed to prove to the people around us that our relationship hasn't gone stale, that we still communicate.

"…she doesn't seem to have the same knack with the customers as the other girls I've worked with over the years…"

At the same time, there is only one topic open to discussion.

"…she's too abrupt with them."

Her work. I just don't get it, I don't know why she has to look at her watch, and I don't know why she wants to discuss work when we're on a trip to France. I just don't get some people at all. Especially Maureen.

"It's not just me…"

Sometimes, what I really want to do is just to stand up and walk away.

"…the others have noticed it as well…"

When I'm in this situation the thing that really gets me is; what are the people around us thinking? What do they make of the conversations that we have?

"…I expect everyone will leave it to me to have a talk with her."

All the time she's droning on, I'm wondering if anyone is listening in. Then I start to feel embarrassed. I'm embarrassed by the conversations we have.

"I think it's because I've worked there the longest."

Or Maureen has. I gave up trying to contribute to the conversation years ago. I did try for a while.

"I should ask for a pay rise…"

But it seemed like anything I had to say was ignored. She didn't listen. She didn't pay any attention to what I had to say. Sometimes she'd even interrupt with a completely different topic half way through. As if what I had to say wasn't important. And once she'd finished talking I didn't feel at ease with going back to what I'd been trying to tell her and so I'd let it drift.

"…I'm expected to do more than everyone else and I'm not complaining, but I should be rewarded for taking on extra responsibilities."

Gradually I'd contribute to the conversation less, and less. There came a point when I stopped wanting to talk to her at all and I'd just let her chat away.

"Tina needs a hip replacement…"

And boy, can she, with her incessant drone, which seems to stretch out into a single pitch and is strung together like one long syllable that reaches out into the horizon and beyond and seem to have no full stop or ending.

"…of course it's been really difficult for her since her husband left…"

Sometimes I wonder how a person can have so much to talk about. Sometimes I wonder whether she breathes at all when she's talking, whether there's space to breathe.

"…he went off with her neighbour."

Sometimes I listen. Mainly I don't.

"I can't believe that anybody could be so cruel…"

Maureen bores me and I came a point a long time ago where I hit a brick wall.

"…they had two children as well."

There came a time where I needed more, where I craved intellectual stimulation. I wanted to sit down and discuss something important in depth. I longed to talk about politics. And history. I wanted to talk about our history, about the history of the world, about where we're from and where our future lies. And what is going to become of the human race. I wanted to consider life. And death. And the quality of life in various countries. I wanted to discuss nutritional theories for babies in Africa. And the spread of HIV. I wanted to explore religious concepts. I wanted to talk about things that matter.

"He left a note on the kitchen table and then walked out…"

I wanted a deep and meaningful debate about global warming. Or to discuss the energy crisis. I wanted to work out how we can find future sources of power. I wanted to compare the price of bread in Europe as opposed to the price of rice. To consider the European Union and what, if any, benefits there are for our country. There's xenophobia, racism, pacifism, Marxism, Communism. There's the class system, the compensation culture, our immigration policy, our pensions crisis.

"…they've gone to live in Devon."

What about the economic imbalance between countries and continents?

"She's taken it badly."

There's superbugs. Bird flu. The future of the NHS. There's war. Religion. Even sex. Petrol prices. The growing population. Our debt mountain. And recycling, of course.

"We ran out of cola on Wednesday because nobody filled the fridge on my day off…."

I wanted my grey matter to be stretched. I wanted to feel interested in something. I craved for more from life. I wanted to talk about worldly subjects. I wanted to explore possibilities. And capabilities. And discuss the news.

"…although the water sold well that day, and we do have a good mark up on that."

And now I make the news.

"Anne wants me to change my bingo night to a Wednesday, you don't mind do you?"

The couple on the next table sit in silence. Not connecting in any way, shape or form. They are together but worlds apart, just two individuals who happen to be at the same point at the same time, marooned onto some blank canvas which has nothing to connect them but a history. As I watch them, I think to myself that it could be worse. Or could it?

"Charlie?"

Then two teenagers walk past the café. They stroll under the bunting, which hangs above the promenade in front of the beach. Both with smiles on their faces. Both with eyes that glow. Both entwined around each other, walking as a single item. All young. And fresh. And happy. All optimistic.

"Charlie?"

I feel a pang of jealousy. Because I do remember those times. And maybe the memory isn't as sharp as it used to be, but it was still there once upon a time. Sometimes, when I'm feeling nostalgic, I wonder if I'll have that experience ever again. If I'll ever feel that desire. And that passion. And that intensity. Or are those feelings only limited to the younger generation. And that we all get too cynical. And too experienced for our own good.

"Charlie?"

Don't we all end up sitting next to someone who we don't want to be with regardless of how it all starts out. Or could there be such a thing as a soul mate? Someone who meets all our demands, no matter at what level. Someone who makes even the most trivial task seem worthwhile. Someone who you can share your entire life with and never get bored. Or am I being unrealistic.

"Charlie?"

I look across at her.

Maureen stares back at me in that funny manner she has when she catches me not listening.

"Sorry?" I say

"I was saying that Maxine wants me to change my bingo night to a Wednesday."

"Oh."

"I really think that….."

Off she goes again.

I met Maureen when I was seventeen and at the time I was a popular guy, I had lots of friends and I went out on a regular basis, I had money in my pocket and I was in my prime, I had it all. I was the only child of Polish parents and they were typical hard working immigrants who were grateful for the chance of reaching hospitable shores. My parents had gone through the Second World War and had experienced incredible hardship as a result they wanted to make life easier for me. In short, I was spoilt. I wasn't expected to pay any keep and my mother couldn't do enough for me. She would wash and iron my clothes, and buy anything I needed, and she'd even give me money to go out with. My parents didn't have any family around, but they had each other. And me. My father was content to work as a bus driver and my mother had a couple of small cleaning jobs. They wanted no more than a meal on the table. In the evenings my father would spend his time down at the local social club and my mother would make a fuss of me. I didn't mind, I was happy to let her. Life was good.

Then Maureen came onto the scene. At first I was in awe of her and was smitten. It felt like nothing else existed, that my life before her had been bland. I'd been nothing more than average. Maureen was intoxicating. She gave me status and empowered me. I thought that by being with her I could take on the world, that I could achieve something significant and I could be somebody. It seemed like those feelings would last forever. We had an old fashioned courtship where we did everything properly. We waited for marriage, I didn't mind, I thought that we had all the time in the world. I thought I made her as happy as she made me. But somewhere along the line it all went wrong, somewhere shortly past our wedding day she started to disapprove. Firstly it was petty things, that I wasn't tidy enough, that I left the toilet seat up, that I squeezed the toothpaste at the wrong point and I didn't take my shoes off when I stepped through the door. And then the list got longer. Then it was that I went out too much, I drank too much, and my friends weren't suitable. Visits to my family were delayed. And then cancelled. Nothing was out of bounds as even my religion got changed. My catholic upbringing was a symbol of my past that Maureen disapproved of and she insisted that we marry in a protestant church, mainly to satisfy her parent's demands but also to satisfy her vision of where we fitted in with society. Gradually I stopped arguing. And I'd rather stay in than have another confrontation. The invites whittled down, the phone stopped ringing and by the time my parents passed away, one shortly after the other, they were strangers to me. Eventually it was just me and her. And it was too late.

I still catch myself thinking that it could be different, that we could wake up and do things, we could be spontaneous, and we could pull together and be happy. But who am I kidding? It's always the same wherever we are. Which is the saddest thing, we could be anywhere in the world and it still wouldn't be right. Nor will it ever be. Because it doesn't matter where we go or what we do, there's not a place on this planet that could repair the gulf between us. We could be in paradise but none of it would mean anything if I'd have to live like this.

The waiter brings our drinks and sandwiches over. Maureen still chats away. The couple on the table next to us still sit in silence. I still sit and brood. The world around us ticks slowly by.

When it all gets like this, I can feel my life ebbing away as if it's being sucked down a drain. Slowly but surely. Inch by inch. There are times, like now, I'm so conscious of it that I could break out into a run. I could stand up from this table right now and run and run and not stop. Because it's when I stop, it's when nothing around me happens, that I'm left to think. When I've got nothing to distract me, it all becomes too much to stand.

That's when I know I'm ready to kill again.

Chapter 14

Number five is the most difficult so far, I hadn't planned to kill today but I'd woken up in a particularly bad mood. From the moment I opened my eyes, a dull pain was throbbing in my head. Like a big black cloud had clawed its way under my cranium. And was pressing down real hard. To weigh down on my thoughts. Knowing that I had to kill four more was beginning to stress me, not in a guilty way, but in the way that you get when you know that you've got loads to do, and that the jobs are piling up and you just want to plough into it all, and get it out of the way so that you can think about other things and get on with other issues. That was where I made my mistake, I suddenly got a rush on. I decided that today would be the day for my next outing. Instead of the murder being calm and planned, instead of taking my time, I chose to go out on a whim. Big mistake.

The woman in question screams.

I punch her in the face, sending her reeling backwards. Her legs stumble, trying to keep apace with her upper body, as her arms flail wildly in search of something to grab. Her shoe catches on the root of a nearby tree causing her legs to buckle and she falls to the ground in a heap. Her head, which is still travelling backwards, connects loudly against the trunk of the tree and rebounds.

For a moment the impact stuns her. She is rigid and still. I expect her to cry. Instead she lets out a dull moaning noise. She puts her hands up to the point of collision and rubs at her head, ruffling her bright ginger hair. Then she looks up at me.

"You fucker" she sneers, her broad Irish accent, gruff and indecent. "You fucking fucker. You're not fucking getting away with this."

"No?" I ask, shrugging my shoulders.

"No fucking way" she spits, her face all mean and pinched and withered and hard.

"No?" I ask again.

"Not while I've got a fucking breath in my body."

"I'm scared" I mock.

"Fuck you" she roars, her pierced lip lisping badly, "you've fucking had it now. I'm going to make you wish that you'd never met me."

"Is that right?" I say, stepping towards her. "Is that right?" I slip my hand into my pocket to reach for my knife. But the pocket is empty. Then I remember, in my haste I hadn't bothered to pick up my knife and it's still in the car. I curse myself for not being tooled up. I thought I could handle it. I got cocky, having all my other murders go to plan I thought that it would remain that way. But now in front of me is a situation I hadn't bargained on. I reach for my scissors, before I get to them, she makes her move.

"You can fuck right off!" She is on her feet in a single movement. And then begins her charge. Before she gets to me, I'm ready for her. I'm ready for her alright. I grab her by the shoulders and twist her round, throwing her onto her back. And then I'm on top of her, punching and punching, a white mist overtaking me, an anger boiling over, anger that my plan hasn't fallen into place, anger at the way that this bitch beneath has dared to speak to me, and anger at Maureen. I vent my rage in an outburst of flying fists, one after another, pummelling against her head, while an urge deep inside of me drives me on, a raging urge, a need to smash her face in, a desire to shut her up, an urge to show her that she can't mess with me. That I don't need to take her filthy language. That she can't look at me with that expression on her face. That I should be respected. That I am bigger. And I am stronger. I'm the very person to teach this bitch a lesson. She's not going to get away with talking to me like that. Not to me.

All the while I'm doing this, I don't see her, all I see are my gloves, the colour of blue, passing my face one after another and landing with a thud beneath me. All I'm aware of is a feeling deep down inside of me, a pulse getting louder and louder and the stress which I have carried around for too long, starting to melt, to become released and absorbed into the punch bag beneath my gloves. All I can hear is a distant whimpering sound gradually tailing off, the sound of deep and heavy puffs drowning it out. I stop.

The woman beneath me has nothing much to say now, her face is a smudgy mass of welts and lumps and blood and gore. A clump of snot clings to the end of her nose and collects in the dent above her mouth. Her mouth is swollen, her pierced lip is rent at the point of the hole and oozes freshly drawn blood. The hoop is nowhere to be seen. Both of her eyes have puffed up and are hidden behind a rainbow of reds and blues and purples.

I catch my breath. Nausea washes over me. My stomach churns at the sight beneath me. More than that, I'm horrified by the enormity of what I've just done. But none of it is for her, she's got what she deserved, I'm just worried for myself, that's all. I'm worried about my situation and for once, I don't feel quite as confident as I normally do. For once I have my doubts.

I look down. I look at my hands. My right hand is clutching a blood soaked rock. Only I don't know how it got there. Or how it's managing to remain there. For my hands are shaking. Then I realise that my body is trembling too. My whole body. Vibrating away. So much so that I have no control over it. I'm in shock. I'm shocked by my own ferocity, but I tell myself she had it coming, that you can't walk around and talk to people in that manner and not expect them to react.

There in the woodland, in the mid afternoon air, the world suddenly stops turning and with it my plans hit a wall. The wall that I thought would never happen. I curse myself. And curse my stupidity.

"Fuck!" I shout out aimlessly into the sky.

The woman beneath me stirs. She groans softly and a hissing sound comes from the newly formed gap in her teeth. I ignore her. There are bigger issues going down at the moment. It's all that I can do to ask myself, what is this path I've walked down? What is this life I've chosen for myself? I'm beginning to wonder, because never have I felt so scared. Never have I felt more exposed and so raw. And so hurt. A bird fluttering above distracts me before I remotely connect to some answers.

I drop the rock and look at her. I inspect the damage which I've inflicted. A crimson line trickles out of the side of her mouth and slides across the freckles on her face and on past her earlobe, forming a drip down to her neck. Her face has swollen out of proportion to her frame. Her nose is now one of a seasoned boxer. Her lips are full to bursting. Her hair is matted with gore. The sight of her is nothing like I have ever witnessed before.

I start talking out loud to myself. I tell myself that I've got to pull myself together, that I can't let this stop me and my plans are still there. What's happened just now is no more than a slight disruption. That, if I've chosen the path I have, and if I am the killer that I think I am, then I shouldn't let anything get in the way. I shouldn't expect to have boundaries. That it's all the same in the end, they all die one way or another. I tell myself, this is nothing I can't handle. But I'm not so sure any more.

I squat over her frame whilst considering my position. She's seen me, which means that she can identify me, and which also means she has to be taken out. But, I ask, do I connect her to my other murders? Because if I do, then it adds a whole new dimension to my crimes. The police will know that I've moved into a different phase, that I've become a different type of killer, a killer who's lost control. And a killer who loses control makes mistakes. I know that. They'll know it too. So the question is what if I let this one go? What if I kill her but don't leave the beads? They won't connect this crime with any of the others and it'll be a separate inquiry. But it also means that, either I have to kill an extra person or I have to change my plans.

The woman beneath me starts to moan, it's a dull and heavy sound. Her head starts to roll from side to side, her eyes flicker and she begins to come round. I know that I can't afford to hesitate, that I can't sit back and risk her gaining consciousness, because if I do then there's no telling what might happen.

I put my hands around her neck and squeeze. The molten mess beneath me makes a choking noise, blood and fluid burble up into foaming bubbles between her lips.

It hits me from nowhere, straight between my legs. The force of her knee thrusts me forward. My arms release and automatically come out to try and break my fall. I land partially on top of her and my knee connects with her face. She lets out a piercing scream, it cuts through the air. Pain shoots through me. I curl my legs up and roll to the side. From the corner of my eye I see her move, her free hand scrambles around on the ground beside her. She tries to move, but I am there before she has a chance. A moaning noise marks at the airwaves, but I'm unsure from which one of us it comes. I push at her face, grasping for her mouth. She cries out one more time and is then silenced. I move myself back over her and clamp both of her arms with my knees. The pain throbbing between my legs is but a minor distraction. I grip her mouth and nose with one hand as mucus absorbs into my gloves, my other hand has hold of her neck. In the end I think she suffocates. To be certain I release her mouth and strangle her properly. I hear the bone in her neck snap. There's no mistaking it, it gives up a muffled cracking sound. And I let go.

I pause for breath. Then take the scissors out of my pocket and start to cut. The woman's underwear is as unsavoury as her attitude, her bra being a dirty grey instead of the white it once probably was. Her knickers are as tatty, with the elastic coming away around one leg. Pierced belly button. Shaven pussy. Appendix scar.

It's as I'm reaching for my bag containing the DNA that I hear the voices.

"I'm sure it came from this direction" says a man's voice.

"No, we need to go this way" counters a woman.

"I think you're wrong" says the man "It was definitely over here".

"Hello" shouts the woman in a high pitched trill "Hello."

"Hello" booms the man.

For a second the sound of their voices paralyses me. Then I move into action. I empty the DNA, a key, on top of her and reach for the beads. All the time the voices get louder. And closer. I guess them to be coming from the east and about 200 metres away. I look down at the woman. But have no time to waste and no time to think. I switch on to autopilot. I open the bag containing the string of beads and hastily drop the contents on top of her. They hit her stomach and roll down the side of her body, falling carelessly onto the floor. I don't wait around to replace them. I stand up and start to move.

Chapter 15

I'm over a mile away and travelling to the north when I hear the scream, it pierces through the air, sending birds scattering from the trees in every direction. I don't stop, I continue through the foliage with ever increasing speed. Cursing myself as I go. Cursing my stupidity, but worrying at the same time. Wondering if this is the day I'm going to be caught. Wondering if I'm going to spend the rest of my life in prison. Because if prison is my future, then I'm not sure that I've got it in me, I'm not sure that I shouldn't speed home as fast as I can and select one of my pellet guns. That I shouldn't just rest it against my chin. And pull the trigger. Then decorate the bedroom walls in a Pollock style frieze, and let someone else do the mopping up. Let it be their problem instead of mine.

My legs move quickly. My brain does too. Switching from one thought to another. Thoughts such as killing myself. Thoughts of how to escape. And questions such as where it leaves my plans. It all cascades through my head at such a fast rate that I can't fathom anything out. I stop abruptly in my tracks as another thought strikes. What if, in my frenzy, I've left any clues behind?

My blood runs cold.

I start to move again. It's too late now, I tell myself. I've got to keep running. But I get to thinking that I've not been quite so clever this time, that I've not really got a grip on today at all. All the while I'm travelling there's this thumping sensation in my chest. There's this lump stuck in my windpipe, making it hard for me to breathe. Adrenaline is pulsating through my veins. Revving me up, pumping me on. Powering me forward. Through the bushes, over the roots, even out onto a pathway into the open for a short while, and I don't care if anyone were to see me. I'm past caring, I'm just looking for the exit, that's what I'm doing, I'm looking for a way out of all of this. And the quickest route possible please. And my clothes, the absurdity of my clothes in the late November browns of the forest. With my dark brown trilby and my two tone purple and blue mod suit. And my pink shirt, with my lace tie flapping against my chest. And my shoes, my winkle pickers, they sure aren't coping with this running very well. I don't know what I was thinking. All I know is that it's all starting to melt.

I reach my car in a sweat and jump into the driver's seat, and then put the car in motion.

I'm twenty metres down the road when I realise that I'm still wearing my gloves. Smears of clotting gore and strands of bright ginger hair are attached to my knuckles. There are visual reminders across my suit too, as blotches of crimson are splattered across it. A lighter red stains my shirt.

I pull my jacket together. My foot hits hard on the accelerator. The car powers forward. I reach fourth gear in record time. I speed like a mad man, throwing the car around bends, wanting to crash, wanting to burn. Wanting to switch off from my life. I drive in no particular direction. All I know is that I'm putting my fuel consumption to the test. I speed from one road to another, coating the asphalt with rubber.

Ten miles on and I start to slow down. I begin to regain my composure and reign in my demons. But not enough to turn me around, not nearly enough to send me home where Maureen is waiting. I drive past my county and into the next. I drive even further still. On, past town after town. Skirting round the edges. Taking one obscure B road after another. Avoiding the roads which might be busy. Or those that might take me near to anyone. The roads pass by in a blur as the darkening sky looms in, bringing the evening with it. Hedges and fields, trees and distant cottages are relegated to the rear view mirror. The car curves and swerves, cutting though the countryside, passing the occasional remote pub and sweeping through tiny villages. I drive for so long that the red on my clothes starts to change colour, it gradually deepens into a dark burgundy. The stains of my gloves crossover to the black leather steering wheel, leaving smudgy stains. Outside, it begins to rain. Raindrops patter onto the roof of my car. And then slide down the windscreen. Distorting my vision. Leaving me at a loss as to where I am and where I am travelling to. I flick the wipers on. And become entranced by the pattern that the water makes on the window. Blurry signposts point down country lanes stating names which have no meaning. My only companion is the tarmac which stretches endlessly in front. On I go. Trying to put a distance between the events that have taken place. Running if you like. But I choose to see it differently. I see it as merely getting away from the scene. Eventually I drive so far that I pass the bad weather by and the clouds in the sky shift behind me.

Cars, looking for an alternative from the rush hour traffic, can be seen in the distance. But I continue. Past fields. Past road signs warning of deer. Past country roads with tree top canopies. Past imposing houses with sweeping driveways. On past fern filled verges. The road eventually breaks into a bleak hillside which gradually winds upwards. At the top, it breaks out into a flat where there is nothing to be seen but for grass and the occasional wind sculptured tree. Eventually I look at the petrol gauge and tell myself to snap out of it. I pull in at the next lay-by and switch the engine off.

The first thing I do is to try and take my gloves off, but as soon as I start the pain gets to me. My fingers don't seem to want to straighten and even before I look at them I know that it's bad, and I don't need the dull light from a single streetlamp to see the blackened bruises forming all over my knuckles, I could feel them before I even looked, I could feel them as soon as I made contact with her face over three hours ago.

When my gloves come off, the sight of my hands makes me miserable. Worse than that, there's a dull ache inside my head. A headache which is rapidly sliding into a fully blown migraine. Whilst all the time there's a voice inside my head, asking me the same question over and over again. 'What have you done this time Charlie? What have you done?' Try as I might I can't seem to silence it. And for once in my life I don't seem to have an answer. All I know is that I've got to starting thinking real quick. Because if I don't...

I begin by reaching into the glove compartment and taking out the bottle of water. I open a packet of tissues and wet them. Then begin to clean. I start with the steering wheel. I scrub everywhere, millimetre by millimetre, the top, the underneath, and the centre, until it returns to its former state. I continue to scrub even after the wheel looks clean. And then I move to the gear-stick. Only the more I look for stains, the more I see places where they could be. On the indicator. On the switch for the lights. On the dashboard. Everywhere.

I scrub and scrub, even cleaning the places I haven't touched, but I scrub them anyway. Gradually the tissues reform as a red stained pile at the side of me.

When I run out of tissues, I take my jacket off and turn it inside out and then clean with that. Eventually I tell myself that it's useless and give up.

I step out of the car and walk to the edge of the road, taking in the coolness of the breeze. It's there with the wind breaching my shirt that I remind myself, if I can feel something then I'm not dead. If I can feel the wind, or feel a sensation, then there's hope for me yet. But my thoughts only grate with the reality. For the reality of the situation has changed. The physical high which normally follows such an outing is missing. Now I only feel depressed. Worse than that I haven't a clue of what to do, or where I am, or what I'm going to tell Maureen.

Beyond, at the bottom of the hillside in the distance, twinkling street lights form patterns, they line into blocks and curves and bends. Around the edges they taper out into darkness. The town beneath me plays out its normal life. I sit on the grass to look at it. I make out a pier stretching into the sea and a string of white lights along the seafront. I spy blocks of flats, one high rise stands out from the rest. The rest of the buildings clump together in an urban sprawl. But they give no real indication of their location. Or mine. Its there, standing above the view, that I make my first decision. I realise that I'm going to have to drive down to the town to find out where I am.

As I'm walking back to my car, I hear the sound of a vehicle in the distance. Headlights on full beam stream in my direction. I run and hide by the side of my car without thinking. Waiting for the car to pass. Unsure that it might even be the police. That they might be coming to get me. I crouch, with my knees tucked in, panting heavily, and struggling with my shirt buttons. I rip at them, tearing the shirt apart as panic overwhelms me. I pull off my top and stuff it under the car and then sit there, my chest bared, shivering with cold and trying to hide behind the density of one of the tyres. Then it gets to me, in seeing the way I'm behaving, it occurs to me that I'm getting paranoid, that the police would never be able to trace me here, that I don't even know where I am, so how the fuck would they find me? The madness of it all gets to me and I start to laugh, I'm squatting beside my car in the middle of nowhere with some unknown car passing by and all I can do is laugh. Laugh at the absurdity. Laugh at the way things are unfurling. And laugh at my craziness. Maybe, I think, that I really am losing it, but in recognising that its all gone mad surely that's a sign that I'm not insane, because if I had gone crazy then would I not know how insane all this is? The car passes on its way. The engine noise neither slowing nor speeding, keeping to a regular speed. It tootles off into the distance. But I'm still beside myself. Laughing, but worrying all at the same time. Finding both humour and horror at the way my life is unfolding.

I roll onto the floor and laugh until tears break out and dampen my cheeks. I laugh at my shirt under the car. I laugh at the high pitched screams of the people earlier on and at how close they came to meeting with me. I laugh at my hands. I laugh at the clothes I chose to wear. I laugh at the town beneath me.

My laughter peters out.

I lay in the light of the half moon, looking at the sky, my bare back being supported by the grit at the road edge. I count the stars above me, but lose track after a while. I watch as the moon rolls behind a cluster of clouds and then reappears a couple of minutes later. I try to make out a constellation but get confused. All the while I hear more cars passing by. But I am beyond reacting. I am in my very own Zen.

Eventually I snap out of it and gather myself together.

I begin by changing my clothes. I take off my trousers and replace them with jeans. I pull on a blue Fair Isle knitted jumper and my slip on shoes and put my soiled clothes into a bin liner and then pack them into the boot of my car. I take out my contact lenses.

I walk to the streetlight and stand directly underneath to inspect my hands.

My hands are swollen and just looking at them I know that it's a major problem as there's no way I'm going to be able to hide these bruises from anyone, not from Maureen, not from Harry, not from any of my other colleagues. Even now, I figure, I can't go anywhere with my hands looking this bad. Not down to the town in front. Not to the petrol station. Not even to an off licence for the drink I so desperately need.

I stand under the glow of the light trying to work out a strategy. The chill of the evening wind sweeps around me. In front, the grass laps at the edge of the road. Pushed by the light wind which is blowing in my face. Making me feel cold and focused. Slowly, a plan starts to formulate.

I reach into the car and grab what's left of the water and then empty the remains over the gloves to try and clean them. Once I've rinsed them, I place them over the vents at the top of the dashboard and start up the engine to allow them to dry. After five minutes they are dry enough to wear and I slip them on. Then I climb back into the driver's seat, put the car in motion and head for the town below.

The town is quiet and the shops shut. The one-way system transports me around the centre. I drive in circles, covering blocks, trying to spot what I'm looking for. I get to a junction and take a left. The clock on the dashboard says nineteen fifty-three. I travel ahead, staying to the left of the dual carriageway. Shortly down the road I come to the perfect solution. A garage. A car sales showroom to be precise.

I park up in the forecourt, take a deep breath, and then lift the lid of the compartment in the centre of the front seats and take out my mobile. Eleven missed calls says the display when I've switched it on, and I don't have to look them up to know who they were from.

Maureen answers on the first ring. "Hello" she says her voice all wobbly and upset.

"Hello" I respond sadly.

"Charlie?" she gasps, her voice cracking with emotion.

"I'm sorry love," I whisper. "I'm really sorry."

Then I go silent. I know that anything I say from now on is going to be greeted with relief, that at the other end of the phone I've put Maureen in a state of panic. That she's not used to me having a life outside of our usual routine and that the events of today will have caught her off guard. I know what's going through her mind at this very moment, she's thinking that I've left her and I'm phoning up to tell her that I'm with another woman. Then she's wondering how I could've met someone else, she's probably spent hours stewing over it and wondering if my trips to Mrs Gibson were for real. Or whether I spent the time meeting up with someone else. Then she's looking at herself in the mirror next to the telephone stand, she's looking at how old she's become and at how she's stopped making an effort recently. She's noticing how her jowls have filled out and how her eyes have sunken and become hooded, at how her clothes are practical rather than glamorous. And she's turning away from the image, she's turning because she feels more comfortable when she's not looking at herself. She'll have spent the entire afternoon contemplating life without me. And it'll have scared her. So any bullshit I come out within the next few minutes will be greeted with relief. I know because I know her that well. I know because there's nothing she can hide from me. Nothing.

"I…I… I thought you'd had an accident" she stutters, her voice straining with emotion.

"No" I reply, letting her suffer for a little longer.

"Charlie…? Where are you…? What's going on…?" she asks her words hesitant but having to be said.

"You're not going to believe this…" I say, feeling the bullshit start to slide off my tongue. All of a sudden I start to talk. And for the first time ever I feel the power of getting one over on her. The gullibility of my Maureen, my poor, stupid Maureen. At the moment she'll believe anything, I know she will. I know because I'm all she's got. I know because she's too old to start again. She's too prim.

Maureen, who has only ever known me. Me, her first and last. Sometimes I feel like she owns me. But on days like this I have to wonder. Because on days like this it's all I can do to stop myself from being really cruel. To stop myself from really hurting her. To stop myself from saying something in spite. Something that'll just about see her wounded for the rest of her days. I remind myself that I don't need to go making any enemies at the moment. That it's the last thing I need. All I need is someone there to keep me level, all I need is Maureen. "…but a guy at work told me about a car that was for sale at a garage down in Eastbourne."

"Eastbourne?" she says in confusion, "What? Eastbourne by the coast?"

"That's right," I tell her "that's where I am at the moment."

"You're in Eastbourne?" she asks, unable to comprehend my words.

"Yes" I retort, getting exasperated, "I'm in Eastbourne!"

"Why didn't you phone me?"

"I didn't think I had the phone with me" I say, "I thought I'd left it at home" and once I'm on a roll, its as if I'm taking on a character "I'm so stupid" as if I'm method acting in a play "I put the phone in the glove compartment instead of where I normally keep it, in the tray next to my seat" that's what its like for me "so when I went to phone you, I couldn't find it" that's what my life is like "I didn't have time to stop off to call you" like one long drama "it's only when I was looking for some water that I realised my mistake" just one long piece of acting. I end my speech with a "I'm sorry love."

Maureen believes me and why shouldn't she, I've been the model husband for twenty two long years, I've fallen in line and I've done everything she's possibly requested, there aren't many blokes who could cope like me, there aren't many blokes who would bite their tongue in the way I have. There aren't many blokes who can stretch to the levels of endurance that Maureen has put me through.

"It doesn't matter" she says softly, now that she knows I'm alright and that I've not run off with someone else. "So what's all this about a car?" she says, her voice getting back to its normal authoritative tone.

"It was Bill," I explain "he told me that there was a BMW for sale at the garage I'm at and that it was a good price, I've driven all this way only to find that it's been sold."

"What? At this time of night?" she snaps.

"It wasn't this time when I set off" I reply sharply "I got lost with the sat nav, it took me down a dead end road by mistake."

"Sorry" says Maureen.

I suddenly feel guilty, it's a rare occasion when I hear her say that word and it brings home what a fraud I am. Hearing Maureen say sorry always has that effect on me.

"I don't know why you're looking at a new car though, our Mondeo is perfectly fine" she says trying to bury her apology as soon as she's said it "you should have spoken to me before you drove all that way, what do we need another car for?"

"It seemed like a good idea" I say, beginning to regret phoning her, "I wanted to do something different for a change, to surprise you."

"To surprise me?"

"Yes. It was going to be a present for you."

"Oh Charlie" she gasps.

"But I messed it up."

"No, you didn't" she coos.

"Yes, I did."

"Are you alright?" asks Maureen quietly now

"Yes. Why should you be asking that?"

"No reason, it's just that I'm worried about you, you've been so distant recently and you seem preoccupied. Is there anything bothering you?"

"No, nothing" I reply.

Then I think about it, I take a look down at the bruising around my knuckles and call me manipulative, but suddenly I start to see a way through all this trouble, because I sure have got myself into a tricky spot this time. And there is Maureen standing with the door wide open. Sometimes life is like that, sometimes a way out can present itself at the most desperate of moments, so when I hear her speak and when I take on board what she's just said, there's only one thing that I can do, I grab the chance that presents itself before it disappears. "It's just that I'm feeling a little bit tired at the moment" I say wearily. "I think I'm coming down with something." Silence from her. "I really shouldn't have driven all this way when I'm not feeling so good" I tell her in an apologetic tone. "I don't know why I did it, it was impulsive of me. I just thought that it would be nice to do something special for you for a change, to show you how much I appreciate you, but this journey has made me feel worse. I think I might have a fever coming on. Maybe I should take a few days off work" I mumble, inspecting the damage to my knuckles. I notice the deep cuts on my right hand which aren't going to disappear overnight. "I think a few days in bed, tucked up under the duvet might help, I have been feeling strained lately…"

"Perhaps you need some rest" says Maureen as if it was her idea all along. "You have been looking pale recently, I think you've been working too hard and I do worry about you. I'm sure Clapton's can manage without you, after all you haven't taken much sick leave since you started there and how long have you been there? Twenty five years? It's a long time. The company must owe you by now. Take some time off, get some rest, and I'm sure that you'll be feeling better soon enough."

"You're right," I agree "I'll start the car and make my way back home. It won't take me long, maybe a few hours, but I'll come home and then go straight to bed. Several of the lads at work said they felt a bit off colour recently and I've probably caught something from one of them. I really shouldn't have driven all this way. I should've consulted you first."

"Your dinner's here, I'll keep it warm for you and I'll make you a nice hot toddy when you get back."

"I don't think I can stomach anything love, I don't think I can look at food at the moment, I just want to climb straight into bed. You don't mind, do you?"

"No" she says. "It's alright, I understand. Just come home. Drive safely, but come back home."

I reach for my ignition key. "I'm on my way."

And for once I don't feel too sore with Maureen, because for once she's made things easier for me.

Chapter 16

Depression hits me hard, leaving me unable to get up from my bed. It's been the same for nearly a week. My hands still look bruised, but the colours are changing, the blacks are turning to yellow and soon they'll start to fade. The scratches are beginning to heal too, but boy do my knuckles feel itchy, they itch just about most of the time and its driving me crazy with wanting to scratch. But I know that I mustn't because it'll set back the healing process. Even without the visual reminders I know that I've got issues, because try as I might, I can't seem to come to terms with my last murder. I've always known that I am capable of murder. I've always known that I had it in me, ever since I was young. I've never had any qualms about squashing a spider, or swatting a fly, I've even been known to pull the wings off butterflies, and as I grew older the knowledge that I might have to go to war as a reserve gave me no moral dilemmas, my training in the Territorial Army gave me a calculated insight to the business of death, so when it comes down to the last man standing, the choices are easy. I've always been clinical in that respect and I've managed to separate the emotions of death into a calculated equation. We live. And then we die. Some live longer. And some don't. The method I use is to turn people into targets as the whole damn business is simpler that way, but what happened last week was different. I got far too involved for my own good. I let my emotions take over. And I lost control. I found myself crossing a line that I'm not comfortable with. Which in turn has made me take a fresh look at myself. Its given rise to some pretty deep questions. The act of violence which spilled out of me has shocked me to the very root of my being. It's given me cause to ask 'who am I?' Because I'm not sure anymore. Before last week I knew, before last week I had it all worked out. But now, I've unearthed a side of me that I never knew existed. And I fear it. I fear it because once unleashed I don't know if I can contain it. Like my decision to commit murder, all it started out as was a small crumb in the back of my mind, but as I started to explore ways in which I could carry it out it snowballed and with each and every idea it only got bigger. All of a sudden the option of whether I did or didn't kill was gone. The act of collecting and imagining and plotting had taken me over and was spinning me towards the conclusion, and I got to the point of no way back long before I stepped in and snatched the first woman. So now I ask myself questions such as, is the man last week who I really am? And, was last week just a glimpse of who I've always been? Because if it is, then I've never really known myself. And that truly is a revelation. Only it's not quite welcome in my life. The knowledge that I've spent time on this planet and have never been aware of my true capabilities, and we're talking real violence here, we're talking something so destructive that it nearly took her face off, well that's just scary.

The bedroom door opens. "Charlie?" says Maureen.

I stay hidden, tucked under the duvet, unwilling to communicate with her. She walks to the side of the bed and says my name again, then waits for a response. When none is forthcoming she walks back out and closes the door. Less than a minute later the front door slams shut as Maureen leaves for work.

I sit up in bed and rub my face vigorously and, as I do, my fingers catch against the stubble across my chin, it makes me wonder what I must look like. But I won't be shaving for a while as I've not gone near a mirror since I last killed. I don't dare look.

My head spins from lying down for too long, or maybe it's the intense thinking that's been going on, and the pit of my stomach turns with an empty hollow sensation which neither food nor medicine can soothe. These feelings are with me constantly, as are the four walls of this room. Only I'm in no mood to get up, I'm in no mood to do anything. Worse than this, I know I'm going to stay this way for a while to come. I'm not going anywhere, not until my fingers heal, not until I can go out with confidence, not until I can walk down the street belying who I really am.

I sneak a look at my hands. There's no change from when I last checked them ten minutes ago. In disappointment, I look away. I reach for the folded newspaper on the cabinet beside the bed which Maureen must've put there when she looked in on me.

The front page still holds the screaming headlines from last week's news. Bold black letters proclaim that the link has been made. FOUR MURDERS, it states. Beneath it are the pictures of four of the women, all of whom I recognise.

The hunt has begun. The reporter writes with alarm. He writes so that I don't even recognise myself. He writes about the ferocity of the last attack. And at the way I was nearly stumbled on. He tells the readers that the people who found her are being treated for severe shock. It goes on to report each victim and the circumstances of each one. It says that a DCI Riley has been brought in to oversee the hunt and that he is experienced in this type of inquiry, having worked on several high profile cases in the past. It discloses that the police have named their inquiry Operation Woodland. The article finishes off by writing that I have been dubbed 'The Woodland Killer'.

I put the paper down and reflect.

It's not how I thought I'd feel, reading about each murder doesn't give me any satisfaction. Seeing the screaming headlines warning everyone to be extra vigilant doesn't make me happy. Maureen's thoughts about the murders don't inspire me either, the way she goes on, of how a crazy loner must be at large, and of how no woman is safe, of how he's out there stalking the streets as we speak, and how she's not even safe going to the shops by herself. Maureen and her opinions. All the while I'm sharing a bed with her. All the while she's stood in the same room talking to me. All the while my hands are tucked under the sheets. It doesn't make me feel any better. Not now that I've realised I'm not the person I thought I was. All I know is that I've got to see it through and get it out of my system for once and for all. But I worry. I worry a lot. I wonder when all of this is over, if I can go back to the person I was? Can I ever return to the me I knew before? Because I don't think so. It's this that scares me the most. Everyday I wake up and I find myself asking the same question, why have I taken it so badly. Why? When I know I'm a murderer. Why? When I know what these hands of mine are capable of. The answer belongs in the violence. It's that which has changed everything.

I lie back and stare at the ceiling, I look at the paintwork, which could do with a new coat. One part of it in particular catches my eye. It's a crack which breeches the coving. It is split and broken into the shape of a cross. The cross starts me thinking about religion.

I wonder whether priests and nuns and vicars and believers really do believe in a greater being or whether they find comfort in handing their life over to some moral constitution, where boundaries are set for them and where their future is taken care of by rules of behaviour, where their life is mapped out in advance. But what's the point in having someone else dictate how you live? And can a person really live to the end of their days and find absolution in giving up responsibility for their entire life? Or is it a cop out? Surely they must feel a tinge of regret at the very end. Surely it's better to live in the flames of danger, and experience, and excitement, than to succumb to the banality of restrictions. Surely it's better to live a life which is laced with the flavour of toxicity, but which gives a person the chance to enhance their life, than to live in one of conform. Can the godly masses really be blessed and be saved for giving up their choices? Can their souls really be pardoned or set free for what amounts to apathy? Can they really find comfort in settling for a life of familiarity? Or do they have times of frustration?

My thoughts of religion lead me to think about death. I think about my mother and of how she gave up her life in the devotion to our family life. I wonder whether she had any regrets about the way she lived her life. I recall her lying in her coffin in the parlour of our home, at how still she was and how serene she looked. She didn't look dissatisfied. Even so, I didn't take her death well. I spent many years afterwards feeling disappointed that we didn't spend more time together when we had the opportunity. It wasn't like she was too busy to see me. I suppose I was bereft for a while. I felt as low as I do this week.

I sit up with a start. Suddenly I see it all so clearly. I come to understand what this week has all been about. And strange it is, how odd, that me, a killer, me, who has murdered other people, and has caused all of this trouble… is in bereavement.

For myself.

Chapter 17

I buy flowers. I'm walking down the street and I happen to look into the florist's window. There behind the glass in a big silver bucket they catch my eye. Blooms of chrysanthemums. All fresh and bright. Their petals having just broken out. The next thing I know I'm in the shop and the woman behind the counter is asking me which colour I'd prefer. White. Or brown. Or pink. Or yellow? I choose pink.

She wraps them in a delicate floral paper and hands them over.

When I exit the shop, I feel good. Maybe, I think, I've bought the flowers because I've caused so much trouble recently and it's my way of trying to balance the sheets, to do something nice for a change. Maybe I'm trying to give instead of all the taking I've been doing. Maybe I'm just feeling guilty. Maybe it's something else. I don't know, but for less than a fiver the flowers make me feel better.

"They're for you" I say handing them over.

The expression on her face is reward enough. Mrs Gibson's smile says it all. But she speaks anyway. "You shouldn't have" she replies gratefully, her smile as broad as any I've ever seen.

"I'll get a vase" I mumble in a sudden rush of embarrassment. I head off to the kitchen and find what I'm looking for on top of the mantelpiece. It is in amongst a group of dusty old pots and cookery books. I reach for it and bring down the multicoloured vase, its glaze slightly cracked to one side, which is holding some plastic roses. I empty them out, clean the vase, and then fill it with water.

When I get back into the lounge I take the flowers out of her hands, open the wrapping, and hold them out for her to see them properly. She gazes at them appreciatively. "They're beautiful" she says.

"I think so too" I agree.

Once she's had a proper look, I arrange them into the vase and place them on the table next to her seat and then sit on the couch.

"I'm glad you've come today," she says "as I've been meaning to speak to you". Only while she's talking to me, her eyes travel between me and the vase, as if she's checking that they're still there. She reaches out and touches a petal and then satisfied she turns back to me. "I think I'm getting near to the end" she whispers.

"Don't talk like that."

"No" she replies, her eyes fixing me with a determined gaze, "I know that it's hard for you, but all the same it has to be said, I don't think that I've got long to go. My body is starting to give up."

"In what way?" I ask. But I don't want to know. I don't want her talking like this. It gets to me. Only I like making conversation with her sometimes, I like to keep her company, and if this is what she wants to talk about, if this is where her head is at the moment, so be it.

"I don't know" she says, becoming confused, "but it's there, I can feel it. It's in my arms and in my hands. It's in my body too." Mrs Gibson looks away. She turns to the window and gazes out at the sky. "I'm not scared," she says, in a pitiful attempt at bravado, "I've had a good innings and I've done everything I could wish to do. I just hope that when it happens I go quickly, that's all."

"Don't be silly. You're as tough as old boots, you are. You'll last forever." Then my mind flashes back to running through the woods, to thinking about blowing my brains out and to thinking that I'd reached the end of the line. For a second I get distracted, I become involved in my own thoughts, thoughts of running and thoughts of why I was running. It strikes me that I was thinking like Mrs Gibson not so long ago. That I was thinking that the end was near. But then I tell myself I'm here two weeks later, aren't I, I'm still alive. "You might even see me out" I tell her. And I mean it, because I know life can be like that.

"I very much doubt that" she responds, turning back to me, "you've got years ahead of yourself, so don't go wishing your life away because it all goes by too quickly as it is."

"I'm not. I'm just pointing out that we don't know when our number is up, it can happen at any time. It's not always about age."

"You're right" she agrees. "But when you get older, and I am in my late eighties now, I'm eighty-seven now, you know, when you get to be as old as me, age does become a factor."

"People live to be a hundred these days."

"They do, but what quality of life do they have?"

"It depends. Some of them are still with it."

"Some of them" she repeats.

"People are living longer and they're having active lives for longer too" I tell her.

"Yes, yes, I know. And I know that there are lots of people out there who are older than me, but I also know that I'm getting weaker and my body can't continue like this forever. Things have felt different for me recently and I sense that I haven't got long left" she says, her voice direct and strong, much stronger than the frail body that it comes out of, "I don't worry about dying, I'm not afraid to meet my maker, the only thing that ever concerns me is that I might lose control of my body."

"I'm here to help you."

"I know, that's not what I'm talking about, I'm talking about if I was really ill, or if I was to get one of those illnesses that old people get."

"What? Like Alzheimer's?"

"Alzheimer's doesn't scare me. And it wouldn't worry me if I was to lose my marbles and go gaga, that would be for the National Health to have to deal with, they'd have to stick me in a home and prop me up and that'd be it, I'd end up as someone else's problem and I wouldn't even be aware of it. No, the thing that worries me is if my body was to let me down, but my mind stay lucid. The thought that I'd able to hear and see everything going on around me but that I wouldn't be able to communicate, that I'd be trapped and no one would know that I'm still in there, the thought of that scares me."

"I think if it were to happen, then it would've happened by now" I say.

"You're probably right," she replies kindly "but all the same I'm thinking about making a living Will. I had this chap visit me recently, he was from a firm of solicitors in town and he was here to update my Will, we got talking and he said that I could make a living Will and that I could request not to be resuscitated in the event of me becoming seriously ill."

"You don't want these solicitors talking you into things like that, they don't do it for charity, you know, its all business for them."

"I know," she replies "but I can't see the point in living if I was to be a burden to other people, I can't see the point in taking up a hospital bed or of being alive if I were to be in the way."

"But you're not in the way."

"Not now, although I do worry that I'm taking up your time, and then there's the district nurse and the man from the wheels on meals, you all could be doing other things."

"We could, but equally we could be at another home helping someone else out. That would be no different to helping out here."

"Maybe so" she concedes. "What I'm trying to say though, is that I've had a good life and I've done everything I ever wanted to do, there's nothing much left for me anymore, all my relatives are dead," she says sadly "apart from you, I think about you like a son. You're part of my family now, which is why I've mentioned you in my Will."

"Don't go telling me things like that," I say "I might be tempted to bump you off."

"Silly" she replies, with a big grin on her face, "You'll do no such thing."

"No, I won't," I say reassuringly, "but you shouldn't leave anything to me. It's not why I visit."

"And who am I to leave it to?" she asks me now. "There is no one else. When my son John died, that was it. He was the last in line and he never had the chance to have any children as he died so young. So there is nobody else, and there's no one else I'd want to leave it to either. If I don't stipulate who I want it to go to, then I'll end up dying in intestate and all what I've got will end up going to the government, that's the last thing I'd want. It'd be swallowed up and spent on the feckless. At least this way I have a say in where my money goes."

I look at her. And it gets me. I let her get to me. Her head with its rhythmic bob, her frail body which is always tucked under a blanket, even on the hottest of days, her vulnerability and that fact that she's right, that she is moving towards the end, we all are, but she more so than others. When you start to smell it, what can you do? There was a point, not in the distant past as it happens, that I'd pass people like Mrs Gibson in the street without even noticing them, it seemed like I was a million miles away from who they were, that I was a different species even. But the clock is ticking and time moves on. Now I can't help but compare. I can't help but think, hasn't it all gone too fast. And, it isn't going to be long. If anything, it makes me even more determined and it adds to my reasons.

"It isn't a lot" she says, "but all the same I want you to have it."

What can you say? What is there to say?

"Thank you."

I say thank you, I don't know why, but I say thank you and although it seems inappropriate in the circumstances, it's the only thing I can think of to say. Mrs Gibson smiles. Sometimes life is like that; sometimes what might seem wrong is actually welcome. She's just told me that she thinks she's going to die soon and she's promising to leave me something in her will and all I've got to say is thank you. It seems to make her happy. Crazy isn't it. What a crazy world it is.

"I had a visitor two weeks ago, which is why I contacted my solicitor, it was Elsie Brannon's daughter, Emma, you remember Elsie, don't you? The one that used to visit me on a Friday."

"The one with Parkinson's?"

"That's right" she nods. "A couple of months ago I'd heard that she'd fallen down some stairs and her daughter came to update me on what's been happening."

"How is she?"

"She's okay, but she's been in hospital ever since the fall. Her daughter was telling me that she only had a broken arm and concussion, but once she'd been treated they wouldn't release her because she was too ill to look after herself at home. She's ended up stuck in there ever since. One of the consultants told her that they weren't allowed to let her mum move back home and that she would have to be moved into a nursing home because she couldn't stay in hospital, he said that she was bed blocking. Emma came to tell me that they've found her a place in a specialist nursing home but because of her illness the bill is over £3000 a month. Imagine that?"

"It can't be that much, can it?"

"Apparently so. I was shocked when she told me, I remember when that was a year's wages not so long ago" she says. "Anyway, she seems to think that Elsie will never be able to go back home again. The social services have stepped in and told Emma that she has to sell her mum's house to cover the bill and that they'll give her a loan in the meantime."

"Don't the social services pick up the bill?"

"They should do, but they're refusing to" she replies grimly. "I don't like what I'm hearing and I only hope that I don't end up in a home because that would eat into any legacy I wish to leave and I wouldn't want that to happen. I can't say that its fair, not when I think about it, it seems like our generation paid into the social security system, that we were the ones who got it going and built it up and in return all we get is a paltry pension, which is barely enough to cover the bills, especially the gas and the electric, we get clobbered with council tax, and if it gets too much for us to cope in our own homes, they stick us in a nursing home and all our assets get seized. Its shocking how the system works."

"It's not right."

"It certainly isn't" she agrees bitterly. "I'm not prepared for that to happen, my late husband wouldn't have wanted that to happen either, he worked hard in order for us to buy this home, it wasn't like it is now, it was different when I grew up. We started off married life living with my parents in a rented house, that was the way it was in our day, and when we bought our own home, which was mainly because of my husband's forward thinking, it was only right that my parents moved in with us. They lived in this house until the day they died, bless their hearts. It's all I want as well." Smoky stirs on her lap. She puts her hand down and strokes his back. He rolls and extends his claws above his head and then stretches his body. "It's not just about me, of course," she says, looking down at Smoky, "this is his home as well."

"Indeed" I nod.

"I can't say that I approve with the way the system runs today, why should the bone idle get cosseted and the people who've supported themselves have to pay again, we paid taxes and our national insurance and then we have to pay again when we're ill. My home is the one thing that my husband and I achieved, it's a symbol of our life together, it was all we ever wanted, our aspirations and our hopes. Which is why you're so important to me, I rely on you and it's the kindest thing possible that you're willing to help me stay in my home. I do appreciate it."

"I know you do."

"So you shouldn't go buying me presents, don't go wasting your money, you've been more than kind already and I'm sure that there are more important things that you could be spending your money on."

I brush away her concerns. "I don't mind" I tell her, eying up the flowers guiltily. "Anyway, they weren't expensive and I thought they would cheer you up."

"They have and it was nice of you."

It's while we're talking that I start to look at her in depth and I can't help but notice that she's looking smaller and her dress is getting looser, that she doesn't fill it out anymore. Sometimes we pass by so quickly I don't see the subtle changes that are happening to her. Then all of a sudden I take the time to be with her. Its then that I realise she's shrinking. Wasting away. The sight of Mrs Gibson makes me question my mortality and I ask myself, is that what the future holds for me? Is that what's waiting around the corner? Because, if it is, I don't like the look of it one bit. Recently I caught sight of myself in the mirror while I was getting dressed, what I saw was shocking. My skin is starting to wrinkle. Subtly I might add. But it's happening all the same. Seeing it was frightening, it only exacerbated what's in the back of my mind. I feel nervous about growing old. The vulnerability of it all.

"Are you alright?" asks Mrs Gibson.

I look at her. "Yes."

"Have you gotten over your cold yet?"

"I'm still a bit tired."

"Perhaps I've picked the wrong moment to have this conversation with you."

"No, it's alright" I insist.

But I'm not so sure. Seeing the old people in the supermarket, the ones that lived through the war and fought in it, the ones that were strong and able, who went through difficult times and are now reduced to shuffling along. The old folk with their walking sticks, or in wheelchairs, or propping themselves up on Zimmer frames. And the smells that emit from some of them. All of them, I tell you, live in fear. Just talking to Mrs Gibson confirms it. So when I start to think about it, I feel scared, and I'm not so sure I want to get there. I'm not sure that old age is for me. But what's the alternative?

"I can prattle on sometimes."

"Its okay" I reply. But it isn't.

"I'm glad to have you back. The woman who was in for the past two weeks was awfully nice but it wasn't the same as having you around."

"Who did they send?"

"It was a woman called Helen."

"Yes, I know her."

"She didn't do much of the gardening because she said she had an allergy to grass, but she did help to clean the house."

"I can see that" I reply, looking around the room "it looks very tidy."

"It won't last" she grins.

I look at her. And then wonder how on earth I got into my current situation. I suppose that it goes back to the past. A few years ago I thought I had all the time in the world. The days just ticked on, one after another, I used to think that tomorrow I'd make it all come good, that I'd sort it all out given time. But that time just ticked away, one day after another. Menial jobs and errands got in the way. But I didn't stop promising myself. Now, I can't help but look back. I can't help but think that my golden age has gone. That any opportunities I could've had have been sidelined by my age. Its stupid things really, but it counts in my life, things like the fact that I don't look the same without my clothes on anymore. And that I can't hold my drink like I used to. Things like, I can feel my body slowing down and I'm not as athletic as I once was. I ask myself, is all that's been happening lately just one extreme midlife crisis? That this sort of thing, or its equivalent, is happening to lots of other people out there and that everyone gets to this stage at a certain point in life. Only my being around Mrs Gibson is giving me cause for concern. She's a signpost of what I fear the most and I worry that she's exacerbating my situation. But I can't walk out. I've fallen into a trap of my own making. I've become involved.

I get up, unable to cope with the conversation any longer. I stretch exaggeratedly and then walk to the window and look out at the grass. "I see the weeds have taken advantage."

"Yes" she replies. "It's a bit of a mess out there. It's probably because of the house at the back, they've let their garden to go to seed and the weeds are spreading over here."

"The house with the students?"

"The very one."

"Someone should have a word with them."

"They won't listen; the youth of today don't listen."

"I don't suppose they will" I reply. "Not to worry, it won't take me long to get it back in shape." I move back into the room. "Do you want to come out and sit in the sun?" I ask.

"No thank you" she replies, looking down at Smoky who is still asleep on her lap, "I'm comfortable here."

"Very well" I say. "I'd better go out and get started, but knock on the window if you need me."

"Will do."

I head to the door into the kitchen and then make my way into the garden. The first stop I reach is the garden shed.

Chapter 18

"I'd like a word with you, if you don't mind" says Andy from sales, walking over to our table and addressing Keith. Only today Andy's not speaking in his superior nature, today he's got the time to patronise us, the manual workers, instead of his buddies in the sales department, so as soon as he speaks it brings the canteen to a halt.

"You're the union rep, aren't you?" he asks, knowing full well that Keith is, and has been for the past thirty years. It's all that Keith can do to look up from his chair with a weary expression and nod. Andy grabs a vacant seat at our table, hitches his trousers up at the knees, and sits down next to Harry.

"It's about the pension fund" he says.

"Oh yeah?" answers Keith despondently, folding the paper he was reading and putting it on the table and then leaning his elbow on it to stop anyone else from taking it.

"I've got a slight problem" Andy continues, as his eyes flicker across the table, taking in the grime which is embedded into the top of it. He slides back into his seat and pulls his face at the offending mess. Then remembers where he is and adjusts himself, "its just that a couple of months ago I decided to move my pension to another company, my brother's been telling me about a pension called a SIPP, it's a self invested pension plan, you know, the type where you can run your own pension portfolio, he seems to be doing quite well with his, and after that brief spell when I dabbled in the stock market a few years ago and made a bit of money, I thought that I could give it a go…"

Harry, sitting next to Andy, leans across the table to me. "Biscuit?" he asks offering me his packet of lemon thins. I glance at the open packet. Normally this is an inducement to talk, but today I'm not in the mood and so I take a biscuit, pop all of it into my mouth and then start to crunch it loudly.

Andy shoots me a look.

I shrug my shoulders and carry on munching and he backs down. He knows that he might be able to have it all his way on the shop floor but in the canteen he's no more a chief than me. He pulls a surly face and gets back to what he was saying.

"...it's just that I've been waiting for a valuation of my pension for a few months now, and the more I wait, the longer I'm having money go out of my wages and into the company scheme. I don't want to keep contributing to the scheme as I'd like to be in charge of my own funds and I've had a word with the Admin staff but they say that they're not allowed to stop taking my money out of my wages until I get it sorted out..."

Harry offers the packet of biscuits towards me again in desperation.

Keith nods sombrely at Andy. But says nothing.

I take three biscuits and place them on the table in front.

One of the young girls starts laughing loudly to catch Andy's attention, but he's too engrossed in what he has to say to notice. "It's my pension... that I've contributed to... and I should be entitled to take my money out at any stage, after all I put the money in, I've earned it" he says, his voice breaking out into a whine.

"Did you watch Big Brother?" Harry asks me, pulling a sulky face.

"No" I reply abruptly.

"What about Love Island?"

"No."

I pop another biscuit into my mouth. And he gives up.

"It's my future that they've got control of and if I can do better..." Andy continues, looking around the table for support.

Harry starts to perspire. I crunch my biscuit. Keith stares with a glazed expression. Mick picks at his nose. Bob eyes up the paper.

"Anyway, I keep waiting for a response from them" he says, toning down his voice as he realises that his visit isn't as welcome as he'd hoped, "I've put my request in writing and so far I've made at least twenty phone calls to try and sort it out, but I keep getting fobbed off. I don't seem to be getting anywhere."

"Hmm" says Keith thoughtfully.

"All I really want is to get my money out, and sooner rather than later."

"Ah" says Keith in a way that you know won't be good.

"'Nother?" asks Harry, pushing the biscuits forward.

I point at the two biscuits in front of me and shake my head.

"Is there anything you can do about it?" asks Andy desperately.

"The thing is…" says Keith slowly drawing out the news "…there have been changes to the way that pensions can be run."

"I need the loo" says Harry, shoving his chair back. It scrapes across the floor, but he is gone before anyone has time to complain. I watch him as he walks away. Harry knows when bad news is on the horizon and it's the last thing he wants to hear. I make a silent bet to myself that when he gets to the porcelain he won't be able to do anything. That's because he only went twenty minutes ago and he's never been that regular. No, I say to myself, he's shipping out before he hears what's coming next. Harry disappears, but its Keith that I'm interested in. Keith pauses as if he's contemplating on how to break the news, as if his brain is searching for the safest sounding sentence; him being the bearer and all. Andy's not going to like what he's about to say. All the while it's written on his face. Its in his eyes, it's in his sombre mood. It's buried in the wrinkles across his forehead. Bad News On The Way. Only Andy, not being one of us, doesn't get the message.

"Which are?" prompts Andy anxiously.

"Which are" Keith drawls awkwardly "that the pension rules have changed and now the company has the right to delay the request for a valuation."

Andy looks puzzled. He scans around everyone trying to make sense of it. He looks around our table, to Mick, to Bob, and to me. Then over to Sally and Kate by the coffee machine. He looks at the empty chair where Harry had been sitting. Finally he looks back at Keith.

"How long can they delay it for?" he asks.

"I believe it can be indefinitely" Keith replies as blandly as he can in order to soften the message.

Mick, who's been following the conversation with interest, moves up in a flash. "What does that mean?" he asks angrily, stabbing his finger at Keith.

Keith, thinking that he's going to get hit, flinches. When he realises that he hasn't been thumped, he sits and flicks his hair as if that was what he was doing all along.

However, it's across the table that the real action is taking place, Andy's looking at Keith with disbelief, as if its personally Keith's fault that he can't get his hands on his money. He flexes his chest and leans forward in a menacing manner. Andy being a good fifteen years younger than Keith, he fancies his chances, and with him being a Millwall supporter, he's not normally the type to debate.

"But without the valuation I can't move my pension" he says in a half question.

"Precisely" replies Keith curtly. "It's not my fault" he says, exonerating himself quickly and showing his palms. He squirms and looks at his watch to see if he has got a get out route. Then he checks around to see if he can hasten the march back to our workstations.

I bask in the enjoyment of the situation. Ever since Keith took on the role of union rep he's walked around the building with an air of self importance, as if taking on the role of extra responsibilities without more pay makes him more important. If you ask me it makes him stupid. The workers are unhappy and anyone in that room can see that the unhappiness is beginning to get to him. I reckon that he got more than he bargained for by thinking that he could move up the ladder.

"They have every right to do it" adds Keith bleakly.

There was a point when I craved to be up there, where all I wanted was a bit of responsibility, when all I desired was a promotion. A leg up the pecking order. But that was in the days when the unions ruled. That was in the beginning before I became ingrained into the system. Then everything was done to rule and the only tune on the hymn sheet was servitude and mastery. But times have changed and now it's all evolved into a different ball game. Now a promotion is no longer about respect, it's no longer a sign of experience, it's more to do with politics and blame and it's the ones in the middle that carry the can. The management at the top can easily step aside with a big payoff. The minions at the bottom are there without any real importance. But the ones in the middle, the ones like Keith, are stuck in a vice of their own making. I chuckle to myself.

"The bloody management are robbing us" Mick shouts angrily throwing his hands in the air and gesticulating wildly.

"You're wrong this time Mick" replies Keith, rolling his eyes.

"Am I fuck!" shouts Mick in a rage.

Keith doesn't react. His voice remains flat but firm. "I think you are. I think that you'll find that it's not the management this time," says Keith, unhappy that he's been turned into a spokesman in support for the company but happy to put Mick right. He turns and addresses Mick personally, finding it easier to tell him than to face Andy whose scowl is now taking on a sinister manner. No, Keith's happy to tell Mick because Mick's a snapper, Mick would take on Andy, or even Andy and his mates any day of the week, he'd be happy to take them on even if he were to lose, a bloody nose and a black eye or two on a Monday morning says he will. Keith knows that if he can convince Mick that he's right then he can extricate himself without the punch up that's waiting on Andy's knuckles, "it's the trustees who get to decide whether to allow members to transfer their rights out of the fund."

"So who are the bloody trustees then?" asks Mick.

"The trustees are the fund managers who invest the portfolio, they're called Maxwell Carter and they get to say where the money goes and who gets to have access to it. I think you will find that they can block anyone under the age of sixty-five from exiting the fund."

"They can't do that" says Andy in disgust. "I've put my money in, it's my money, I've earned it and it's for me to decide where I want to put it." Andy in his smart pinstriped suit with his heavily gelled blonde hair which is sticking up into spikes is starting to look ruffled. His top lip curls in dismay.

"It's to protect the fund" Keith tells Mick.

"Protect the fund?" shouts Andy, pushing up his sleeves, "Protect the fund? How's that when the fucking fund is falling?"

"It's there to pay for the workers who've been at the company for a long time, that's what it's set up for. If people take money out of the pot before they retire then it'll balls it up for everyone else. That's the way pensions works, the younger ones fund the older ones."

"Fuck me" says Andy. "You can't be fucking serious? How can that be? I'm fucking stuffed! There's more fucking pensioners in this place than in a fucking bingo hall!"

"I didn't make the rules" says Keith.

"But you're the union rep, surely its up to you to it sort out?"

"I wouldn't want to even if I could" mutters Keith.

"You what?"

"I said I wouldn't want to even if I could" he repeats cautiously.

"Are you for fucking real?"

"I'm here to give people advice" says Keith, continuing to address Mick "and my advice is that it would be too costly to try and challenge the trustees and there's no way you would win. My advice is that the trustees would be able to use the pension money, our money, which we've put in, in order to defend their position, and that could have an affect on our pensions. I can put it to the union but I'm pretty sure that they wouldn't support such a move. My advice would be to accept that your money is in the pot and to let the trustees get on with investing it."

Andy crunches his knuckles and glowers across the table.

"Yeah" says Mick standing up and suddenly changing his tune and agreeing with Keith.

Keith looks on in surprise that for once Mick sides with him. His face breaks out into relief, having Mick on his side just about gives him the edge because with Mick's support he gets the rest of the canteen on his side as well, Mick's the type of bloke that no one disagrees with. Not even a supposedly hard man like Andy.

Andy backs down, he knows when he is beat. He throws a sneer to everyone around the table and stands up, pushing his chair heavily. It falls over and bounces off the floor. But he doesn't bother to pick it up, he kicks it instead and then turns in anger, "well you lot are fucked anyway" he snipes spitefully, his face turning red in rage, as he steps over the collapsed chair.

"You what?" asks Mick, squaring up to confront him.

"You lot, you're fucked" seethes Andy, "the management are in talks to move the plant over to Bulgaria, of course they'll need their sales teams based back here, but the rest of it, well, work it out for yourselves."

With that, Andy pushes past Mick and marches to the exit. He reaches the door just as Harry reappears.

Chapter 19

I approach her on the darkest of nights, the sky up above is filled with angry clouds which are heavy and low. I look up to the biggest cloud directly above me and wonder whether it'll hold out. It is dark and full and threatening. The signs don't look good. I consider abandoning my plans for another time. But, when you've taken the trouble to turn out in the way I have, what's a few clouds to spoil the party? I tell myself that if I'm quick this should be easy. Which means no messing, be focused and don't prevaricate. Even with this in mind I walk steadily.

The time is shortly after six pm and the evening has already set in. I scan the street before striking. The streetlamps cast a lazy yellow hue, barely lighting the scene. On each side of the road the houses are shielded behind closed curtains, tucking the occupants in and keeping them out of view. All the cars in the road are parked up for the night and are stationary and silent. A man ahead of me slips around a corner and out of sight. The street is left with two occupants. Me. And her.

I step onto the pavement as the woman passes me by. She is lost in thought. I interrupt.

"Excuse me dear" I say, in a hesitant voice. "Could you help me?"

The woman swings round, her impatience at being stopped evident. And then her face changes upon seeing me. Her features soften but retain a puzzled expression, as if she knows that there's something not quite right about me but she can't quite work out what it is. "Are you alright?" she asks me in a patronising manner, leaning forward and peering at me as if talking to a child.

I shuffle back a few steps. "I seem to have lost my dog" I say, turning and holding the empty lead in the air.

Her eyes sweep over me in the dusky light. She studies my floral dress, with its thick starched collar that conceals my Adam's apple. And then takes in my crumpled beige handbag, which contains my necessities, my knife, my scissors, my DNA and my beads. She wears a pitiful grimace as she notices my thick dark support tights. And then scowls as she looks up at my wig, with its light brown curls sticking out of the old green crepe hat upon my head. My pea green coat to match gives her no sense of joy.

"It's not the night for losing a dog, is it?" she says.

"No" I reply, stooping to try and reduce my height.

The woman looks at her watch.

"I'm sorry," I say softly, my voice barely a whisper, "are you in a rush?"

The woman consults with her conscience. "No" she replies. "Nothing that can't wait."

She glances over me again, and then takes a step forward.

"What's the dog's name?" she asks.

"Fluffy" I reply awkwardly.

"Well I'm sure Fluffy can't have gone far" she soothes.

I glance towards the place I aim to take her. The alley beside us is so narrow that it barely spans the width of one person, it's the perfect setting. It gives me the excuse to move in on her without her becoming suspicious. It's an alley with a start but no ending, having a curve halfway down it, bending to accommodate the row of shops and their courtyards with which it parallels. It leads to a river a block away but few people have use of it. One small street lamp halfway down gives light to the concrete passageway and the bits of debris which litter the route. Multi-coloured graffiti proclaims the names of the few that have dared to venture through. The woman follows my gaze and then catches her breath as she sees the mess.

"When did you last see him?" she asks me hesitantly.

"He slipped his lead a few minutes ago" I croak, "and he ran off down there."

I point to the direction I've no doubt she'll take, I point down the alleyway beside us.

The woman grimaces as her eyes take in the pile of fresh dog dirt which lies at the entrance. "Do you live nearby?" she asks.

"I live in Charlton Street, two blocks away."

"Do you think that he might have gone home?"

"No," I falter "he went in the opposite direction. He probably went to the river, he likes it down there."

"I see," says the woman.

"I'm sorry," I say, my voice becoming higher. "It's just that I worry about going into alleyways in the evenings, you hear of all sorts of things like muggings and murders. The streets don't feel safe for an old woman like me anymore."

"Here, here" says the woman gently "don't you worry, I'm sure that we'll find him. He can't have gone that far."

With that the woman falls into my trap, she turns and steps straight into the alley.

I follow behind, taking one faltering step after another, finding it difficult to walk in women's shoes. The front of them squeezes against my toes and the bridges press down harder, the chafing at my heel is worse. I sense the beginnings of a blister taking shape.

Ahead of me the woman calls out. "Fluffy" her voice echoes, in a cut glass accent which is strangely alien in its surroundings. She stops at a gateway and then pushes back an old wooden gate. Her head briefly disappears as she checks the courtyard. She reappears and continues forward. "Fluffy". Every few paces she looks over her shoulder in order to give me a reassuring smile. "Fluffy" calls out the woman. "Fluffy."

"Fluffy" I mimic, hobbling behind.

"What breed is it?" asks the woman.

"Breed?" I query, taking another faltering step. My arm reaches out to touch the wall in order to give myself some support, but it makes no difference, it doesn't stop the shoes from hurting. The tightness of them has my feet in a vice like grip and they're becoming more and more painful with each successive step. "It's a terrier, a small brown terrier."

"Right" says the woman.

A sharp stabbing pain shoots from my feet through my body. I feel the irritation move upwards into my system. Boiling to the surface. I sense the need to unleash it. To let it all out. To let off steam. To vent the rage. But I warn myself not to go down that road again. No, I tell myself, I'm not going to lose control this time and I'm not letting this situation get out of hand. This time I'm going to make it easy.

"Is it a Yorkshire terrier?" she asks.

"It's a crossbreed" I mutter.

I am three paces behind her. Keeping a distance, but being close enough. Close enough to know that she is within reach. Close enough to know that there's no way out for her. Close enough to get a backdraft of her expensive perfume.

"Are you sure he hasn't run home?" she asks.

"No."

I watch transfixed at each step the woman takes. Her hips moving smoothly. But it's her trousers that really have my attention; they crease and level out with each step as she moves graciously down towards the bend which leads us out of view of the street. The trousers are a light cream. I find myself worrying about what kind of mess they'll end up in, with them being such a light colour and this being an alleyway. But then I guess I might have to cut them anyway. I might have to if they don't come off easily.

"Has he done this before?"

We round the bend with me taking each step gingerly and her ahead treading easily.

"He likes to run down to the river and bark at the *ducks*."

The last word I use is the last word she hears; it intones my usual manly voice. A baritone syllable breaks from my mouth. There can be no doubt. She turns in shock. It's there, where the light from the lamp is brightest, that she realises. It's there that her face changes colour and she gives out a gasp. One hundred metres into the alley her life ends. She knows it before it happens. She realises as she looks straight at me. And sees me for who I really am. She concedes defeat before I even lay a finger on her.

I throw my hands around her neck and pull her into a small siding. I force her behind a black plastic wheelie bin of all things and it's there that I bring her life to an end. There in the mid evening dusk. There, with my wig itching, and the crotch of my tights slipping down my legs, there, in Mrs Gibson's floral dress and her woollen coat. With my face smeared in make up and my shoes pinching at my toes. With a handbag swinging from my arm. And my calloused hands doing their thing. There, witnessing her every disbelieving expression, I take her life away.

When she is gone, I drag her body into a doorway and bring out my scissors and begin to snip. I cut straight through her expensive woollen top. Then pull down her trousers. I run my blade through her matching lacy panties and bra. I expose her finely couture clad body to the elements of the mid evening frost.

She lies in the shadows, with her head propped up against the brick wall of the yard and her arms drooped beside her and her legs slightly askew.

I open my handbag and bring out some tissue. I pick up her hand, wrap her fingers around the tissue, and then, once it contains her prints, I drop it onto the path nearby. I put the beads onto her bellybutton.

When I'm finished, I pause to bend down the backs of my shoes. Then step out of the doorway and into the night.

Chapter 20

The man looks bedraggled. His grey hair is combed and gelled into place, his clothes are neat, and his suit is his Sunday best which has been starched to perfection. His shirt is crisp and smooth, his tie is perfectly placed, and he is recently shaved and well turned out. His face however conveys his inner turmoil. It is ridden with agony. He tries to speak. He opens his mouth but the words combine into a mangled gasping hiss, it's a sound which curls and evolves and stretches until it forms into an unsightly sob, which takes him over and wracks through his body. The blonde teenage girl sitting next to him throws her arms around him and he collapses into the hollow of her neck as his tears flowing heavily.

The cameraman sensitively swings him out of view and focuses on the boy sat beside him. The boy, with the same elongated features as the man, gulps and speaks slowly into the camera. "My mother would help anyone… she was popular… and in the prime of her life… it was two days before her 46th birthday… and she was taken away from us when we least expected it." He stops, and is briefly unsure of himself, unsure of where to look, or of what to say. He breathes in deeply, holding his breath for a few seconds, mentally counting because he remembers that that is what his mother taught him to do to control his emotions. Count to ten, she used to say, and so he does. But as he does, he's painfully aware that he's not going to get any advice from her ever again. He wonders how he will cope without that advice and without her there to remind him to wash his shirts and to brush his teeth. He holds back the salty water that threatens to dampen his cheeks and then continues. "This man needs to be caught… if anyone has any information… no matter how small… then please, please, report it."

A second camera focuses on the man sitting alongside the family.

In the mixing desk behind the scenes the assistant producer touches a button and transmits a pop-up card. The card appears across the television sets throughout the country. Detective Chief Inspector John Riley states the words.

The man leading the investigation sits forward in his seat and stares straight into the camera lens.

"Firstly I'd like to say that Mrs Curtis-Hayes was attacked and killed in what can only be described as unpleasant circumstances. We as a team offer our sincere condolences to the family at this time. We have reason to believe that Mrs Curtis-Hayes was lured from her usual route home to her death and we implore all members of the public to be on their guard. If anyone is approached, for whatever reason, please bear in mind that this man is out there, is dangerous and needs to be caught…" he says, each word echoing the steely determination inside him.

Deep down he reminds himself that he's got a small task force and a low budget which he doesn't know how to spend to best effect. That the laboratory reports are beginning to confuse the inquiry, because despite having managed to get DNA from several scenes, none of it fits together, the only real things to link the crime scenes are the beads but there's little information coming from that source, he's had squads going round the churches and he suspects some of the beads may have come from abroad, but other than that there is nothing. So far there have been no witnesses. Nor any firm leads. The man has struck in prime daylight and in popular locations so how can that be, he asks himself. He tells himself that there must be someone out there, someone who doesn't even realise it yet, who might've got a glimpse of him. He's got thirty seconds of airtime to find a witness, thirty seconds to convey the devastation of one family's grief then to make his plea, to stop this person before he kills again, and while he is sensitive to the family beside him, he needs to get his message across, he needs all this time and more, all this time to reach out and stop him. Before it's too late. "We have already linked him to several other murders which have occurred over the recent months and we now strongly believe that he will strike again. This man is a danger to the public, in particular he is a danger to women, he won't stop until he has been caught and safely locked away. I implore anyone with any information, no matter how small, no matter whether you might feel that it is trivial. I'm asking you to come forward and you will be treated in the strictest of confidence. We believe that several people were in the vicinity of the River Cherwell at the time of the most recent attack and those people have yet to come forward, we need those people to get in touch with us. The area that this took place is known as a courting area, I want to state now that we're not interested in the reasons that these people were in the area, any reasons will be treated with the strictest of confidence, and all we need is to eliminate them from our inquiries. We can be contacted directly at the Surrey police station where we have set up an incident room. Alternatively you can go into any police station around the country. Remember," he says as the technician begins his countdown "it's vital we stop him before he strikes again."

Chapter 21

Iask myself, am I mad? I think not. No more than anyone else on this planet. I'm sure that deep down everyone else has similar thoughts to me. Anger, bitterness, hurt and rage, all combining in a sense of disappointment that someone has let them down. And then thinking the worse, wishing someone was dead and hoping that the police will turn up at the doorstep, to lead them into the front room where some young bobby with a sympathetic lull would break the tragic news. Then how softly one would cry.

I'm sure that every adult around the world has thoughts like these and have even rehearsed their reaction to receiving such news. From a brother to a lover. From an angry wife to an ex seeking revenge. All no different to me. All wanting their pound of flesh. All secretly wishing for the grim reaper to call.

What is this world in which I exist? I'm caught in a world where people conform. Where we're reared into being nothing more than clones of everyone else. We're human robots who have been programmed by society's demands, from the style of our hair, to the clothes we wear. From the way that we talk, to the social life we lead. Our look has become no more than a uniform. Our life is in everybody else's hands. We must do what everyone else expects of us. Must have friends of a certain type. Must have correct model of car and home with at least one dinner party a month. All I see are ants. Ants scurrying around. All on the same journey. All of them judging. And the newspapers want to print that I'm insane. We have to say please. And thank you. We have to hold open doors. And stand in a queue. And everyone does it without question. A gold ring around your finger so that you belong to me. Holidays that count. Two point four children. Hamsters on a wheel. And god help us if we're different. But I'm not different though. Not from the outside. Nor on the inside either. The only difference with me is that I choose to act on my impulses. How many people have the guts to do that? The world is the same everywhere you go, because every country has its own set of rules. But when it boils down to it, it's all the same. Must walk the same way. And eat the same food. Pasta in Milan. Noodles in Hong Kong. Curry in Bangladesh. We must look the same. And act the same as everyone around us. Individuality? Not on this planet. Use the wrong blend of butter and you're trouble. And what is work? It's a grading, that's what it is. How many people have I met who immediately ask me what my job is. A lot. A classless society? I don't think so. Blue collar? White collar? Professional? Graduate? Does it matter? Yes. It matters. It matters to the people who need a label. It's a sticky tag to enable us to group. Just beware if you try to change category. No road sweepers on this side of the town thank you very much. No, I'm not mad. Everyone else is. Must remember to use the correct knife and fork. And live in a house exactly the same as everybody else. Boxes. Rows of them. All in a line. All with the same mass produced green velvet curtains. Hands up those who've owned velvet curtains in their lifetime. See! And our high streets, which are the same from one end of the country to the next. What town am I in now? Does it matter? No it doesn't because Vicky in Newcastle, with her teenage pregnancies behind her, is as cynical as Tina from Cornwall who can't stop shagging her best mate's man. How do I know? I've seen the daytime television. It's all out there. With the self absorbed tears. And the pitiful whining. It makes for good ratings though. Then there are the celebrities who will eat worms for the attention. Or those who court the paparazzi and then, when they become famous and they get the publicity they wanted, they complain. There are the politicians who speak of duty and fairness and change for the better, ask me if they're corrupt after a year in office, ask me if their principles meet with their aspirations. We all want. We all crave for something more. And at some point we all stop and ask ourselves why. Why? Why, because we've sold ourselves down the river, Why? Because we follow what everyone else does. Why? Because we've bought into the nightmare and now we're too scared to do anything about it. But I'm not scared. I've been liberated. I'm swimming against the tide of public opinion and I don't give a shit what the papers print about me, they're wrong, killing is the sanest thing I've done in a long time. It's given me a purpose. And it has set me on the right track. I've been given a future. That can't be wrong, can it? Then, when I've completed my crimes I know that I'll sit back, well away from the rat race, I'll sit in some corner of the world that's not polluted by traffic fumes and that's not built around what extras have been added to your car, or the latest modernisation that's been added to the house, that's not built around those little imaginary boxes that cut off the circulation and stifle and limit. Those boundaries which we cram ourselves into like cornered vermin. And that everyone's too afraid to step out of. I'll sit in my own little space, away from the stink of manipulation, away from the cog wheels which bind into nine to five, away from the envy and the spite. From the jealously and the discontent. From the crowds of the half witted population. From the pushing and the pulling. The tugging and the snatching. Well away from the greed. The demanding. The wanting. And the whining.

And I'll laugh. I'll laugh at all the bastards I've left behind.

Chapter 22

Iknow exactly where to stand. I wait inside the bushes at the side of the path which leads to the pond and then stay as still as I possibly can. My green jumper and my black trousers mix into the foliage becoming the perfect camouflage. I'm not taking any chances this time. I'm here to do what's necessary. I'm here to connect my past with its future.

I stand frozen, barely daring to breathe. My eyes, the only things with any movement, are firmly placed on the pathway ahead. After a while even the birds don't notice me. They come and sit on branches nearby. Tweeting and fluttering. Hopping from perch to perch. They don't distract me. There are no distractions for me today. All I can do is wait. And hope. Hope that she comes my way. Hope that no one else is around at the same time. And hope that everything goes to plan.

Before long I spot her. Walking heavily. Swinging her hips from side to side. Her red coat, bright and loud, like a flag to a bull. Her blue trousers, neatly starched with firm creases down each leg. Her cream Macy's shopping bag by her side. Her hair perfectly set after a trip to the hairdressers. She casually strolls down the empty pathway as if she has all the time in the world. And how I, in that instant, feel joy. How I laugh. Without even moving a muscle.

I wait until she is directly in front of me and then jump out and grab her. I go straight for her mouth. And clamp it firmly. And then I pull her sideways into the trees. I spin her round. And let go. She opens her mouth, with the intention of screaming. But, in seeing me, her eyes only widen. The sight before her takes her breath away. She looks at me in astonishment, her face a glorious mixture of horror and shock which mingle together to create an expression which I've never witnessed before. In seeing all of this, in witnessing it first hand, it's enough to throw me into fits of hysterics. It's enough to wipe me off my feet. It's enough for me to guffaw in her face. But I don't. I suppress my urge to laugh. And instead I smile.

"Hello" I say, beaming happily.

"What the...?" she responds, her words petering off.

"I wanted to surprise you" I continue with a giggle, as if what I've just done is the most normal thing in the world.

"Surprise me?" she asks in confusion.

"Yes."

"Well you've done that alright" she says sharply, throwing her shoulders back and bristling angrily. Only there's something else beneath her irritation, something deep down which she can't quite hide. Perplexity. It's just how I expect her to be. Angry. But curious. "For a second I thought I was going to be attacked" she huffs.

I start to laugh. "Don't be silly," I say "why would anyone want to attack you?" But as soon as the words have left my lips I know that I've made a mistake, that she's taken my remark badly, her face immediately drops into a deep seated frown as she takes umbrage with my words. It wipes the smile off my face in an instant.

"Charlie? What are you doing here?" she asks me abruptly.

"I've got a surprise for you" I stutter. And I have. Only now I'm not quite as sure of myself as I was a few minutes ago. Now something inside of me says that this time I might have bitten off more than I can chew. That this time my plans might be harder to execute. That there's still time to put a stop to all of this before it goes too far. So I ask myself, is this really what I want? But I know alright. I've known it for a long, long time.

"A surprise?" she questions as her eyes sweep across our surroundings taking in the scenery before us. She scans the autumn leaves and the woodland setting. The gold's, the oranges, the reds and the deep dark greens all intermingling into picturesque postcard scenery. Nothing unusual. And nothing frightening. There's nothing wrong with this scenario at all. Not even with Maureen. She's exactly how I expect her to be. She's her usual bolshy self.

"Yes."

"Where?" she asks, holding out her hands in exasperation.

"It's not here" I say pointing through the branches towards the centre of the park where the pathways don't connect. "It's back over there, I've hidden it amongst the bushes over that way" I tell her. "But, because it's a surprise, I'm going to have to cover your eyes until we get there."

"Nonsense" she retorts, unwilling even for once to let me be in charge. "Neighbours is starting in twenty five minutes and I haven't got time for this."

She takes a step away.

"Don't" I retort.

Maureen looks back at me, the anger in her face. She gives me a withering look to let me know that I've spoken out of turn and that I'm in trouble when I get home. But she's never been one for public scenes. She waits, and brews, she plots, and holds the thought, but as soon as the front door is closed she really lets me have it. Which is why I rarely cross her. But cross her I have and I can see from the expression on her face that I've given her a dilemma, on the one hand we're outside, but on the other hand, there is no one around and I can tell that she's tempted to berate me. "Don't ruin my surprise" I say sadly, before she's had the chance to consider what to do, "It's taken me ages to prepare."

"What's going on Charlie?" she asks.

"Nothing, I just wanted to do something different for a change."

She opens her mouth to speak but then stops and furrows her head. "What's that jumper you're wearing?" she asks.

"It's an old one" I reply.

"I've never seen it before."

"You bought it for me, don't you remember?"

"And those trousers?"

"You know these trousers. I've worn them on many occasions. You've definitely seen these before."

"Hmmm."

She pulls her face, but she remains in the same spot. Hesitating and loitering, as if about to leave. But she's not going anywhere. I know it, she knows it, and I know that she knows that I know it. The fact is Maureen has to know everything and the notion that I could've hidden something from her, and that I know something that she doesn't, it's almost too much for her to bear. I see it in her eyes, the indignation. And the anger. That opening my mail and going through my pockets, that looking in my wallet, and checking my phone, that all those sly manoeuvres and I've still managed to keep a secret from her. It's consuming her. Though she may look all demure, though she maybe all shy and playful at the moment, that churlish manner is still transparent.

"Don't ruin my surprise, it's taken me a long time to prepare" I say sadly. All the time I'm talking to her I know that Maureen is watching me, that she can't help herself, that she's playing a game just as much as me, that it's all one big power struggle, but power struggle or not, I've not spent all these years with her and not got to know what makes her tick. All it takes is a little bit of a tease. "All I want is to cover your eyes and walk you to my surprise. It's not very far and I'll be careful…"

"Do you seriously expect me to go traipsing through all these branches when I've just had my hair done? And with you steering me as well?"

The implication that I might not be capable of such a task wounds me. I want to put her straight, to tell her that I've done it before. With great success as well. But I don't. I don't because this was exactly what I was expecting; this is Maureen right down to the very core.

"I want to make up for what happened the other week when I wasn't able to get the new car. I feel like I owe you a surprise and I thought that it would fun to do something different," I say, edging the conversation forward, "to come up with something, a bit like a treasure hunt."

That's all it takes. Maureen's face lights up. Her eyes shine greedily in response. Maureen was never one to resist the lure of a present. But Maureen being Maureen, she takes some time to consider it. She takes some time, but there's no doubt what she'll do. When she turns to me in a more convivial manner and smiles that smile, I know that she's hooked. But then I knew it all along.

"Can't I walk on my own?" she asks me coyly, tilting her head to one side and smiling in a girly manner that does a woman of her age no justice.

"No, you can't see anything until we get there because it'll spoil the surprise."

"Please" she begs.

"No."

Maureen hesitates. She cogitates. She mulls. She even has time to check her hair. Finally she gives in. "Ok" she says eagerly. "But be careful."

I move towards her and caress her arms to reassure her. I rub her cheek. Gently. Lovingly. One last touch. I stroke her hair and cup the nape of her neck. To give myself one last chance to see if anything is left between us. One last chance to try and give it another go. One more attempt at trying to stoke the embers of what once was there. But there is nothing. Or am I wrong. Does emptiness count?

"Turn around" I say.

She turns gracefully and I slip my hand over her eyes. I place my other hand across her body and pin her against me. And in my mind I am strengthened. This being the hardest thing I've ever had to do. But this being the most right.

"Do you have to be so rough?" she says in a whiny voice. Reminding me. Just reminding me.

"Sorry. I thought that if I kept you close then it would be easier for me to direct you as we don't want you to fall, do we?"

I walk her along in an exact re-enactment of my second murder, only this time it is played out with the willingness of my victim. Her feet shuffle beneath her, leaving behind a trail which echoes the pattern of someone being marched along. I've thought of it all.

At this moment I want to lean forward and whisper in her ear, to tell her that she's cost six women their lives so far. And that I've also got to kill another woman in order to ensure that every victim looks like a random attack. That this is what she's going to be, just a single murder in the midst of a lot of others. That the police will come along and find her, that they'll find the rosary beads and that they'll connect her death to the killing of all the others. That they'll then analyse the crime scene and put it down to the work of the same man who's been responsible for all those murders in the past. That they'll go into the laboratories with their DNA, which must be quite a collection by now, and that they'll scratch their heads. I've spent eighteen months planning how to kill her and many more hating. Today is what it's all come down to. The process of committing a murder which wouldn't outwardly be linked to me. I'm going all out for the perfect crime. As for the others, I'm sorry, I'm genuinely sorry. But she was just as responsible as me. If it weren't for her then I wouldn't have had to kill them. But I needed to build a framework.

I lurch sideways and walk her into the branch of an ash tree, making sure that it snags her hair.

"Hey," she says indignantly, her hand coming up to pat down her hair again, "watch out, I've just had my hair set."

"Sorry," I reply "I didn't see it."

Her hand comes up to smooth her hair back down but in doing so she loses her balance and falls against me, probably leaving scuff marks where she stumbled, I applaud myself for my ingenuity in being able to manipulate her. Her being Maureen and all. Her thinking that she knows it all, and thinking that she can tell me what to do, thinking that she has all the answers. Well it just so happens that I've got an answer too.

"Is it much further?" she asks.

"Not long now."

"Can I stop for a second?"

"No, we're nearly there."

"Is it a big present?"

"I would say so."

"Can I guess what it is?"

"No."

"Can I have a clue?"

"No."

"Is it a car?"

"I've already told you, wait and find out."

I lead her into the part of the woods that will give me the privacy I need. In the middle of the bracken we come upon a disused brick and concrete electricity building. I know that its disused because I've already done my homework, I know because I've left nothing to chance. I know that there's absolutely no chance of being disrupted this time. There's no chance of messing it up. I know because Maureen won't let me.

I guide her round to the back of the building. "We're here. This is where you're going to get your surprise" I say. "But before you do, you have to do as you're told. You've got to keep your eyes closed and count to ten and then you can open them" I say, propping her against the brickwork. "And no peeping. Is that understood?"

"Yes."

As soon as I take my hand away it's as I expect, Maureen automatically tries to open her eyes.

"No" I insist, covering her eyes again. "Count to ten first."

Maureen closes her eyes and starts to count. "One… two…" she says, rushing in anticipation.

I remove my hand and take one last look at her. I look at her light blue eye-shadow. And hate. I look at her sagging jowls. And at her crooked nose. And I hate. I stare at her unkempt eyebrows. Then at the lump of skin growing on her left cheek just below her cheekbone. And hate. I take in her big frame, all thick and lacking in the femininity that I once admired her for. And hate.

"…three… four…"

Before the count of five I strike.

Maureen's eyes spring open and her mouth drops in shock. A mixture of horror and hurt combine in glorious absurdity across her face.

"Yes" I tell her quietly, as my hands continue to clamp tightly around her neck, "you're right. What you are thinking is true. I'm going to strangle you and you've only got seconds to live. I'm about to kill you Maureen and it won't be difficult because I've killed before. I'm a killer and I want you to know that, I'm the woodlands killer. All those women who've died around this area in past six months were killed by me, I strangled them. You might be in denial at this very moment but I'm telling you the truth, it was me picking them all off and then coming home to you. I snuffed them out. And now it's your turn."

Her eyes grow wider. With fear. With sadness. With disappointment.

I compress on her neck. But hold off from squeezing too hard as I don't want her dead just yet. I've got a few more things to say to her before she departs. Things that she should know. Things that I've held back on for a long time. I've planned this day. Oh, I've planned it alright. Right down to the very end. So I know what I'm going to tell her next. And tell her I will.

"It's your fault," I say to her now "they were all your fault, because if it wasn't for you they wouldn't be dead, you see you've never really known me, you've never really been able to understand me, you've never been able to give me what I need. Look at me now, look at what you've driven me to, look at what you've created." I am millimetres away from her; in fact I am so close I can smell her breath. Onion salad for lunch again. For once it doesn't repel me. "You're responsible for all of this."

Maureen doesn't put up a struggle, she doesn't fight back. She doesn't put up any resistance whatsoever. Its as I suspected, Maureen would sooner die than live with the knowledge that she'd married a killer. She'd sooner be killed than have to walk down the street with people pointing their fingers at her. I've always thought that it's tougher for the relatives of murderers than for the perpetrators themselves. The killers get sent to jail but it's the ones that stay behind that are those who have to live with it. For Maureen, that's not something she could bear.

Her face starts to change colour which shows that she's moving onto the next stage. I move a fraction closer.

"I want you to know that I'd sooner spend the rest of my life in prison than live it out with you. And that I'd sooner kill you than have to fork out the money on a divorce. I've got you insured up to the hilt and once you've stopped breathing I'm going to cash the money in and I'm going to have myself a real good time. Let me tell you darling, that once you're gone I'm going to have something that I've hankered after for many, many years, I'll have my freedom, freedom to do what I want… freedom for when I want it… and freedom to come and go as I choose."

Maureen's eyes close. A single tear trickles down her cheek. But I've got one more thing to say before I put her out of her misery. I press on her throat a little bit harder, forcing the pain through her, just enough to get her to react, and to let her inner senses take control. Her eyes spring open instinctively. They bulge with the pressure. Once I've got her attention, I tell her my final message.

"I want you to know" I say, leaning up as close as I can get without connecting to her, leaning so close that she cannot fail to hear me out, "that if we both end up in the same place in the next world, don't, whatever you do, come near me ever again."

With that I kill her off.

Chapter 23

For a single second I wonder what I've done. For a second panic flickers through me. And then loneliness. In seeing her dead, in seeing her waxy expression and the harmless look on her face, in hearing the quietness all around us, the stillness, and the emptiness, it's an experience that I've never encountered before when being in her company and it only goes to magnify the situation. I feel a lump in my throat. A deep sense of sorrow envelops me. You don't spend so many years with a person and not feel at least one pang of regret when they're gone, not even if you're married to the worst person in the world. There's always a gap whenever something is moved. Displacement. That's what it is. For a fleeting moment I let it get to me. But my sadness doesn't stay around for long. It soon withers, it shrivels up as I remind myself just why this had to happen and what she was truly like to live with.

I open my palms and let her fall and she slumps to the floor and lands with a thud, her body sprawling in a crooked Picasso like mixture of angles. I stand above her, staring down at the figure lying beneath. I stand there in amazement, amazement that I never thought I'd see this day. Amazement that I pulled it off, amazement that Maureen, my Maureen is down on the ground. Dead.

A single leaf flutters past and drifts to the floor to add to the carpet of leaves which surround her body. It seems touchingly poignant as the decaying leaves only go to mirror the events of today. As I take in the autumn scene, I can't help but think that this is the way of the world. That this was all meant to be a long time ago. A long, long time ago. Even before I ever thought of it. It was all an accident waiting to happen.

I take a deep gulp of air.

Then steady myself.

I focus my mind.

And set to work.

I pull her coat aside, exposing her top. Her beige blouse from the outsize department of a local store tears easily. It exposes her domestic use bra which is thick and cumbersome with pointed cups, and is starched and white, a well washed white. I snip at the middle and then slice through the strong elastic. I release her ample chest. Then look. I look because it's something I've rarely seen of late. I look because it signifies everything that our relationship became. I look because something inside of me wants to find out how depraved I really can be. And how much I can defile her. It's all about revenge. Nothing more.

I move down.

I pull at her elasticised trousers, dragging them off until they meet with her pop socks. Then look. Her pubic hair extends beyond her knicker-line and sprouts down the insides of her legs. It's just how I remember her to be, with her mass of jungle which I always hated and which was rarely groomed. I cut her support knickers.

Once free, her belly moves from the bottom of her ribs back to its natural position. Across her stomach zigzag lines made from the impressions of the now defunct knickers are etched into her fleshy rolls in the most unpleasant of ways.

In seeing her exposed, a deep sorrow hits me. I am sad. But I don't feel sorry for her. Or me. All my sympathy goes in another direction. I feel sorry for the policeman that has to deal with her. That he has to look at her and then he has to come and speak to me. That he has to witness how grotesque her body is and then look me in the eye. I feel uncomfortable for him, embarrassed even. So much so that I get urges like never before, I get impulses that are hard to contain, I want to hide her, or mutilate her, to shred and to cut. To desecrate the sight before me. I want to torch her body, and change its form, so that the policeman won't have to witness what she really looks like without her clothes on, with her lumps and her bumps and her varicose veins. Everything flashes through my mind. Thoughts of annihilating her. Thoughts of hacking. Of cutting. And sawing. Then I think about the blood. Of how easily it spreads. And of how, once it gushes, it begins to clot into those big scarlet lumps. I get to thinking about what my state of mind would be like afterwards and that now more than ever I need to keep it all together. That soon they'll come knocking at my door. That they'll be breaking the news and then watching me. That they'll be waiting to see my reaction. That's when I'll really be tested.

Leave it alone, says the voice inside my head. I listen to that voice.

I dip into my pocket and pull out the plastic bag. It contains a piece of paper. On that paper is some writing. That writing, in sprawling inky loops, relates to part of a thesis. That thesis is about the Merchant of Venice. Act IV, Scene 1 precisely. I drop it carelessly beside her and watch as the paper flutters to the ground.

I place some beads into the folds of her belly. I take one last look and say a silent prayer.

"Please God," I say as I look up to the sky above "don't ever let me see her again."

Chapter 24

The two of them stand sombrely at the door, both holding their helmets in their hands, both looking equally uncomfortable, each waiting for the other to speak. Finally it's the woman who plucks up the courage. "Mr Scanlon?"

"Yes?"

"May we come in?"

My nod is my reply. I swing the door open and we walk into the lounge.

My response is different from what I'd rehearsed. All along I'd imagined what it would be like, of how I'd have to try and act out my grief. Of how I might wail. Or sob. Of how I would fall to the floor in despair. Or stand silently still in shock, unable to comprehend the news. Worrying that they'd see through me. That I'd be transparent. That they'd know. But when it comes down to it my feelings are real and no stage play in the world can come close to the reality. The whole sorry scene is touching, the young man and woman, with their fresh faces and their sadness, are moved by the news that they bring and I am touched. And I am saddened. I feel a stir in my soul as they tell me. I feel a genuine hurt.

I bow my head, unable to look at them any further and sit in silence. Outside a car drives past and the roar of its engine penetrates the room, but the silence inside the room is louder.

"Mr Scanlon?" says the policewoman softly, breaking into my thoughts, "Mr Scanlon, it might be better if you sit back in your seat."

I look at her, with her big blue eyes and her mouth which is turned down. I look at the way she tries to hold eye contact, only for her head to keep rolling away to the side of me. She refocuses and then slides away again in the opposite direction.

I look at her and then realise that it's not her who is moving, it's me. I'm swaying. That's what I'm doing, I'm actually swaying. And no part of me is putting it on. I'm not acting this time, I swear I'm not. It's really happening. Her words make sense now. Her words connect. I grab hold of the side of the chair and sit back into the seat and then look around the room.

This room is where it all began. It was many years ago now but the memory is still fresh in my head. It's as fresh as yesterday's events and as sad as the events of today. It was such a trivial thing that started it all off. But maybe it would've happened anyway.

It began when I got home from work. I had had a particularly stressful day, the workload had been pressured and all I wanted to do was to unwind and to relax in front of the television. Maureen had other ideas that night, she wanted to talk, she wanted to gloat, and she wanted to interrupt my thoughts. It was the way that she was dancing around the lounge, showing off her latest purchase, it was the way that she scowled when I asked her how much it cost. It was the way that she dismissed my question. That's all it took. It was then that the thought came to me, and it was the most fleeting idea. I'd say it was no more than a two second notion. But later it came back to me. From then on, every time she did something irritating, and every time I disapproved, it was there. Gradually the thoughts came more often. Now the policewoman is looking lost, and the man is glancing around the room unable to look at me. Now it has all resulted in this.

"How?" I ask.

"We're not sure yet."

"Where?"

"She was found in the local pack, The Rye, late this afternoon."

"She only went out to have her hair done" I mutter blankly.

The policewoman shuffles.

The man beside her stares over to the dining area.

I'm aware of the ticking of the clock. It's something I've never noticed before and it makes a strange noise, pulling at my attention.

"Do you want me to get you a drink?" asks the woman.

"No."

"Is there anyone we can phone? Or anyone that can be with you?"

"No."

"What about relatives?"

"No."

"Did Maureen have any relatives?"

"Yes" I reply. "But I don't want them here."

"We're going to have to contact them at some point" she says in her softly softly whisper "unless you wish to inform them yourself."

"Oh" I reply. "Right. She's got a sister."

"Do you want to talk to her, or shall I send someone round?"

"I'd rather not if it's alright with you."

"Of course" says the woman, reaching into her pocket and producing a notebook.

"What about any other relatives?"

"There weren't any."

"Parents?"

"No."

"Children?"

"No."

"What's her sister's name?"

"Tina Blackthorn."

"Do you know where we can contact her?"

"Yes. She lives at number 16 Granger Close, in Bexleyheath, it's on the new build estate behind the library."

She opens her notebook and jots down the details. "We'll get someone round there straight away" she says, standing up.

She leaves the room and can then be heard talking into her radio in the kitchen. The other PC sits in silence. I focus on the carpet. I find myself checking the pattern, which is made up of interwoven squares and red paisley shapes. I start to look at it from different angles, but whichever way I look at it, it all falls into line at some point and I've checked the carpet so many times over the years that I know this as fact, but I still check anyway.

"Where is she?" I ask, when the WPC returns.

"She was taken to High Wycombe General shortly after she was found" the woman replies.

She looks at her colleague, widening her eyes, as if passing on an invisible message. He ignores her and turns away. She hesitates before speaking again. "I know that this is hard for you, but there is something we must inform you of," she says quietly "she's going to have to be identified."

"Might it not be her then?" I ask.

The policewoman closes her notebook. "We have reason to believe that it is."

At the hospital I get to meet the man leading the investigation. Detective Chief Inspector John Riley. I get to see him. Face to face. We are less than two feet apart with only a Formica table and a heavy air of intensity to separate us. He is different in the flesh to what I'd expected. He is smaller. And thinner. And wearier. A whole lot more wearier. Fatigue is ingrained into his whole being. Physical exhaustion, and even clearer, mental tiredness is hanging from him like a big neon sign. And nowhere, not anywhere, do I begin to think that he suspects me. There isn't a trace of it on him. Not even the remotest of notions. All there is is the disappointment that another one has slipped through the net. That and the fact that he's answerable to it.

"I'm sorry" he says, his words coated with dejection.

I want to tell him that I'm not, and that I'll get over it, that it's not the worst thing in the world, me not being with Maureen, and the house being quiet, it really isn't so bad at all. Nor is it a problem not having to come home when she expects me to. In the hours in which she was missing, I've come to enjoy my own company. I quite like the freedom. It's been good having the space to breathe. I'm starting to get used to it. I want to tell him but I don't. Instead I stay silent. My eyes flicker past him to the wall of the side room that we're in. One leaflet in particular catches my eye. CRIMESCENE says the bold letters. Underneath it warns that pickpockets can strike anywhere and at anytime. I look back to Riley.

He is looking back at me in sadness. "There's no easy way to tell you this" he says, shuffling uncomfortably in the hospital standard seat, "but we have reason to believe that Maureen's death is linked to several ongoing inquiries which we've been undertaking in recent months."

I stay silent, eying him closely.

He loosens his tie at the front of his collar. His top lip has a hint of moisture and he wipes it away. The air in the room is heavy, the heat too warm for a conversation of this nature. Riley struggles to remain composed. The fold above his lip starts to glisten again. He gets back to what he is trying to tell me.

"I don't know if you're aware of a case that we're currently working on" he says, as his voice starts to thicken, "it has been reported in all of the papers. There have been several murders recently which all point to being the work of the same person."

"Not...?"

Riley makes an oversized nod and then confirms it in words. "We have reason to believe that Maureen was a victim of The Woodlands Killer."

"What makes you say that?" I ask.

Riley squirms, as if the pertinence of my question is getting to him but he answers anyway. "At the scenes of each crime there have been specific details which all point to this being the work of the same individual. At this point in time I'm not at liberty to divulge what those details are, but it is clear that we are dealing with the same person in this case."

"How did she die?"

"We believe it was by strangulation" says the detective. "The autopsy will confirm it."

"Was it quick?"

"I believe so."

"Did she suffer?"

"It's hard to say."

"He didn't..."

"No" he says firmly.

"Christ" I say, slipping my head into my hands.

A sob unexpectedly reaches my throat and I am taken aback by it. It's as if everyone else's feelings are rubbing off onto me and I can't seem to stop myself. The policewoman at the side of us shuffles.

"Why?" I ask.

"We don't know at this stage" admits Riley, as his hands fiddle with the folder on the table in front of him. I look at it. It is a thin brown cover filled with pieces of A4. It is already yawning. I wonder what's in there. Then I wonder if any of it relates back to me.

"I'm ever so sorry Mr Scanlon" he says pitifully.

"I know" I respond generously.

"We're doing everything we can" he says, bending the bottom corner of the file. But his words convey his lack of ability. His words are empty and hollow. "I aim to catch this man and bring him to justice."

I nod.

The policewoman suddenly starts coughing, as if her surroundings are having an effect. I wonder whether people cough more when they're in hospital. My eyes flicker across to her and then back to Riley. He is stuck for words.

"When will her body be released?" I ask.

"We can't say at the moment."

"Will it be soon?"

Riley looks uncomfortable, his brow breaks out in sympathy with his top lip. He reaches for a tissue from the box on the table and wipes at his face. "Because of the circumstances of the situation, Mrs Scanlon's body will have to undergo a detailed examination" he says, brushing at the side of his neck. "We aim to conclude all our tests in the shortest time frame possible, but given the nature of what has happened it's impossible to state exactly how long that will be."

"She was a god fearing woman detective" I tell him "and she believed that people pass on to another kingdom, she also believed that her destiny was in heaven, I for one would not want to impede her on her journey."

"We'll take that into account" he replies "but the more time we have to conduct our tests, the more it will go towards helping with our enquiry. I'm sure you understand it's important that we get as much evidence as possible."

"I do detective," I say, acknowledging his concerns "although I'd like to hope that Maureen can be put to rest as soon as possible. It's what she would've wanted."

"Of course" he accedes. "I will be keeping you up to date with all stages of the investigation. In the meantime, we will be assigning a family liaison officer to you. She will be available to talk to you at any time should you have any concerns or questions. Her name is Sally Curtis and she'll be working alongside me. I'll let her know of any relevant news which you should be made aware of as soon as possible and then you'll be up to date with our enquiries."

"When do I meet her?"

"She should be along shortly" says Riley, looking at his watch, "I've asked her to meet me here but she does occasionally get held up."

"Right."

We wait in silence, Riley fidgeting and drifting off to some world of his own. Me, staring at him. The policewoman coughing. "Would anyone like a drink?" asks the WPC, after a particularly bad hack.

Riley declines. I ask for a coffee and she leaves the room. Riley shuffles his file together.

Eventually a tall woman with plaited hair and a plain face appears at the doorway.

"Ah right," says Riley "this is Sally."

"Hello" greets the woman gently.

I nod.

Riley gets up and they leave the room together. A muffled conversation takes place out in the corridor. I look at the folder but don't bother to touch it. On the front is written OW. I wonder what if the letters refer to Operation Woodland. The policewoman returns with a drink and then stands near the wall again. Eventually Riley returns with Sally. As soon as she steps into the room, she comes over to the table, puts her briefcase down, and touches my shoulder.

"I'm so sorry" she says. At the other side of the table Riley is gathering his file together. He breaks into Sally's sympathetic speech.

"I'm afraid I've been called away urgently and I'm going to have to leave you with Sally" he says. He turns to the policewoman. "Can you make sure that Mr Scanlon is escorted home?" he asks. She nods.

Then he looks at me, his face grave and intense. "Before I go, I want to make it clear that I intend to do everything possible to catch the perpetrator of this crime, I want to make sure that he doesn't get away with it" he says. "I promise you Mr Scanlon that I will do everything I possibly can and I won't rest until this man is caught."

Then he is gone.

Chapter 25

I find myself doing things which I've not been entitled to do for such a long time. And it feels good. I pick my nose. And stick my hand down my pants when I'm slumped on the sofa. I leave the toilet seat up. And forget to shower. I order takeaways every night. And eat when I feel like it. I don't shave for days in a row, until my stubble thickens into something more substantial, until it hides the face in the mirror. I like the look so much that I decide to grow my hair long to match. I buy porn and discreet brown envelopes come delivered to my door via the postman. I spend my time wanking. I sit in the dark with my thoughts keeping me company, thoughts of just how far my life has taken me and thoughts of how my life might have turned out without the interference of Maureen. Thoughts of whom I might have been and of who I could be in the future when all of this is left behind. I think about all the murders so far, I replay them in my head, but find no disappointments in the actions I have instrumented. All I find are reasons to square with what I have done. I arrange for a satellite dish to be installed and then keep the television on continuously. I sit glued to the screen until the early hours of the morning, channel-hopping from one station to the next, flicking to all the programmes that Maureen would've disapproved of, from programmes about sex, to programmes about crime. I watch football matches, and macho action movies, broadcasts which flicker into the lounge, the sound buzzing away. All of the time I am lost in a fog of confusion, confusion of what to do next, of whether to spend the rest of my life going back and forth to work, and staying inside the safe environment which I've built around myself for the past twenty years, or whether to abandon everything and head off into the sunset, which has always been purpose of my plan. But now, having come this far, my courage wavers, the thought of drawing a line and going out there by myself seems daunting, it seems more scary than the events which have propelled me to this moment in the first place. Which is bizarre. But not as bizarre as the life I'm leading. I sleep on the sofa and wake up with backache, but fail to move anyway, preferring it to the marital bed. I pile all of Maureen's stuff into the cupboard under the stairs. All of her gels, her clothes, her makeup, her jewellery and her ornaments, everything that could possibly remind me of her is shoved into that tiny place and boarded over with some pieces of ply and timber. I drink. I have whisky for breakfast and Port for lunch and copious amounts of Vodka. I drink a glass of wine in one mouthful, glugging it as if it is drinking water, not even tasting it really, but benefiting from the numbness that it brings. I buy cigarettes and smoke one in each room of the house, carelessly flicking the ash onto the carpet and then making sure I tread it in. I smoke until my head hurts and I get a migraine, sickness rumbles at the lining of my stomach and my bowels start to churn, but I continue anyway. I continue in the hope that she's out there somewhere, watching and disapproving, but not being able to do anything about it. I want her to know what it feels like, I want her to feel the pressure, I want to bundle up all my years of exasperation and frustration, to shove it aside, to plant it firmly on top of her. To weigh her down. To get her back. To show her how it really feels. And why I had to do it. I still want my revenge. The act of killing her hasn't yet smothered the burning torch of hatred. The hate is still ingrained into everything I do.

I buy rock music and play it at full volume. I headbang in the middle of the lounge, wanting to regain my youth. Wanting to catch up. Or start again. I'm unsure of which. I buy shirts from a trendy surf shop, shirts which wouldn't look out of place on a beach in Hawaii, shirts of all shades, of bright yellows and azure blues, of vivid pinks and funky purples, all of them with tropic designs, of beach settings and parrots and palm trees. Along with the shirts I invest in some shorts, some with pockets on the sides, some plain, some with logos, some so tight that they squeeze at my balls. I complete my look with some wraparound sunglasses and open toe sandals and then wear them out in the winter weather, to the consternation of my neighbours, and the amusement of the local kids, who group at the corner of the street and holler as I walk on by. All along, every time I venture out, I see people avoiding me. I see them slipping into shops, or pretending that they haven't seen me, I see them swerving, or looking in a different direction, unable to face me, unsure of what to say, embarrassed even. So much so, I vow to myself I'll tell the first person to come up that I killed her. But it doesn't happen, the British stiffness stops them from coming. Or maybe it's the lack of eulogy for Maureen. I don't know. But they don't come and I am alone. Apart from one visitor, that is. Sally. Sally, my family liaison officer. With her permanent fixed expression. Sally who lends an art to looking sadly sympathetic. She sends letters through the post, and leaves garbled messages on my answer phone. She sometimes calls by. Mainly she keeps me posted on everything the police are doing and all the publicity which the case is receiving. I find myself being unnerved by her presence, as if scrutinized. I find her shock at the gradual descent of my living accommodation unnerving, so much so that I tell her that unless a major development occurs then I'd rather have some space to grieve. She nods understandingly and then leaves. I contact the insurance companies and set in motion the process of applying for probate. I even contact the criminal injury compensation board and am told that I am eligible for a claim and that they'll send me the appropriate paperwork. I rifle through drawers in order to find any more policies which I might've forgotten about. It's there that I stumble across the one thing that changes everything for me. Stuffed into the back of the bureau, partly hidden by some tissue paper, I come across an old dog eared savings book. On closer inspection, I notice that the book is made out in Maureen's maiden name. But that it was opened several years after we got married. I am stunned to realise that it contains details of deposits spanning back some twenty one years. Money I didn't know about. Savings that had obviously been salted away during the course of our marriage. In total, I'm staggered to read, it adds up to more than twenty five thousand pounds. But it's the last transaction that takes me most by surprise. I look at it in disbelief. An amount of £200 was deposited shortly before our trip to France.

Then I'm back through the bureau, rooting through all the sealed compartments. I tear through all of Maureen's orderly filed papers, frantically searching. Until I find what I'm looking for.

The papers show it clearly. The total cost of the trip to France is exactly two hundred pounds less than the amount she told me it was. I move to the previous deposit. I go through them one by one. After half a dozen I give up. All the evidence is there. All the deposits add up to money which I had given to her.

Infuriated by her deceit, I launch the book across the room.

It bounces off the front window and then hits the floor with a pathetic plop.

I spend the rest of the day in a daze.

I reach for the bottle, hitting it harder than in all the recent drinking sessions I've had of late, needing the comatose effect. I drink. And think. But the more I drink the more I think. Then I get to wondering what else she could have hidden from me. What kind of secrets could she have possibly kept? Why would she want to hide the money from me? What did she need that much money for anyway? It's not as if I didn't give her enough. It gets to me so much so that I get to thinking that maybe Maureen wasn't the person I thought she was, and that maybe I never even knew her. So much so that I know I won't rest until I've eased my suspicions. I move back to the under stairs cupboard. I start pulling. And searching. And checking. Unsure of what I'm looking for. But knowing that it's in there somewhere. Nothing passes my fingers without me scrutinizing it properly.

I come across a necklace. A pearl necklace to be precise. One that I don't recognise and one that I certainly didn't buy for her. It's something that I've never seen her wear. It is sat in a cushioned jewellery box, but there is nothing with it to suggest where, or who, it came from.

I convince myself that Maureen bought it for herself and that the only reason I didn't get to see it was that she didn't want me to know that she'd spent the money. But I hunt a little further. I hunt because I can't shake this feeling of doubt. I hunt because I no longer feel that I'm in control. I feel the life that I had with her is beginning to dissolve and that I've stepped onto a seismic plate which is taking me in two directions.

I get more and more agitated. With increasing anger, I ransack through. Knickers and waxes. Blushers and creams. I wade through all sorts of woman things, things which I'm uncomfortable touching even. But I keep going anyway. Wanting to assuage my fears. Or wanting to prove them. All I know is that I won't stop until I can understand. But what I don't understand is the perfume bottle with the inscription yours forever on the bottom. And then I find two valentines cards made out to Mokins stuffed into an old handbag.

Suddenly I feel sick. I need an explanation. I want Maureen back. I've got some questions for her to answer. I want to know from where these things have come? And for how long has she had them? More importantly, I want to know if Maureen is the person I thought I knew. I want answers. I want them but I'm not going to get them. In disgust I throw the cards in the bin and pack her things back into the cupboard.

In this solitary night everything changes for me, the bedroom no longer seems sacred and Maureen is no longer held in regard. I move the television upstairs and go to bed for the entire weekend with only a crate of lager and some cold pies to keep me company.

For the next week I fall asleep in the afternoon and stay awake at night. The toilet roll runs out, the milk in the fridge curdles, the floor is sticky when I walk on it, and I run out of plates to use. The phone rings but I don't answer it. I stay off work, spending my time flipping through brochures to far flung destinations. I belch. I break wind. I cut my toe nails and leave the clippings on the floor. I lie in a bed full of crumbs. The house begins to stink. It's an unhealthy pong which intensifies in odour as the days tick by. Eventually I have to admit to myself that all these things don't feel quite right. That all of these things are alien to me. That I've been so ingrained to Maureen's way of living it's become a part of who I am. Even without her here, I still find it hard to snap out of those little boundaries that she built around me. After two weeks of furious masturbation, I stop and pull myself together.

Chapter 26

When they finally release the body, the funeral is a quiet affair. The coffin cheap, the service solemn. Her friends from the bakers. Her sister and her family. A few distant relatives and an old childhood friend. Not many to account for her life on this planet. It makes me wonder if I'll get such a poor attendance. Or does it really matter, because once you're gone, you're gone. The vicar of the crematorium says a few pleasantries of how she lived a clean lifestyle. Of how she went to church on a regular basis. Of how helpful she was. Of how tragic events culminated to this day.

The congregation weep.

Mrs Gibson makes an appearance. In black of course. She sits at the rear of the crematorium, venturing no further than the last pew. She closes her eyes and presses her palms together as the man in the dog collar speaks charitably.

I turn back to the view in front, my eyes focusing on the box which almost blocks the middle of the aisle. The man says a prayer. And then the air is broken by music. Elvis's Love Me Tender pipes out of the system. Maureen's favourite record plays as the coffin passes through the curtains at the front.

It's as I'm watching it disappear that I suddenly become jumpy, I get the urge to stand up and run over to the coffin, to rip the lid off. I suddenly need to see, to make sure, only to double check that Maureen's in it. To make sure that no one's made a mistake. To ensure that she burns at a very high temperature. Only to ease my mind that she's out of this earth for good. I keep imagining that I'm in the set of a horror film and that she's going to wake up any minute now. That she's going to sit up from that creaky coffin. And then look across at me and point her finger.

But it doesn't happen. The music plays. The mourners grieve. The coffin slowly slides out of view.

Watching the coffin move behind the curtains and disappear, the enormity of it all hits me. That this really is the end. That it's the final closing scenes for Maureen. Suddenly I want to laugh; I'm overwhelmed by the desire. I start to laugh. Then, remembering where I am, I change it into a sob. I bend forward and cover my face with my hands. Whilst my cackling sobs rock my body. A hand or two reaches forward to pat my back. But I'm not interested as I don't need the comfort. All I'm aware of is the voice going through my head. I'm free, it says, I'm free at last. I throw my arms up into the air and scream. A wailing sound echoes around the walls and then reverberates in the recesses of the room. A gasp of horror comes from those around me. Shuffling feet back away.

I can't control myself any longer, I leap up and then turn and jump over the back of the pew in one fluid movement, my eyes transfix onto the door at the back as I make a dash for it. I run, in a burst of drama, out of the room and into the lobby of the chapel. Then on beyond. Out of the pointed double doors. Out to the rest of my future. Out without a second to spare. On the steps of the crematorium, the few guests who'd been too embarrassed to stay in the room with me, part as I move past them. I spring down the concrete steps in one long leap. And then run across the gravel yard. I race down the path to the north, past all the headstones, past the plots of rotten corpses, past all the wilting flowers and the weather beaten teddy bears. I pass the fading pictures of relatives who no longer visit. A few people, tending graves, look up in astonishment. The gravediggers stop and stare. One or two elderly people, pottering along between the rows of stone, look round in confusion. I ignore them. "Fuck 'em all," that's what I say. The death which surrounds me makes me want to live the rest of my life without a second to spare. I power up that path as fast as my legs will take me, out towards the iron gates at the end of the path, out to the road beyond the ten foot high brick walls, the walls which separate the living from the dead. Out, away from the charring remains of my past. I run away from the oppressive atmosphere of the church. My feet thudding one after another, beat the ground beneath me. Moving as fast as my legs can carry me. I reach the iron gates and speed straight through them.

And I don't stop running until I get home.

Chapter 27

"I did attend the church service" says Mrs Gibson warily.

"I know, I saw you" I reply.

Mrs Gibson is sat in her usual chair in front of the electric fire with two bands on, with her blue winter blanket tucked around her knees instead of her pink summer one. Only the room inside the house still feels colder than the late autumn afternoon outside.

"I didn't want to intrude" she says hesitantly "but I felt it was my duty to turn up."

"I understand."

"How are you coping?"

"I'm managing" I tell her, unable to look at her in the eye. I stare at the cross on the wall. The cross is simple with just two inter-joined pieces of wood combining. Simple but effective. Making its point. Addressing all who step into this room. Reminding them that this house is above sin. That the person to whom it belongs believes in a simpler life, a simpler life than mine. "I'm taking each day as it comes. There's nothing else I can do" I tell the wall.

"You shouldn't have come here today" she murmurs "you don't have to bother about me. I can take care of myself."

But we both know that this is a lie, that her arthritis gets worse when it rains. And it hasn't stopped raining for several days. The blackness of the clouds outside have cast a shadow which reaches into the room, dulling it, even with the main light switched on. Under that florescent bulb her house is particularly untidy. The plate sitting next to her from the meals-on-wheels is still wearing its metal cover. An uneaten dinner. And there's no sign of the usual clutter of spent coffee cups that normally surround her. Only dust and grime. And the lingering smells of cat food which has been left out for too long.

"I'm sure you can" I agree, plucking up the courage to look at her. "But I've got to get my life back into order."

I sit down on the couch next to Smoky.

As soon as I do, he gets up and wanders off.

"I was concerned when you left the church" she says, pausing, "as you seemed to be in a bit of a rush."

"I needed some fresh air."

"I tried phoning."

"I unplugged the phone."

"I understand."

Mrs Gibson is cautious, sparing me too many questions. I feel grateful for her company. The awkwardness which is constant around other people is not an issue here. Here, there are only the words of kindness of a type which belongs to bygone days. They draw out a response from me.

"I needed some time to think about things, but I can't sit at home anymore, I've got to have something to keep me occupied, sitting at home all day only makes me ponder on everything" I mutter quietly.

"Aren't you working then?"

"I was on compassionate leave because of the funeral, and then I booked some extra time off to extend my leave. I thought it would give me time to get my head around everything, but it's not helping, all this time off is making me think too much."

"You're always welcome to come round here if you need the company. You can call by anytime, day or night. You've got the key. You know that you can come and go whenever you please. You don't even have to speak to me if you don't feel like it. But I'm here if you need to talk."

"Thank you."

"You can phone too. Just remember that."

"It's good of you" I say.

"One good deed deserves another" she replies.

Mrs Gibson looks up at the pictures upon her mantelpiece. Her eyes sweep from one end of the row to the other and then rest on one particular frame. The silver frame that holds a photograph of her husband. Her face melts into a pensive expression. "The first six months are the worst" she says in a hushed tone, staring at the picture. "It's hard adjusting to being on your own. The best advice I can give you is to find yourself a distraction, you need a hobby to take your mind off things. I found crosswords therapeutic." She moves her blanket away from her knees and drapes it on the armrest. And then eases herself up to her feet, wobbling in the process.

"Do you want any help?" I ask.

"No, I can manage" she insists, clinging to one side of the chair until she has her balance. She lets go and begins to shuffle to the corner of the room, touching various objects as she goes. And comes to a stop in front of the bookshelf. Her hand tremors as she reaches for an item on the third shelf. "Here" she says, struggling to extract a book, "let me give you one of these." Mrs Gibson gives it a tug and it slides out. "It's a crossword book. I've got plenty of these, and sudoku books too, they've been filled in with pencil and so you can rub the answers out and start again." She places her hand onto the top of the television to regain her balance, and then makes her way across to me and holds it out.

"Thank you" I say, taking the book from her even though I know that I'll never use it.

"I've got more of them if you want to help yourself" she offers "I've been meaning to have a clear out."

"I'll see how I get on with this one first of all" I reply, tapping the book.

She makes her way back to her seat and pulls her blanket back over her knees, then pats it down.

"You never forget" she says. "But you learn to live with it." She tucks her water bottle into the front of the blanket. "Time is a healer. Of course my experience was different to yours and I was a lot older than you when I lost my husband. The circumstances were different too. But when my son passed away…" she lets out an audible sigh.

"You must have been around my age."

"Yes," she replies sadly "but I remember it as if it were yesterday, I remember it all so clearly. I was forty five. And John was only twenty two."

"I can't imagine what it's like to lose a child."

"It's the worst thing in the world. Apart from your situation" she nods. "You never expect to outlive your child. There was a long period when I thought I'd never get over it. But you have to find faith and then you can come to terms with it."

"I suppose I'll get over Maureen eventually."

"It's never easy. These things are never easy" she says wistfully. "Of course when John died, it was different, it was expected, and it was welcomed in some ways, the cancer had made him very sick. And he was in a lot of pain. If I could've swapped places with him then I wouldn't have hesitated, I would have gladly gone before him. He was ill in the days before the medical advances that are available now and there was nothing we could do to help him. We could only standby and watch."

"At least Maureen went quickly."

"It shouldn't have happened though" she maintains. "I don't understand what life is about, here I am, waiting to go, and others would be blessed to live as long as me."

"Life is a game of chance."

"Life's a complicated journey. But there must be a reason behind it. I'm sure God has his reasons" she says looking up at the cross.

"Who knows?" I mutter.

We sit in silence. Both respectful of each other's thoughts. Her eyes flicker to the picture on the mantelpiece again, concentrating intensely on its image. Her face suddenly furrows in momentary expression of pain and she turns away. She is quiet for a couple of minutes.

She pulls her blanket higher. And eventually she turns to me. "Are you eating properly?" she asks.

"I could ask you the same question" I say, gesturing over to the covered plate.

"There's not as much of me to feed" she replies, patting her stomach.

I rub my bulging tummy which has increased in size and remind myself to cut down on the alcohol.

"Yes, I'm eating. I'm probably eating too much. I'm living on ready made dinners, it's amazing what you can buy at the supermarket these days."

"They can't be good for you in the long term."

"No. But they'll do for now."

"If I was younger, then I'd be helping you."

"There's no need. We modern men have to know how to cook" I say. "And we can boil a kettle and use a microwave."

"Good to hear it" she says.

On cue, I stand up. "Coffee?" I ask.

"Yes please" she replies understandingly.

I head for the kitchen and make her a drink.

When I carry it back through, I put it on the table. "I'll get on with the gardening, if you don't mind."

"Not at all" she says, reaching for the mug. "Only do the things you want to do and leave the rest, don't worry if you don't get it all done, the gardening can wait, it's you that's important."

"That's nice of you to say, but I think I need to get myself into something."

She nods. But says no more.

I head for the door and retreat to the garden shed.

The shed is damp and cold, the gaps between the timbers leak the wet autumn weather. A small trail of cobwebs bounce around one wall, half stuck and half blowing in the gusts of wind. I reach for the big box and pull it down.

I settle it on the workbench. And look inside.

The box is almost empty, apart from a few remaining clothes which have taken on their damp surroundings. A musty pong rises from them, assaulting my nostrils as I pick my way through. I spread them out onto the workbench and then think about what is left to do. I have one more crime to commit. Then I'm a free man. Free to start my new journey in life. Free to move on. I think about Riley. I wonder how wet his top lip is at the moment. And then I wonder whether he is as fraught as the last time I clapped eyes on him. And whether he's any closer to catching me. The thought of Riley being out there, Riley having to make do with the DNA, Riley with the initials before his name. I'd like to tell him that initials might matter in some circles, but who's really running the show? Because it sure isn't him, that's a fact. He doesn't look so clever right now, but I'm not convinced that I'm so clever either. Everything has changed for me recently. Life without Maureen is different to how I'd imagined it to be. In some ways it's easier. But sometimes...

I look at the dwindled collection and contemplate my last act. My mind flickers through all sorts of ideas and all sorts of ways to give Riley one last chance. One last ray of hope, because that's what the victims are to him, another one equals another crime scene. And another chance to get to me. And I hate to disappoint. There is so much I could do, I could commit the most heinous crime in the world and not get caught, I could butcher, I could slice, or I could go for a select victim. I could pick my prey carefully, even someone he knows, perhaps a relative or a colleague. But then as I start to think and I decide that all that matters is that I bring it all to an end. That, with one more victim, Maureen becomes an equation in amongst them. That Riley won't know what has hit him, he won't even begin to understand why, and no amount of initials at the front of his name is going to crack it, because, how can it? How can you select eight victims and know which one, if any, is the link? How can you know which is the odd one out? The answer is simple, you can't. Maybe you can look into the last one more thoroughly and try to reason why it stops there, which is why I have to kill again. But what has Riley really got, other than corpses?

I scan the outfits and then come to the conclusion that it really doesn't matter which one I use as all are equally suitable. The only important thing is that I keep to my routine. That I wear a cap with my hair tucked in. And that I wear gloves. That I swab my victim with disinfectant afterwards. And that I leave the beads.

I take a jumper off the top of the pile and mix it with a dark pair of trousers. I take out a pair of gloves, a pair of socks, and a pair of shoes. I pick a hooded waterproof jacket with toggles. And then pack them all into my holdall.

From the second box, I choose a piece of DNA which isn't on any database nor will it ever be. It's a small piece of fluff that is barely visible to the naked eye. It is probably no more than three strands of fibre, but its enough. It's a piece of lint which I teased off Riley's jumper when I met with him at the hospital.

I bundle what is left of the clothes and the DNA into a single box and stack it onto the shelf. But as I do, I make a promise; I tell myself that there are to be no more. That one last killing will finish my crimes for good and that after the next one, it all stops. I tell myself that in future I'm going to use my time to find a new person inside of me. That, whatever happens, I'll find a new road to walk down. That Riley will have to get used to not knowing why. That Riley will have to live with what I've done. That a brighter fate is beckoning.

Chapter 28

"Mr Scanlon?" says Riley, who is stood on my doorstep holding out his identity card. But I don't need to see the card to know who he is, I remember him more than he thinks I do.

"Mr Scanlon?" repeats Sally, the family liaison officer, standing short of DCI Riley, wearing her weary expression. "I did ring, I left several messages on your answering machine, but I didn't seem to get any reply."

"Did you?" I mumble vacantly, playing for time and trying to fathom what they're doing on my doorstep. "Yes, I think I remember hearing a message from you. I was going to phone you back…" But Riley is having none of it, before I can finish my sentence, he interrupts impatiently. "I'm sorry to be calling at this time of night" he says, the urgency in his voice apparent, "but it's important that we talk to you."

I look at him and wonder whether he knows. Then I wonder how much he knows and whether all this is some kind of test to watch my reaction. I think about my penknife in the glove compartment of my car, which is sitting on the tarmac of the driveway that Sally is standing on. I think about my outfit and the fluff which are in my holdall in the hallway in view of where they're both stood. All my dry mouth can utter is one strained, arid syllable.

"Right" I croak.

"May we come in?" asks Riley, looking into the entrance.

I nod and usher them through the door.

"May we…?" asks Sally, gesturing to the lounge.

I nod again as I am unable to speak. Cold fear gets to me. Bile reaches the top of my throat. I swallow hard but the taste doesn't move. The acid burn clings to the back of my tongue. While the unpleasant flavour mingles into my saliva, biting into my taste buds.

I turn and follow them into the lounge. Each step I take is accompanied by strains of panic. A nerve under my eye begins to twitch. Deep down my stomach stirs. I wonder at this very second if the food inside prison is as unpalatable as I've been led to believe and of whether it's been all worth it; a mere six and a half weeks without her. And those weeks haven't been as heavenly as I'd hoped. Oh no, not by a long shot.

I reach my chair, gauging how to respond. My head still searching for a way out. Even now it's not all finished. I'm still looking to absolve myself. I'm looking for an excuse for my behaviour. I could collapse. Or act insane. Or take my punishment like a man and hold my head up high and let them bang me up. Let someone else take responsibility for my life, because without that someone, I'm kind of drifting, I'm not getting it together very well. At all.

In the event I don't need an excuse and I don't need to fake. When we reach the lounge Sally politely asks if they can sit down. Once she says this, and once I realise that they're not wearing their hats, or being overly formal, I know that they're not here to arrest me. When I realise that I'm still a free man, I'm capable of speaking again.

"Have you caught him yet?" I ask.

"I'm afraid not" responds Riley meekly.

He turns and glances at the couch before sitting down and placing his folder onto his knee. Sally sits alongside him. Both of them wearing the same weathered look. Both of them looking forlornly at me. Both of them unable to comprehend that which has little meaning.

I slump into my chair.

"What's going on then?" I ask in irritation that they caught me unaware, as I glance at my sole companion for what was going to be a long night ahead. The lid of the Whiskey bottle sits idly by, the bottle itself has a large amount missing.

Riley notices it as well. He furrows his forehead as he scans it. And then he refocuses and begins. "We're sorry to be calling by so late in the evening, but it's very important that we speak with you. We did aim to get here earlier, but Sally got held up along the way. I hope that we haven't disturbed you."

"No" I reply a little too curtly as I lean over to the table and pick up the bottle. Drink?" I ask.

"Not while we're on duty" Riley replies.

"I can make a tea or coffee, if you prefer."

"No thank you."

I look across to Sally.

"Not for me" she says.

I pour myself a large measure, lift the glass to my lips and swallow the amber liquid in one gulp. Riley briefly focuses on the glass. His eyes narrow in guilty disapproval but he doesn't comment. Instead he coughs, clearing his throat, while waiting for my full attention.

"Mr Scanlon" he says formally, once I've put the glass down, "we're visiting you tonight to update you on everything which has been happening recently. I believe Sally has been keeping you up to date with most of the information…"

"I have had a few problems getting hold of you" says Sally interrupting and looking rueful and then guilty. She eyes at me in desperation. "I left some messages on your answering machine and I was hoping that you'd get back to me."

"My phone's not working properly" I lie, in order to help her out.

But it makes no odds to Riley, and he turns to her in disgust.

"When was the last time you spoke to Mr Scanlon?" he asks.

"It was a couple of weeks ago."

"Have you got an attendance form?"

"I'll look for it" she replies, reaching for her briefcase. She pulls it onto her knee, springs the locks and then flicks through her papers. She takes out a pink slip and hands it to him. He peruses it grimly. At one point he tuts. Once he's read it, he addresses me. But it's obvious that his words are aimed at Sally. "Because you haven't been updated in a while, what I'll have to do is to take you through everything that has been happening overall and then we'll move on to more recent developments." He pauses and looks down at the sheet again, contemplating the notes intensely, and then finds his entry point. "I'm going to pick up from our last meeting at the hospital, that way you'll be fully informed of all the progress we've made" he says, as Sally winces. He looks up. "Since we met at the hospital, there have been some fundamental changes to the way we've approached the process of this operation, I want to make it clear right now that we've been working tirelessly to try and make headway and as a result of an internal review, a selected team from our police force in Cheshire have combined with a specially picked squad from Greater Manchester. We believe that this will create a more effective task force and that by integrating this group of personnel we'll be able to collate all the information quickly. So far we've employed more than 500 man hours to this case, and it's been given top priority. I'm doing all that I can to oversee this operation and I'm now able to tell you that we've managed to recover some forensic material from several of the crime scenes. These are being analysed by our laboratory technicians at the moment and we're hopeful of a breakthrough" he says, the disappointment in his voice all too real. "It's all a question of time."

I look at Sally. She is gazing around the room, taking in the emptiness of it and then feeling sorry for me. She notices me looking and stops. I pour myself another glass of Whiskey.

"If anything we've upped our inquiries recently" continues Riley desperately "we have had some success with what could possibly be a DNA sample and we're running it through our database, but so far we haven't made a match."

I put the bottle back onto the table.

"What have you found?" I ask.

"We can't release any precise details at present" Riley tells me enigmatically "but I can tell you that what we recovered was found at the scene of one of the victims and that we've already established that the sample has no connection to the woman, as we've managed to retrace her movements on the morning that she went missing and we've tested everybody who she came into contact with. We're satisfied that it's an important step forward."

I pick up the glass and knock the Whiskey back. The alcohol tears at my senses. A burning sensation sinks down my gullet and bites at my stomach. My eyes smart from the sensation. I blink the water away. Riley continues.

"Which gets me around to our present position" he says bleakly. "With a case such as this, it's always important to have as much public awareness as possible. We as a police force feel that we'll have the most chance of catching the perpetrator through awareness and identification and as is normal with a case such as this, the general public do become vital in solving these types of cases. So far we have managed to keep up a lot of media coverage but we haven't had as much feedback as we would've liked. This brings me round to why we're here tonight." He stops and scrutinizes the pink form again and then slips it into his folder. "With a case like this we have to try every angle possible. The man that we're dealing with is an elusive individual who has managed to commit multiple crimes so far without consequence. The type of terrain he chooses to strike in makes it difficult for us to find potential witnesses. However, we feel that we have had a recent breakthrough. A member of the public has come forward and has been able to help us with our inquiries. We're treating this potential witness very seriously and he's already given us a statement…"

"When you say witness" I interrupt "do you mean someone who has seen something?"

"We believe so."

"What?"

"That's what I'm coming to Mr Scanlon" says Riley puffing out his chest. "The person who has contacted us was abroad on holiday when we made an appeal for information and has only recently returned to the U.K. He has been able to give us a statement and a description of the assailant and although his description was vague, in view of our position, we've decided to make a reconstruction of that particular crime for television."

"Of Maureen?" I ask.

"No, it wasn't Maureen" he replies. "It's a woman called Bridget Curtis-Hayes. She disappeared over two months ago and was found about twelve miles away from here near the River Cherwell. We consider the information which he gave to have vital implications for our case and that is why we've decided to do a reconstruction of that murder."

"And it's going to be on television?

"Yes"

"When?"

"We've recently held talks with the producers of the Stop Crime programme and I have to say that it hasn't been filmed yet, but it is scheduled in to begin filming next week. The programme will be shown shortly afterwards" says Riley firmly. "Mr Scanlon I have to tell you that the man who has come forward as a witness gave us some disturbing news, he was fishing at the reservoir on the night Mrs Curtis-Hayes was killed and has been able to give us some specific details. I can tell you Mr Scanlon that we've been left baffled as to how Mrs Bridget-Hayes came to be lured from her usual route but we now have reason to believe that the perpetrator was dressed up as a woman in order to coax her away."

"Christ" I gasp.

"Furthermore, we have found a foundation type of make-up on the clothes of several of victims and in addition we found traces of lipstick on one person's jacket."

"Oh God" I mutter.

"Mr Scanlon?" says Sally getting up and walking over and then bending next to my chair and stroking my hand. "Are you alright?"

"Yes" I reply as I gulp furiously. I brush her hand away and reach for the whiskey bottle, but my eyes remain firmly fixed on Riley.

"We believe that we've been given a good description of the clothes he wore that night and our officers have been making discreet inquiries throughout the gay community to see if the description matches anyone who is known to cross-dress, we've covered transsexual outlets and mail order catalogues and our inquiries are continuing."

Sally continues to squat beside my seat, she puts her hand onto the armrest to steady herself, I turn away. I try to remember back to that night, but the awful thing is that I don't remember much after killing her. I remember crossing the bridge, but I don't remember the finer details.

"Mr Scanlon" says Riley, breaking into my thoughts "I know that this must be a shock for you, but we believe that this is the best approach. Of course any filming is likely to bring fresh interest from both from the newspapers and the news channels and there's always the possibility that the reporters might try to get in touch with you. We will be letting you know before the programme is broadcast, but it might be a good idea to try and make some arrangements for when it happens. Is there anyone you can stay with for a few days?"

"No" I say shaking my head.

"It is advisable."

"No."

"Very well" he says.

"Have you seen the bereavement councillor yet?" asks Sally quietly, from the side of my chair.

I turn to her. "No" I reply tersely.

"It might help."

"No."

"Would you like me to make you an appointment?" she persists.

"No."

"I could accompany you."

I shake my head.

"Sally is there to help" says Riley "but we understand if you want to deal with it alone."

"Who is this witness?" I ask

"We can't say."

"Can they help?"

"We believe so."

"What else have they told you?"

"We cannot divulge the full details at present."

"They said it was a woman?"

"A man dressed as a woman."

I stand up. "I'd like you to leave" I inform them abruptly.

Riley looks surprised. Sally stands and makes her way back to her suitcase in disappointment. I walk to the doorway and wait for them to gather their things. "Very well" replies Riley, picking up his folder and standing up. "In that case we'll be in touch soon, although I do recommend that you make one day a fortnight available for Sally as it'd be beneficial for you if you kept to a regular meeting."

"Mr Scanlon?" says Sally, looking at me with her doleful eyes, "is it alright if I pop in next week?"

"I have a lot to do."

"It'll only be for a few minutes."

"Try phoning first."

"Of course" she nods. "But if you need to speak to me in the meantime then give me a call." She reaches into her handbag, brings out her card, and then hands it to me. "I'll give you one of these again and if I'm not in my office then leave a message and I'll ring you back as soon as I can."

"Right" I say, taking the card.

"There are people out there to help," she continues "you only have to ask."

I show them out. As soon as they've gone, I rip the card up and throw it in the bin.

Chapter 29

It doesn't matter when I kill, I am alone and so I don't have to come up with any excuse, I can kill whenever the circumstances are right. I could for instance finish work and notice someone as I'm driving home and then if the inclination gets me, I could turn the car round and follow her. Or I could go out at midnight and leap out of the bushes, and snatch someone off the streets, maybe even a stupid girl who is too mean to pay for a taxi home, and let her be a lesson to all the others who think they're invincible, that it'll never happen to them, that somehow they are different. Well let me tell you, they're not. No one is safe. Not anybody. Not anywhere. There's always something out there. Even if it isn't me. There's always a car accident waiting to happen. There's always a contagious disease, or a time bomb in our genes. Something always gets us in the end. Death is a fact of life. It's the only certainty of living. It'll even happen to me at some point. But I'm getting to the stage where I don't want to kill again because now that Maureen is gone there seems little point. I've done what I set out to do, which is gain my freedom. But with it, I've been given something else. I've been given a different life. Only I'm not sure how to fill it. Before I killed Maureen I hadn't taken the time to think about how much my life revolved around her and how big a void she would leave behind. Because it is one damn big hole, and it's taken me by surprise. For once in my life I don't feel so sure of myself. Late last night I got to thinking about how much everything has changed. Then I got to wondering; I got to considering that maybe Maureen was my rock.

That she was my purpose. That she gave me a purpose. A pretty silly one, I must admit. But, nevertheless, the clock always managed to tick with her around. She always had the ability to move life forward in one way or another. There was always something that needed to be taken care of. Or she had some idea of what she wanted to do next. Without her, the hands on the clock have ground firmly to a halt. Everything has become like a film I watched several years ago. Groundhog Day. I seem to be caught in a few frames with the same day replaying over and over again. This is my life now. It's the same, day in and day out. Get up, eat cereal, get dressed, go to work, work, come home, eat cereal, go to bed. Somehow the days are ticking by, one after another, without me getting anywhere. Deep inside me I know what I want, and where I want to be. It's just that I'm having trouble moving from this stage to the next. There are obstacles in the way. Mainly in the form of Mrs Gibson, but I also have to assess the appropriateness of putting the house up for sale so soon after the funeral. Like, I'm a killer and suddenly I give a fuck about what people were to think if I sell the house. The strange thing is I do. Or maybe I'm just looking for an excuse because I've been a little scared lately. I've been a little bit uncomfortable. What with the visit from the detectives and the way that people treat me. Even Harry. They all treat me differently. It's in their eyes. It's in their voices. The sadness. And the pity. All I want to do is turn away. Only I seem to be caught in the middle of a huge crossroads. Sometimes I think that I could be making a huge mistake by selling up and moving on. And then sometimes I think that I could be making a huge mistake if I don't. This is where I am right now, stuck in a state of indecision. Just lately I've been feeling pretty mixed up. Like really confused. Right now I wish that none of these things had started at all. I want my old life. My life where time just ticked by. My boring existence where I didn't need to think and I didn't need to do anything at all, not if I didn't want to. My old life where the decisions were taken from me and made for me. All I want is that different kind of bored, which Maureen ladled out easily. I want some mundane conversation to break the silence. I want the monotony of 'do and don't'. I want someone to be there. All I really want is steak and kidney pudding. But it's too late now.

Chapter 30

I sit in the darkness with only the flickering light of the television to illuminate the room, to hand is a large scotch on the rocks, the bottle is within reach. My head feels light and woozy, like the kind of feeling you get when you've had too much to drink. Which I have. In fact, if the truth be known, I've had more than a few. I've had enough to make me feel dizzy and nauseous and everything looks distorted and out of focus. Maybe I need to be this way. Maybe it just numbs me, maybe it takes the edge off my life, maybe I've drunk too much on purpose, and maybe it's the fact that the television is on and right now the red light of the video recorder is pulsating away. Maybe it's the way that the digital numbers on the front of the screen are clocking up as it records the programme of my choice. Only I've got the same channel on as well, because I can't help but feel that I've got no other option but to watch. Part of me can hardly bear to look, and part of me cannot stop myself. It's like I'm drawn, like a moth to the light, I'm enticed by those small microdots which have the ability to reach out and spread their message around the room. I'm mesmerised by that transmission, which has the power to reach out to me and to reach into a million other houses too.

The woman walks down the same street which I took her from, she is similar in appearance and her clothes are the same, her height is identical, her hair is shaped into the same bobbed hairstyle, but her face is harder and more cynical, her lifestyle less privileged than the woman which I killed. A subtle difference, but nevertheless an important one. Then near the alley an old woman appears. Only when the camera angles in, it's clear that the woman is in fact a man. I sit up with a start, giving my full attention to the screen. It sobers me up in an instant. For it's the clothes that strike me. The hat is similar and the coat is damn near the real thing. The shoes are completely wrong. The high collared dress underneath is close in style but different in pattern. The wig is similar to that which I wore. The camera flicks up and down the length of him and then pans out. The man is shorter than me and more masculine in his behaviour. He threatens the woman and marches her down the alleyway to the place where I killed her. It's here where the voiceover tells the viewers about the man angling on the reservoir and of how he witnessed the figure moving across the bridge only yards away from where he was standing.

A silhouetted figure speaks *"I'd been out angling all afternoon at the River Cherwell and it was getting cold and dark. I hadn't caught anything for a while and so I decided to call it a day. I packed my things away. It was as I was carrying some of my equipment over to the corner of the bridge that I heard someone crossing up above me. I instinctively looked up and saw what looked like an old woman moving over the bridge in my direction. But there was something not quiet right about her, I think it's because she was moving too quickly for her age, it was her hastiness which made me suspicious. As she got closer it was obvious that it was a man dressed in women's clothes, from the way he was walking. His shoes didn't fit properly, the backs of them had been bent down, and he was hobbling badly.*

I'd say I was no more than three feet away at my closest point but I'm fairly sure he didn't see me, I got a good look at him though, I suppose its not every day that you see a man dressed as a woman and that's what made me take notice. I'd describe him to be around 5'7, he was stocky, and I'd guess middle aged, around his late 40's to early 50's but it was difficult to tell. He was wearing a floral dress with a green coat and a matching hat. He had flat black shoes on and was carrying a beige handbag. He crossed the bridge from Baxter's Way and walked towards Atherton Close. When he got over the bridge I saw him disappear into Leslie Street. That was the last I saw of him. I didn't think anything more of it.

I went on holiday to Spain a few days later and it wasn't until I got back that I heard the news. When I heard about what had happened I immediately alerted the police to what I'd seen."

The programme returns to the studio.

The female presenter is handed a piece of paper, she holds it out of view and then turns and looks directly into the camera.

"In the studio we've been joined by DCI Riley from the Metropolitan police force who is leading the investigation" she says, before turning to the detective. "First of all I'd like to ask you, what are you appealing for tonight?"

Riley focuses on the presenter, addressing her instead of the camera. He stands upright and rigid in his full uniform. His face is sombrely adjusted and has a hint of authority.

"We're looking for information and are trying to trace anyone who was in the area of the River Cherwell on that particular night."

"We're talking about the 30th September at around half past six in the evening. Is that correct?"

"That's right."

"To jog people's memories that was the day when an autumn fair had taken place in the church near the town centre less than a mile away from where this attack took place" says the woman, looking at the paper.

"That's correct."

"DCI Riley, what information can you give us about the person who perpetrated this despicable crime?"

"Firstly I'd like to say that this person has been linked to six murders so far and we are dealing with an individual who is both cunning and conniving. He is a danger to the public and we ask that all members of the public to be alert, we'd also ask that if anyone sees someone acting suspiciously near trees or woodland, then for them come forward and to contact the police."

"You've had an offender profile done, what can you tell us about that?"

"We believe that this person might have a regimental background and he could possibly be married because we believe that he might be using somewhere other than his home to store his clothes, small spores of mould have been found at the scene of each crime. In addition to that we have found another detail which links all victims together but as of yet I am unable to disclose the details. We believe that the suspect could be using an allotment or a garden shed or some kind of lockup, possibly a garage, to store his clothes in. We have reason to believe that he has use of a rough oak bench. Apart from that we've been following several leads but we need to know more."

"DCI Riley, you say that he has been linked to six murders so far, can you tell us more about those crimes?"

"Yes. I can tell you that all the victims have been women, all of them have been between the ages of 17 and 46, and all the crimes have occurred near wooded areas, hence the suspect being referred to as The Woodlands Killer. Also I'd like to point out that the suspect has struck both in the daytime and at night as well."

"Are the crimes sexually motivated?"

"There's nothing at the moment to suggest a sexual motivation, but we cannot rule out that possibility."

"And in each circumstance you've had no witnesses come forward apart from the angler, is that correct?"

"Yes. Each crime has been perpetrated in quiet areas, we believe that all the women were snatched off pathways and we are asking the general public, in particular women, to be on their guard and to take care when walking through parks or down the street. If possible, we're advising women walking by themselves to stay on the outside of the pavement or to stay away from verges and bushes."

"How significant are the clothes that he was wearing on the night that Mrs Bridget Curtis-Hayes died?" asks the presenter.

"We'd like to trace the clothes that he wore in this particular case and I'd ask anyone who either works in a charity shop, or who might have these types of clothing around the house, to try and recall if they recognise these clothes and to check their belongings to see whether they have anything missing. The clothes are an important clue. Additionally, tonight we would also like to release further information and make an appeal for information regarding a brooch that we found near to the crime scene on the night that she was killed."

"Do you believe the brooch may be of significance?"

"We're unsure of the importance of it at the moment, which is why we're making this appeal. The brooch may or may not be evidence and we're asking for further information on it in order to rule it in or out of our inquiry."

"What can you tell us about the brooch?"

"I can tell you that the brooch is a flower shaped design made up of blue and white rhinestones, it is set into a copper frame, and it carries the manufacturers name on the reverse. It was designed by a firm called Matisse who made costume jewellery in the early part of the last century. We believe that it is old and was possibly made around the 1940's. We're asking whether anyone recognises it or whether any antique jewellers have sold a brooch of this description recently."

"For the viewers at home, we have the brooch in the studio" says the presenter, holding up a small cushion as a camera moves in and focuses.

There, in widescreen, is the brooch. Which I recognise. For a second my heart misses a beat. Momentarily, the air just about stops travelling through my body. Everything freezes. As soon as I see it, I know that I'm in trouble. Even through the cloud of alcohol the realisation dawns on me that it's this and only this which will change everything for me.

"Is there anything else that you can tell us about it?" asks the presenter as the camera hovers over it.

"Yes" says Riley firmly. "Matisse created mass produced jewellery and were famous for their copper set pieces. We believe that this is a significant clue because obviously there are bound to be less of them about nowadays, which gives us a good chance of tracing it. It must be stressed that at the moment we are unsure of whether this has any connection to our case, but we would like to hear from anyone with any information about it, and anyone who can put it together with the description of the clothes, in order to eliminate it from our inquiries."

"To recap then, we are looking for anyone who was in the vicinity of the River Cherwell, who recognises the clothes he wore, or indeed anyone who recognises the brooch to come forward."

"That's correct" says Riley.

"Thank you" says the presenter before turning to the camera and settling her eyes on the autocue.

"If you recognise the brooch in question or know of anyone who has had access to the clothes that the suspect wore, or if you were in the vicinity of the River Cherwell on the evening of 20th September, then please do call us either at Stop Crime on 0800 000 999 or you can call directly to the incident room which has been set up by the Metropolitan police on the number which is shown across the bottom of the screen at the moment."

Chapter 31

I see it in her eyes. She doesn't have to say anything but I see it. Sometimes you can just look at a person and know. Sometimes words make the whole damn thing more complex than it needs to be, because sometimes looks manage to speak volumes more than a few consonants and vowels linked together. This is one of those times. I see it in her eyes.

"How are you?" I ask

"How do you think?" she answers me bitterly.

"Is your arthritis bothering you?" I ask, probing a little bit further.

"It isn't my arthritis that's bothering me" she replies. "Although, now you mention it, my hands do hurt. Do you want to know why?"

But I've already guessed. Even before I set foot in her room. Even before I saw it in her eyes. From the hall to the parlour. Clothes are scattered everywhere. All her items have been rifled through and none of it has been packed away again. This being the day after the Stop Crime programme. There's no doubting what she was looking for.

"No, I know already."

"I know as well" she replies emphatically.

Her eyes, which seem more watery than ever today, burn into me. They stare hypnotically, leaving me paralysed. All I want to do is to turn and run as fast as I can. I want to hide from the shame of her accusatory gaze. But my feet are leaden. They are firmly rooted to the spot. As if stuck with glue. I am unable to escape. For fear. Maybe. Or worse still, because I know that I've got a problem to deal with.

"Have you told anyone?" I ask.

"Not yet" she replies shaking her mop of white hair from side to side. "You're alright for now, I want to speak to you first of all, I want some answers, and I want to know why."

From the kitchen I hear the familiar drip dripping of a tap where her hands have been unable to turn it off properly. I know that after today I'll miss that sound. I also know that after today nothing and no one will ever reach me in the way that she did, I'll make sure of it. That life is much simpler when relationships with other people don't get in the way. That friendships lead to only one thing. Obligations. And I haven't got the patience for that anymore. No, I tell myself, I'm better off alone.

"I'm not sure that I've got an answer" I tell her.

"I've got time to wait" she replies.

Her long spindly fingers gesture to the couch opposite. I sit down in response. Out spills the first thing that comes into my head. "It's like this…" I say "…I didn't mean for any of this to start… it wasn't my fault… it began as an accident… it's true… I was jogging along when I slipped and fell into her… she lay on the ground… there was a bump on her head… I didn't know what to do. I panicked and I dragged her into the bushes… then I left her there. I ran off. When I saw in the news that she'd died, I couldn't believe it. I was devastated."

I find myself telling her one lie after another. Of how I didn't want to do it but that it was an urge that built up inside of me.

"Then I started getting the voices… at first it was only in the night… they would come to me in my sleep. And then they started in the daytime too… the voices urged me on. I was taken over by something else, I was demonised. I couldn't stop it. I wanted to. But I couldn't. It was like I had no control over what they said to me. I couldn't escape. They told me to kill, I was powerless."

All the time, when I'm telling her this, I feel transparent. I feel that she can see right through me, as if she's looking into my very soul.

"If I'd realised how ill I was… how sick… then I wouldn't have done it."

She knows, and I know, that it's all a just a game. That it's all just bullshit. It's all a long and winding road of nonsense. All played out for both our sakes. Not just mine, but hers too.

"I never meant to harm anyone."

She could've just called the police. There's nothing to stop her from reaching for the phone on the table beside her chair. Oh, she could've phoned them alright. But she didn't. She didn't because that would've left her alone.

"If I could turn the clock back."

She didn't because she thought that what we had was worth more than that. She thought that she could help in some way. Perhaps guide me. Perhaps cure me. Perhaps even forgive. But what does it all really mean in the long term. It means that she would own me. That she would have a hold over me. That she would just replace Maureen. If I told the truth.

"I should've tried to get help...."

But I tell myself I'm not prepared to do that, not even for her.

"...even if it meant that I'd be committed, or locked up... at least I wouldn't have been prey to those voices..."

I bullshit. And make up the wildest stories going. I give her the works. The lies. And the sob stories. The fantasies and the delusions. But eventually I get to the point where I'm tired and maybe it's just the look on her face. But maybe it's something deeper than that.

"All I wanted to do was escape from Maureen."

The truth gradually starts to leak out of me. Little by little. In between the lies at first. Little bits of honesty. Truths that I've never even acknowledged to myself before. Let alone uttered.

"That's all that was behind it... I couldn't stand her... something drove me to do what I did... I wasn't behaving rationally... but it wasn't just a desire to kill... I've asked myself countless times if I would've killed anyway if I hadn't been with Maureen. I don't think I would have, but I can't be sure."

Then the truth takes over, replacing the lies with how I really feel. I tell her about my feelings for Maureen. Of how I spent so many years just hating her. Of how I spent my time planning. Ten long months, I tell her. It wasn't just a whim. No, I spent ten long months of carrying it around with me.

"It took me a long time to plan… so I had plenty of opportunities to change my mind… but I didn't want to though… my need to kill was greater than anything else I've ever experienced in my life."

Here I am suddenly telling Mrs Gibson, of all people, of what it's really like to kill.

"Perhaps Maureen was an excuse… maybe that's who I really am… I don't know… all I know is that I was consumed by it…. and it stayed with me day and night. I knew I wouldn't stop… right from the beginning…"

Her face watches me in interest, as if observing something freakish.

"…you see I got lonely when I was with Maureen… I was so lonely that I'd think too much… all I could think about was getting rid of her… and gaining my freedom."

I don't know what kills her in the end. But it isn't me. I swear it isn't me. I don't lay a finger on her. I don't touch her. I just get to a point where I've told enough lies, where I feel exposed by those glinting eyes. And I tell the whole truth.

"The planning made me feel alive… the killing did too… when I wasn't out there, I ached for that rush. I've actually killed seven so far, one hasn't been found yet…"

Maybe that is what kills her off, I don't know.

"She was a prostitute called Chrissie. I buried her, after I'd strangled her, of course, I didn't bury her alive, I wouldn't do anything like that. I'm not capable of that sort of behaviour, really. She was number four. I thought that by hiding her it'd give me some space to be able to move on to the next one without the publicity and the police hot on my trail, it's all about keeping one step ahead. I thought about it all carefully, right down to the finest detail, I even made up a collection of clothes to kill in. Then there was the issue of DNA…"

It's as I tell her of how I'd even gone to the lengths of using the Salvation Army as a cover to hide my collection. And that that collection is less than two metres away from where we are both sat. Her face starts to crumple. Her hands come up. And begin to grope at her chest. Her long bony fingers skirt around her lifeline, that big red button which is hung around her neck. But it's like she's holding back. Like she can't quite bring herself to press it.

"I did it all."

It's as if she's heard enough.

"I killed them all."

She isn't prepared to save herself. She doesn't want to. She looks away from me. And turns to the cross on her wall. Her face starts to turn red.

"I have no one else to blame."

But I can't stop talking. It's like a dam has burst straight in the middle of her parlour, the words are tumbling out of me. I've reached a confession box and for once I'm able to unburden my thoughts onto someone else. And they are words that are taking me by surprise. Never have I talked so much. Never have I been so lucid.

"I don't know who I am anymore."

All the while I'm watching her.

"I don't know what's to become of me."

But it seems that I can't find it in me to help.

"Life without Maureen isn't quite how I'd expected it to be."

I don't know why.

"But I don't regret anything."

Maybe it's because I'm afraid of the things she now knows.

"I've asked myself; do I need to kill in order to feel alive?"

Maybe it's the knowledge that I've just changed her life for the worst and I don't want her to have to live with it.

"I ask myself some crazy questions sometimes."

Or maybe it's because of the world that we live in, that it's cruel and it's harsh. And that I think she's better off out of it.

"My head hurts with the pressure."

Maybe I just want rid of her. That she's the one thing in this whole damn town that still holds me back.

"Its not easy being a killer."

That she's amongst the line of commitments that I don't want to be there.

"I don't sleep so well any more… but I'm not ready to stop yet…as I've planned to take another one."

Maybe, I think, that it's about the will and that she's made me a beneficiary. But I know deep down it's not. I know that I'm not quite like that. But I'm unable to help. And this is the thing that I'll regret forever, this is the one thing that will haunt me until the day I die, I don't get to tell her of how much I enjoyed coming to visit, I don't get to say that she stopped me from leaving this goddamn town behind. And that it's my visits to her which have stopped me going over the edge. That my visits have been the only highlights to my life in recent years. That I do really care for her and she's touched me in a way I never thought possible. That she's changed things for me, she's given me peace, she's made me believe that for every bad person out there, for everyone like me, there's someone decent. There's someone better and kinder and more wholesome. I tell her that I really believe the world needs more people like her. But it's down to others to fill the gap.

"I do love you" I say.

I tell her afterwards. But it's too late. She's stopped listening.

"I wish things had been different."

Once she's gone, I clear out the shed and then phone the emergency services.

Chapter 32

With Mrs Gibson gone I am truly left alone. When I get back home, the first thing I do is pick up the phone and put a call in to the estate agents. Then I set about moving bits and pieces into the garden. First to go are my slippers. I carry them out to the end of the garden where the tilled soil no longer holds any of the home grown vegetables which Maureen specialised in. I place them in the middle of the dirt patch on top of the weeds which are starting to take root. And then begin the journey back and forth.

I rip off the ply and board which blocks off the pile of Maureen's belongings under the stairs. And then empty it. I move from room to room, clearing out everything but the basics. Out go ornaments, drawers are cleared, cupboards are emptied, and boxes of unused kitchen appliances get to see the light of day. A bread making machine, which never baked, a sandwich toaster, which made too much mess, and a blender, that is as clean as the day it was purchased. Twenty years of knick knacks are dispatched to the ever growing pile at the end of the lawn.

I load the clutter until it teeters precariously and threatens to overspill. Then, when it can take no more, I stuff it with a few firelighters. A single match sets it alight.

The fire takes a while to take hold and I watch in fascination absorbing in the cathartic effects as it gradually builds. Once going, the orange flames twist and turn, licking and billowing and then retreating to leave scorch marks. It burns unevenly, one side being more exposed to the slight wind and burning that much more intensely. The fire spews out smoke and hisses and spits. It consumes. And owns. It threatens. And destroys. It minimises. And melts. As it does, the heat intensifies. A neighbour several houses away angrily slams a window shut. I am unconcerned. I don't care for anyone else's opinion of my fire, for I am beholden, I am engrossed in the glory of the crackling heat.

After a while I go in search for more things to add. I shuffle back and forth, bringing with me a variety of objects, from cupboards, from mantelpieces, from windowsills. From the kitchen to the bathroom. Anything and everything. Clothes, shoes, a shower brush, a bedside lamp, the doormat. I spend the evening stoking the flames. And basking in the heat.

I open a cupboard and pull out a paper box. The box contains a collection of photographs. I take them outside and then sit beside the fire, and in the glow, I take one last look through my history. There in rectangular captures are memories of all descriptions. They come in all forms, in black and white, to colour, from photo booths to processing labs, from Polaroid to digital. They span Maureen's and my childhoods, to our wedding day and beyond. They log our holidays, and chart our lives. The faces on them tell a story. Of love. And of loss. Of childish belief. And of grown up disillusionment.

I gather them up, and then stand over the fire and drop the contents onto the top. A shower of photographs fall from the case. Photographs of me and Maureen scatter down in a sprinkling of colour and are quickly engulfed. A picture escapes and floats down to land at the side of my foot. I bend and pick it up, then take a look.

It's a photograph of Maureen and me shortly before we got married. We're both standing in front of my first car, a white Ford Cortina. Her parent's house is in the background. Both of us with dated hairstyles. Both beaming into the camera. Both happy with expectations which sadly went unfulfilled. I place it onto the fire.

The neighbour comes out and leans over the fence.

"It's not bonfire night" he says dryly.

"Isn't it?" I reply, without looking at him.

A flame reaches out and curls around the picture and it immediately changes into a dusty charcoal black. Small wisps of charred paper float into the air. And disappear, carried by the breeze. I pick a piece of wood up and prod at the remaining cinders, whilst pointedly ignoring the neighbour. After a while he takes the hint and shuffles back into his house again, closing the door behind him.

Eventually I get round to burning the last items that I've been holding back. I go in search of them and find them in the hallway cupboard. I pick up my holdall and carry it out into the night.

I hold it open and tip the last items from Mrs Gibson's shed straight onto the pile. The fire consumes them greedily.

With the final items dispatched, I sit on the ground. My face burns. And tingles. And glows. But I don't move. I stay. And watch. And stare.

And wait for it all to disintegrate.

Chapter 33

With the house up for sale and Mrs Gibson gone, the fog which had surrounded me has lifted. Everything is gone. And there's nothing left to hold me back. I hand my notice in at work but the redundancy letters have been typed anyway. Everybody understands, they all know that things have changed for me. The Management offer me a place at their new factory if I'm willing to relocate and if I'm willing to take on the going rate in Romania, which they emphasise is a good salary over there. They include a car and an apartment in the package. I decline for I have other plans. Part of me wonders whether they are offering it to me out of sympathy. Or maybe it's because I am single now and am able to make the move. But, it really doesn't matter why, I turn them down. I'm just not interested anymore. I've given them some good years, maybe even my some of my best, I don't know, but I've given them a lot and that's enough for me. I agree to keep in touch with Harry and some of the other blokes, but I doubt if I mean it. I don't think I want anything to remind me of my past, all I want is to let go and start anew. I want to become that different person I've always yearned to be. I say goodbye to a chosen few and then walk out of the door without looking back.

The first place I go is to the bank to deposit the cheques from the insurance companies. In all it totals over £240,000. It's an awful lot of money in the right circumstances; it's an awful lot for a person with no responsibilities. The sum doesn't take into account the house proceeds and any possible redundancy payoff, plus the inheritance from Mrs Gibson, and I smile to myself as I'm filling out the paying in slip. I am equally cheery to the bank teller. The woman behind the counter asks if I am in need of financial advice. I tell her, no. No is the right answer, I don't need anyone else to tell me how I'm going to spend it because I know exactly what I'm going to do with the money.

After banking the cheque, I spend a bit of time walking around the shops. I spend time in a record store and then potter around a computer shop. I become absorbed in looking at all the computer games on offer. I wander over to the gadgets and find myself fascinated with the choice and the quality. The technology of it all. Voice recognition packages, inter-active packages, and on-line connections to play games against strangers. If I were to stick around then this would be the place for me. But I've committed myself to the next phase in my life and I leave the shop without purchasing anything.

It's on the walk back home that I stop off at the newsagent.

As soon as I walk in I spot them, every paper is emblazoned with screaming headlines.

NUMBER SEVEN.
MURDERED.
ANOTHER BODY FOUND.
HE'S KILLED AGAIN.

I pick up two papers, a tabloid for the sensationalism, and a broadsheet for a more rounded view, and after paying, I take them home to read.

Reading the paper brings it all back to me. The article states that the police suspect the latest victim was buried alive, it then goes through each victim, recording all the details which it knows about the inquiry so far. Above the print is a line of photographs, from the first woman, to the photograph which I chose to release of Maureen. Maureen's happy face when she was younger. Maureen staring out of the page at me. Maureen mingled in with all the others. Just another black and white. I turn the page and the picture on the next page is of the forest cordoned off by ticker tape. Only the forest looks different during the day, it looks less imposing, and less eerie. The trees have lost their density as the winter has closed in, the deciduous ones having bared their branches and the ground below is bleak. The forest has given up its secret. My wild card has come in.

For once I have a different perspective of what has happened and I can empathise with whoever is bereaved. But as I look at it, I remind myself of what it was all about and of how it all started and how it was supposed to pan out. I remind myself of the promise that I made before I started all of this, that I'd see it through no matter what. It's then that I feel a stab of incompletion and I know that I can't rest until I kill again. I know that one more time is waiting in the wings and one more victim is waiting to bow out of this world.

Chapter 34

Number eight is to round things up. I didn't have to do it, but I guess I was missing the action. There's something exciting about those minutes leading up to a crime. When I'm skulking in the bushes. With the unknown beckoning, and I'm all hyped up. When I'm waiting for the right person to cross my path. I could stand between those bushes and have people walk by all day long and ninety nine per cent of them won't be right. Ninety nine per cent are too risky to kill. But that one per cent, and let me tell you that in a country with our population, that's an awful lot of people, I know that one per cent is just right. I can't begin to tell what it is that makes them that way, I can't begin to understand what makes some people different to others, and what makes me know that they're different, I just know it. Something happens when I see them approaching. I get an explosion of nervous energy and it triggers a rush of chemicals through my body, from the tip of my head to end of my toes. It's an energy that nothing else can produce, like every neuron and every nerve ending is firing away in synergy. At that very instant I am hit with a desire like no other. I am hit with an urge which commandeers my body. And then takes me over. At that point all the punishments in the world don't seem enough to stop me. So when I see her walking in my direction, and when I feel that twitching deep in my body, I know that it's going to happen again. Sure enough it does.

I sweep my arms out and grab her straight off the street and then I'm dragging her past some trees and over a muddy patch of grass. We stumble over a deserted cobble stoned courtyard and fumble our way towards an abandoned warehouse. I am over her, pushing her down with my weight. I am tussling. And bustling. She is wriggling and squirming. I push her in the direction of an old doorway. The door is long gone, with just a sheet of timber covering the hole where it once stood, but thanks to me casing the joint earlier, it is no longer secure. I open it, push her through the gap and follow on behind.

The doorway leads us into the shell of a factory. Only, gone are the machines, gone are the people, gone is the life and soul of the building, all that's left is a dusty wasteland which still holds the heavy smell of oil.

The girl takes a look at her surroundings. And dissolves into tears.

"Get over there" I tell her, pointing towards an archway which leads to another room.

She shrinks away from me. "I can't" she sobs.

"You can and you will" I shout, grabbing for her arm. She moves it swiftly.

"What's happening?" she cries

"We're just going to talk."

"Can't we talk in the street?"

"No" I reply tersely. "Now move."

The girl takes two paces forward and then turns to me. "Please" she begs.

I grab her arm and drag her along, forcing her into the next room.

The second room is as empty as the previous one; its only objects are stone pillars which stretch from the floor to the ceiling. The rest of the space is a vast area of nothingness. It is lit by dull rays which breach the opaque panels of glass. The glass is set into black metal arched framed windows. They cast a shadowy inspection over the dusty floor. I lead her to a pillar near the back of the room and push her up against it.

The terror on her face is worth the risk. The horror of her expression is like nothing on earth. A hit of fervour rushes through my veins. As I look at her and contemplate what I'm going to do. Only now I don't have to rush. Now, I've got no one to answer to.

And no other place to be. For once I am in complete control and not dictated by the time. That control gives me options. Let me tell you that that control, well, I can keep her alive for the next ten minutes, if I want. Or I can string it out for the next ten days.

The girl looks around the building through her tears as she thinks about how she's going to make her get away.

"Don't even think about it" I say, cancelling her thoughts.

"I don't understand" she cries.

"You don't have to love" I reply, pointing to the ground. "Sit."

She does as she is told.

It's here that her tears flow more freely. Choking sobs rise to the surface. The noise builds up in intensity.

"Why are you doing this?" she asks, through the blubbering sounds.

"It's not for you to know" I respond.

"Please," she begs, gulping dramatically "let me go."

"Let me think first."

But I cannot think, for her crying only grows louder. She snivels and gasps for air. And snorts. And wails. It's a noise which gathers pace with each successive breath. It gets louder and louder, building up to a crescendo, until I can stand it no more.

"Shut up" I scream.

"But you're… you're …going… to… kill… me…"

"I will if you continue with that noise" I quip.

She doesn't find me funny. She doesn't get the joke at all.

"I want my mum" she wails.

"Do me a favour," I say "do us both a favour and shut the fuck up."

She tries to stifle her tears. But has trouble in controlling them. She takes great big gulps of air. Her body wracks into convulsions as she gasps and dribbles. Gradually she starts to calm. The noise begins to unwind. A few snivels escape and she manages to suppress the rest. She continues to cry, but it is void of any sound. With the noise no longer a distraction, I take a look at her.

She is huddled into a ball with her school uniform askew, and I don't know what possessed me to take her in the first place. She is young, probably only sixteen at the most and suddenly I feel bad for her. I feel really bad. I don't know what I was thinking of. Only that I wanted to kill for one last time. Only that the memories of the other women were starting to fade and that late at night I couldn't seem to be able bring those feelings back. All I wanted was one last experience, so much so I told myself that this time I would make every second count, that I would etch every emotion to my brain. That I would take in every sensation. And store it. So that it would sustain me for the rest of my life. Then I'd never have to kill again. One last victim, that's what I thought. Only when I look across at her, with her blotchy red face, and the way that she's cowering, it's not panning out in the way I wanted it to. Maybe I want her to put up a fight. And maybe I don't. Maybe I knew that she was as young as she is. But maybe, just maybe, I miss Maureen. Maybe she's left a gaping wound, and it's a wound that's taken me by surprise. Maybe I'm doing all of this because it gives me something else to focus on, something other than thinking about her all the time. I just don't know any more.

The girl moves her leg and her shoe scrapes along the ground.

It nudges me out of my thoughts. I look at her and realise that she's stopped crying altogether. She's staring at me. With her eyes fixed on me. Those eyes, which are big and wide. Suddenly I can't stand it any more; I can't stand her eyes. It reminds me of those dreams. The dreams that keep me awake at night. The dreams that won't let me rest. The dreams that plague me as soon as I try to sleep. All I ever see when I close my eyes, are eyes staring back at me, bulging eyes, blue eyes, green eyes, and bloodshot eyes, vicious eyes, accusing eyes, and eyes of hate, all moving closer. Then moving in on me. Looking into my very soul. And burrowing into my skin. They slip and crawl and writhe around my body. Making me want to itch. And making me want to scream. Every time I fall asleep, it happens. And every time, I wake up in a sweat. In the times when I'm awake, I tell myself that it's not real and that they can't get me. But it's real enough when I'm dreaming. Oh, it's real alright. Maybe that's why I do it. Maybe I can't stand her eyes any longer, but the piece of pipe is close by. And all I want to do is rid myself of them.

I bring the pipe down over the top of her head. I hit her with force. More than once. I lash out. To annihilate those piercing blues. And the colour crimson visits me again. It weaves into her hair. And begins to trickle down the side of her face. I hit her until I knock her out. It's then, when her eyes are closed, that I'm able to put my hands around her neck. It's then that I'm able to feel her skin beneath my gloves. And I'm able to feel the power for one last time.

I look at her freckly face, with its black smudged make-up around her eyes. I look at her. With her full lips that have yet to turn thin and mean. With her pale complexion in it's youthful prime. With her skin which is all fresh and pure. And her body, which is firm.

I memorise her face, and memorise her fright, even in the unconscious. I memorise the blood. And my feelings. And the danger. And the excitement. I contain the thrill of the energy into my memory, and the worry that someone might just catch me. It all filters into my nerves until they're taut. I memorise the smell of oil which lingers in the air. And I squeeze.

After she is dead, I lay her out.

This time I don't expose her body; there are some standards I like to keep, even for a killer like me. I keep her body under the cover of her uniform, but I do touch her. I have to. I bend forward and slip the beads into the waistband of her skirt.

Then I sit next to her. I sit on the crusty ground as the light outside begins to fade.

I'm still there when the orange streetlights are switched on. I don't want to be alone. I don't want to go back to my house, and be by myself, but there's no one else who I can be with. And so I sit next to her. And I talk. I tell her that I'm sorry. I tell her that I won't do it ever again. I tell her that I hope she's in a better place. I ask her to say hello to Maureen for me and I ask for her forgiveness.

Way past midnight, way past the darkest part of the night, when I think that the eyes won't get to me, and when I think that I can make it to the morning light without nodding off and dreaming those dreams. Way past midnight, when the birds are singing sweetly, and the rumble of a milk float goes by. With the signs of rigor mortis beginning to set in. When all that's left is just me. Sitting in a derelict space, and lost inside it. Way past midnight, I make my way home.

Chapter 35

I tell the wood panelling exactly how I feel. I tell it of how I can't sleep at night, and of how they are always there. Always haunting me. Always following me. Always with me. Every time I close my eyes, and every time I'm awake, and all those hours, and minutes, and seconds in between, they're there. The panelling is heard to sigh; it gives up a gasp of disappointment. Quiet, barely audible, but detected just the same. I tell it about Mrs Gibson and at how seeing her die has affected me real bad. That her, more than Maureen has, much more than Maureen ever could, left a wound. It's a deep wound which goes right to the very heart of me. It cuts into my very core. Nothing can distract me. And nothing can compensate. I've tried, I've tried so many things, I've come up with trick after trick, but nothing, not nothing, can distract from what I've done. Worse than that, I know that nothing I ever do is going to heal that which has broken. I know it and I've known it for a while. It's this, more than any of the other things, which now makes me regret the things I've done. It's this that is a stain on my sheet of life. It's the one true regret which I'll take to my grave. I can taste the salt. But I can't seem to stop it from falling. For it isn't why I've come here. Even Mrs Gibson is not exactly why I'm here, though I do feel closer to her when I'm here. I know this is unfair of me, and I know I'm the last person to ask for this request, but I'm here to seek help. I'm here to find a solution as I need to find a way out. I think that if I can be saved then it'll all be alright again, that my world and the world in which we live will be a better place. That's why. You see, I've recently got to thinking that my life is cursed, and that by having so much death around me, it's had a negative effect. I've begun to feel that I'm blighted. Deep in the middle of the night, and in the daylight too, it doesn't matter where I am, or what I'm doing, I can feel that I'm being watched. I sense that I'm not alone. I've got a ticket in my pocket and I'm prepared to go anywhere to escape. I'm prepared to go as far as it takes, but first, I want to exorcise these demons. I want to rid myself of any evil that surrounds me. Or is inside of me. Or has become me. That's why I'm willing to take the risk. That's why I feel that this is the only option left.

"Father, does God forgive everyone?" I ask now.

"My child" says the voice from the next cubicle "God has room for everyone."

"What about a sinner father?"

"God will always forgive a sinner, no matter what he's done" he replies. "God will always forgive, as long as the sinner repents."

"I want to repent" I tell him urgently "I really do."

And I do. I can be the best person in the world, if that's what it takes. I can believe, I always have in a way, I can believe so much that I'll become the most righteous person on this planet, if all that it takes is to say sorry for the past. I can repent, I think I already have, because I can't hack another night like the last. I can't cope with those dreams and those eyes. And it doesn't matter what I do, I can leave all of the lights on, I can remove all the lampshades, I can buy dozens of lamps and mirrors and lights and coat the house in foil, so that the rooms glare under the brightness of all those reflected bulbs. But it doesn't make any difference. I can walk round and round in circles, even putting obstacles in my way to keep me alert. It changes nothing. I can open all the windows to accommodate the winter frost, to let the house freeze, so that I keep awake. But no one stays awake forever. They always get me in the end. I've tried drinking. I've drunk myself stupid. I've drunk beyond drunkenness until my body rejects it. Only, it doesn't matter what kind of state I get myself into, they always visit me. Every noise counts. Every howl of the wind. Every creak of the floorboards. Every pipe. Every timber. Every slate. It's all there to make me aware. It's there to stop me from forgetting.

"Can a killer repent?" I ask now.

"There is always room for forgiveness in God's heart" he replies wearily.

"Even the worst killer in the world?"

"Everybody has the capacity to find goodness in themselves."

"Does that mean that nobody is completely evil?"

"My child, we are all born out of the love of God. And God is always ready to embrace everyone, no matter what" says the shadow.

I take a deep breath, then turn to address the grill.

"Father, I need to repent" I say.

"Then my child" comes his voice with much sadness "what is it that you wish to repent?"

Chapter 36

I turn the corner and hit the bright winter midmorning sunlight full on. I reach for my top pocket and pull out some sunglasses and slip them on as I'm rushing along. I head for the nearest taxi rank, as I do thoughts go through my head, thoughts like, what if he's on the phone right now, thoughts like I shouldn't have gone there, and I shouldn't have confessed, and that the dreams were all they were, just dreams. That I needn't be afraid as all the women really are dead. They are long gone, I'm sure of it. I keep telling myself that I'm going to be half way across the world pretty soon and no one will be able find me. I'll probably not even know where I am even. With any luck I won't. I'll be some kind of drifter with no past or future. That's all. I'll be an inconsequence. Only now I'm thinking that I might have to go back, I might have to make sure that the priest doesn't tell. But all I really want is to get as far away as possible from the silent disapproval which greeted my confession.

I reach the taxi rank and slide into the first taxi on the row.

"Where to?" asks the taxi driver, as he moves the gear stick into first.

"Take me to Heathrow airport."

The guy takes a quick glance at me from his rear view mirror. And then he looks again. It's a real double take. A puzzled expression slides across his face, as if he recognises me but doesn't know where from. It's a look I often get since my appeal on the television for help in catching Maureen's killer. I put up a big reward. But the police have failed to trace him. And even if they cotton on now, it's going to be too late.

"Going on holiday?" asks the driver.

"Not exactly, I'm moving abroad."

He moves the taxi out into the traffic. "You haven't got much stuff" he says, edging the car in front of a bus. I pat my hand luggage beside me and smile.

"No" I tell him "I'm leaving it all behind and starting again."

"Lucky thing" he murmurs, speeding up. "I've always wanted to do that but I've got a wife and three young children, maybe when they're older, you never know." The guy in the driving seat looks wistful. His face changes into a faraway look that I've seen on many people's faces since I broke the news that I intended to sell up and make a fresh start. He slips into a daydream. But I don't feel sorry for him. I don't have any sympathy for him at all. The bloke in front is stuck inside a piece of tin, day in, day out, sitting in traffic jams, listening to other peoples stories, pressing the accelerator, depressing the clutch and the brake. Going round and round. Following the directions of where others tell him to go. Living a set life. But that's his choice.

"Where are you going to?" asks the man.

"I'm doing a bit of travelling for a while" I tell the reflection in the mirror. "I might visit a few places in far flung locations and then perhaps settle somewhere in Europe."

"Are you starting off anywhere nice?"

"Puerto Rico. I'm booked to stay in a hotel for two nights and then I meet with a cruise ship which docks there. It sails around the Caribbean for a couple of weeks and then travels down the east coast of South America. From then on I'm not sure."

The driver pulls up at some traffic lights. But there's no masking his look, his face curdles with envy. But he is magnanimous enough to say "Sounds fantastic." After saying it, his face falls again.

"Yeah" I reply, turning to look out of the window. I look at the grimy streets. I see the grim people. The ones in their cars looking frustrated. The ones on the pavement all cold and fed up. The greyness. The bleak. The dirt. And the litter. And I smile. I sit back into my seat and start to relax.

No sooner am I comfortable when I'm aware of a hotness radiating from the empty seat next to me. I look at it. And nothing.

Nothing but the feeling that there are more than two of us in this taxi. I turn away. And focus on the view out of the window. The car is back in motion again. The streets are whizzing by, the skyline is starting to get smaller as we move away from the urban sprawl. The pedestrians become sparser. A patch of green appears. The concrete jungle disperses.

I wonder whether things will be different when I'm gone. Whether people will forget. Or whether it'll take time for them to wander back into the parks. I wonder how long it'll take before people, especially DCS Riley, realise that I'm no longer out there.

"Gone a bit chilly" says the driver.

"Yeah."

Only now I'm not hearing him properly. Now my mind is concentrated on other things. Other things like the icy blast of air which seems to be circling me.

"Will you miss England?" asks the man.

"Not at all" I reply. I mean it too. No. The sooner I get on that plane and get away, the sooner I'll put it all behind me. Then I'll be free.

Outside, the rain clouds gather.

The presenter on the radio cracks another innuendo over her co-hosts sex life, to which the co-host cackles loudly. The world ticks on. The driver accelerates and the coldness stops. I settle back into my seat and imagine everyone's faces on the shop floor when they receive the postcards from all of the exotic locations which I intend to visit in the next few weeks.

I look at the time. I've got three hours before my flight departs.

As we turn onto the A40 I hear the wail of a siren in the distance.

"What time does your flight leave?" asks the driver.

"Three-thirty."

"Plenty of time" he says.

The presenter on the radio announces a request for two back to back records for Sonia Harding who works at a hairdresser's in Beaconsfield called 'A Cut Above' from her boyfriend Trevor who loves her very much.

Above the noise of the radio and the traffic, the wail gets louder.

My mind briefly flickers. It wanders to parts which are no good for me. I wonder if they've worked it out. Or whether the priest has been busy talking. But I don't think it's possible. Then I try to remember what I exactly told the priest. Did I tell him about my journey? Did I confess to my escape? The trouble with conversations such as those, you become embroiled in the honesty of it. You become wrapped up in the notion of obligation and I felt obliged to tell him the truth just because of where we were. I became lippy. Maybe it was because it had been so long since I had someone to listen to me. But I don't think I told him everything. Or did I?

"The traffic's busy this afternoon," says the driver "but it'll get better once we're on the motorway."

"That's okay," I mumble "I've got plenty of time. As long as you get me there."

The driver laughs. "Don't want to be missing that flight, do you?" he grins.

"Certainly don't" I say, whilst discreetly crossing my fingers.

The record playing out of the speakers is one from Sting. His voice is distinctive. His lyrics are crisp and rounded. Each word is perfectly formed into a melodic note. He sings of being amongst fields of gold, I listen to the words of the lyrics and imagine the heat of the sun when I step off the plane. I pat the traveller's cheques in my jackets breast pocket.

The siren gets closer.

The driver signals and drives onto the slip road for the M40.

"Had many fares today?" I ask.

The record slips easily into another number. As soon as the first bar strikes up, I recognise it. Every Breathe You Take.

"I've had my fill" says the bloke wearily. "I started at six this morning and it's been non-stop ever since with this cold weather. I'll probably clock off soon" he says yawning at the thought of it.

I look at the case beside me. A change of shirt. Some underwear. A silver St. Christopher medallion which my mother gave me on my eighteenth birthday. Not much to carry, but I carry most of my life in my head. It's all there. Neatly stored into sections that no longer needs exploring. It is built into partitioned walls.

"Got your passport?" asks the driver.

I nod.

"You wouldn't believe how many people forget" he says to himself.

The siren gets louder. I catch sight of a blue light in the passenger's wing mirror. The taxi moves into the middle lane to make way for it. The police car catches us up in no time. And then edges to the side of the taxi. The policewoman in the passenger seat glances across at me as the vehicle overtakes. I watch the car intensely, focusing on the tailgate indicator. It remains unlit. The car continues on the outside lane at speed.

"He's in a rush" says the driver.

"Yeah."

I watch as it drives on and continues down the motorway.

Once it is out of sight, I switch off.

The taxi reaches the M25 and follows the route displaying the sign to the airport terminals. Up above the sound of a plane roars over our heads.

"Won't be long now" says the driver.

"Can't wait."

When we get to the airport I tip him well. He earned it. Just for getting me here. The driver smiles grimly and nods. His meter has stopped. The office is already buzzing him to give him his next job. He's managed to work out where he's seen me before. The look on his face says so, and he's no longer so envious. Instead there's only pity.

"Thanks mate" he says sombrely. "And good luck with the rest of your life."

"You too" I reply.

I watch as his taxi disappears and once he's gone I enter the airport terminal.

Chapter 37

I ask myself, was I lonelier when I was with Maureen? Or am I lonelier now? The truth is I don't know. But what I do know is that I felt more isolated when she was alive. That, in just being with her, she made me want to withdraw. Which is what I did, I withdrew from everybody and everything. I withdrew from life itself. I sat back and watched the clock tick by. It's only now I realise that it was nothing more than a waste. In seeing how all those people lost their lives, in witnessing it first hand, well, it only brings home how little time we have on this planet. And realising that life is short only goes to magnify the opportunities I let slip. There were so many chances I could have explored. There were plenty of meaningful looks before I settled with Maureen. There were plenty more jobs options before I took my place alongside Harry. When I think of just how many, I feel angry with myself. Sometimes I can't believe how I let the time pass by. Or why. But it was such an easy thing to do. I blame it on my youth, and on ignorance, and confidence, and thinking that I had more time than was actually true, I thought that I'd catch up eventually. But the truth is the only thing that catches up is time. Isn't that a bitch? But would I change things if I had the chance to live my life again. Who wouldn't? How many wouldn't sidestep their mistakes and cherry pick their triumphs. Who wouldn't brush aside the clangers and wallow in the better pauses. For all of that I still don't have any regrets. Regrets are only for perfectionists and I came to terms with my imperfections a long time ago. I came to terms with who I am, and I came to terms with other people's opinion of me. So

I don't feel disappointed, not in myself, I only yearn to live those days that I wasted again, to have them back, to make use of them. To fill them up. And make every second count. I can't have them though; all I can do is make use of the ones before me, that's all. But a heavy weight has gone from my life and now that it's been moved I can see more clearly. Life is simpler now. There are fewer issues. There is less of everything. I seem to have lightened my load. I'm nothing more than a snake which has shed its skin.

I meet her in the overspill of the café. She is sat at one of the outer tables with her body carefully positioned underneath an open umbrella which dwarfs the table beneath. Her dark tan legs are neatly arranged and stick out into the full light, whilst her face is in the shade to shield her make-up from the direct heat. The table is to the side of a makeshift stage. Two men stand on it. They both look in my direction as I walk towards them. One nods easily, while both continue to play, idly strumming their guitars, singing Spanish lyrics disjointedly to the sparse audience beneath.

Her face lights up as soon as she spots me. She has already ordered the drinks, hers a frothy cocktail of luminous pink, and mine, a San Miguel dripping in the heat of the mid-afternoon sun. I kiss her, continental style, on both cheeks and then take my seat beside her.

It's been three and a half years since I boarded that plane and left behind who I was, I left questions unanswered and I left a puzzle unsolved, at least in Riley's eyes I did, I left behind the person I was. I drew a line and altered my life, not to everyone's approval, I admit, but I did it. Now it seems almost a lifetime away from the person I was. There are times even when I feel like Maureen didn't happen. Only when I go to the bank to make a withdrawal, then there's the evidence. Sometimes I feel that it wasn't me, that it happened to someone else, only that someone got inside of my body and took me over for a while. Now, here I sit. I sit next to her. We bask in the Spanish sun.

I pour my beer into the waiting glass beside it and then take a sip. The flavour is strong and satisfying, the coolness refreshing against the heat of the day. It caresses my throat with moisture that is welcome. When quenched, I lean over and place the glass back onto the table. As I do, I take a look at her.

The woman beside me turns and smiles in my direction. It's a smile that is both open and mysterious. It hints of promises and has an undercurrent of kindness. It unnerves me. The woman beside me loves me, I'm in no doubt about that, and I love her too, in a way. But when you've gone through what I went through, when you've skidded through the wrong side of the tracks, when you've seen… and experienced… and participated in…, when you've got to know just how unpleasant…., when you've lived on this planet for the time I have and you've seen and done all the things that I've done, then there's little you can give, there's always a barrier that keeps you separated, there's always an invisible wall that stands in the way of wanting and having.

The music stops briefly and then gently slips into a new tune. The flamenco music reverberates around the courtyard. It fills the air with exuberance. It hints of promises of passion. It's an intoxicating rhythm which flickers into the very edges of the body. Making the extremities tap. And the heartbeat quicken. The perfect setting for some. The perfect atmosphere. Only I still feel detached. Maybe, I ask myself, that the way I feel is just the result of the things that have happened on the road of life that brought me here. But maybe this is just a part of who I've been all along. Only maybe… just maybe… I think that what drove me to do the things I did has become a learning curve for me, and by that I mean that I've come to realise that it's the things that I did which now stop me from getting what I truly want. Which is an irony. I know that everyone will think that I did it for the money, I know that they'll think it was all just one big calculated action, what from setting up all the insurance accounts, to cashing it all in, they'll see it as no more than that. But the money was just a byword; the money was nothing more than a bonus. No, all I ever truly wanted was love. To be in love, to taste it, and to be enraptured by it. That's all. But Maureen stood in the way. There's some that might ask, why not divorce? Why not separate? There was a time when I'd have to answer that divorce and separation is no means by which to go forward, I'd have just had a history. I'd have had ties, and a whole lot of my lifetimes work and income would have been lost, and then I'd have been obliged to pay her maintenance, which meant I'd have had to work for the rest of my life to support her. We would have been inconclusively woven together. So it wasn't the money, it was the continuation, and by continuation I mean that she would've remained in the shadows of my life. There would be no escape. I thought that it was no way to be starting a new life. And to be starting out with someone else. I thought that death would make it all a lot less complex. And I have to say, of late, I've come to find that the sympathy vote is a sure fire aphrodisiac. It sure as hell stirs up the hormones when you tell them that your wife was murdered and I can't say that I've not benefited as a result, I can't say that the women don't just emote when I come to confide in what happened. I can't say that I haven't milked it for all its worth. But it still doesn't add up. The sum never squares. What went on stops me from making that connection, it holds me back, it counters my emotions, and it measures my every breath. What went on casts a shadow over my future. It reaches. It goes far. And beyond. You see, it's only now that I realise that in order to find that special someone then there must be those extra special ingredients. That in order to sustain a relationship there must be truth. That's something I can never do. I've come to realise that it's all very well starting out on one level but there always comes a time when things move on. There always comes a time when feelings start to get deeper, and the sex doesn't fill each waking hour. There always comes a time when you have to look someone in the eye. It's something I'm incapable of doing any more. And I've tried so hard, so damn hard, but I always waver. You see, there are always those eyes looking back at me. Always those eyes looking on. Always those eyes boring into me. It's not just the eyes. I can never be honest about my past, I can't ever tell the truth. And all women like to dig. They all want to know everything. They want to pry. And ask. They all have a million questions whizzing around their heads or dripping from their tongues. When it comes down to it, they all like to own. I've found there is only one answer to their questions. There's only one way of getting out of it. That is to get rid of them. My past doesn't allow me a future. And committing murder to be able to love again has, in turn, meant that I'll never be able to love again. I've got a secret buried inside of me and there are occasions where I forget about it and I come to enjoy the moment. But all it takes is one small event, a smell, a question, a woman walking along the street wearing similar clothes to Maureen, all it takes is something trivial, but that something rings a bell inside of me. And it's at that point I know that I can never ever truly love. And that love will never find me. So it's as I say, that the very thing that set me free, turns out to be the very thing that holds me back. There's some that might think I'm being ungrateful, and that I got away with it, that at least I didn't go to prison. But believe me I did. My prison doesn't have walls; there are no limits, no curfews, and no barred windows. But my prison is just as effective. It's just as crippling.

The music plays on and the woman beside me slips her hand over mine. She goes on to caress each finger gently, gradually working her way forward, inching her digits until she gets her way, until her hand smothers mine and she has got a firm hold. She looks at me and smiles. In return, I turn and look up at the stage. The men come to the end of their song and I relieve my hand to allow myself to appreciate the performance. I clap enthusiastically. And, in turn, so does she.

I've spent the last few months dating Christy and there have been moments of pure enjoyment. But they don't last long. Christy loves, she cares, and she empathizes. There are times when I want to tell her who I am. But I don't. The risk isn't worth it.

We meet three or four times a week, we idly chat, we listen to music, we sometimes lie on the beach, we meet for lunch, sometimes for dinner, we meet up with other ex-pats, we do all the normal things that normal couples do. All the time I'm aware that the day will come. Today we'll take our time to share some drinks before walking off to an afternoon siesta, maybe we'll be holding hands, maybe share a kiss, maybe even share body fluids, sharing everything but the truth. We might spend a year together, and if we're lucky, we may get to more than that. Then what? The questions will out. The answers go silent. The disappointments get noticed. Lately I've come to ask myself some frightening questions. The answers I give myself are just as scary. There is one particular question that I fear the most. I ask myself, are we all just a sum of our past? If what I now believe is true, then it means I'll never be free. When I started out I saw my actions as an equation. It's only after the event I realise my equation for murder has changed. And there were more victims than I'd accounted for.

The duo play on. They make sweet harmony. They compliment each other. And do not complicate. They play a number which is recognisable as a song by The Gypsy Kings. Christy hums to the tune. She is serene and happy. She wears a look of contentment. Christy is a big time loser in love. Last night she asked if anything was troubling me. I stopped myself from answering her. She let it go. There will come a time when she won't be so obliging. There will come a time when she'll resent the silence. There will come a time when I won't be around to meet the questions. So it's as I say, although she doesn't know it yet, although she looks like she's the happiest person around, although she believes that luck is on her side, she's a lousy choice of character. She couldn't be more wrong.

So far there has been Frieda, a German woman who I met in Brazil. Emma, a Brit backpacking in Cambodia. Manuela, who was Spanish and who could speak and understand more English than was good for her. And now Christy. All looking for love. And all ending up with me. Every time, right at the beginning, I manage to convince myself that this time will be different. I never take love lightly. I always convince myself that the person I'm with will take me at face value. And that I'll have no need to explain myself. Only it never pans out like that.

What can you tell a woman who doesn't understand the intricacies of life? What can you tell a woman who doesn't know the depths of human nature? The truth is you can't. You can't ask them to share a burden like mine. What can you tell a woman who doesn't know you're dead, and who doesn't comprehend that there is a sum total for everything? Including love. And especially murder. There is nothing you can say. There is nothing that will undo the mistakes of the past. There is nothing that will hide the skeletons of my existence. Not countries. Not timeframes. Not lies. The past is always with me.

So, although she doesn't know it yet, although she's happy to have dreams that are nothing more than foolish, although the woman beside me is grateful for what she thinks is a mutual affair. Although the woman next to me thinks that we both have a golden future to look forward to. Christy is a sure fire loser in the loving stakes. For my days with her are numbered. She doesn't know it yet.

But I do.